W9-AGH-022
10/2018

THE CHINESE ORANGE MYSTERY

ELLERY QUEEN was a pen name created and shared by two cousins, Frederic Dannay (1905-1982) and Manfred B. Lee (1905-1971), as well as the name of their most famous detective. Born in Brooklyn, they spent forty-two years writing the greatest puzzle mysteries of their time, gaining the duo a reputation as the foremost American authors of the Golden Age "fair play" mystery.

Although eventually famous on television and radio, Queen's first appearance came in 1928 when the cousins won a mystery-writing contest with the book that would eventually be published as *The Roman Hat Mystery*. Their character was an amateur detective who uses his spare time to assist his police inspector father in solving baffling crimes. Besides co-writing the Queen novels, Dannay founded *Ellery Queen's Mystery Magazine*, one of the most influential crime publications of all time. Although Dannay outlived his cousin by nine years, he retired the fictional Queen upon Lee's death.

OTTO PENZLER, the creator of American Mystery Classics, is also the founder of the Mysterious Press (1975), a literary crime imprint now associated with Grove/Atlantic; Mysterious Press. com (2011), an electronic-book publishing company; and New York City's Mysterious Bookshop (1979). He has won a Raven, the Ellery Queen Award, two Edgars (for the *Encyclopedia of Mystery and Detection*, 1977, and *The Lineup*, 2010), and lifetime achievement awards from Noircon and *The Strand Magazine*. He has edited more than 70 anthologies and written extensively about mystery fiction.

THE CHINESE
ORANGE MYSTERY

ELLERY QUEEN

Introduction by
OTTO PENZLER

**AMERICAN
MYSTERY
CLASSICS**

Penzler Publishers
New York

Published in 2018 by Penzler Publishers
58 Warren Street, New York, NY 10007
penzlerpublishers.com

Cover image: Andy Ross
Cover design: Mauricio Diaz

Paperback ISBN 978-1-61316-106-7
Hardcover ISBN 978-1-61316-110-4

Library of Congress Control Number: 2018904872

Distributed by W. W. Norton

Printed in the United States of America

9 8 7 6 5 4 3 2 1

THE CHINESE
ORANGE MYSTERY

INTRODUCTION

OFTEN CALLED the Golden Age of the detective novel, the years between the two World Wars produced some of the most iconic names in the history of mystery. In England, the names Agatha Christie and Dorothy L. Sayers continue to resonate to the present day. In America, there is one name that towers above the rest, and that is Ellery Queen.

That famous name was the brainchild of two Brooklyn-born cousins, Frederic Dannay (born Daniel Nathan, he changed his name to Frederic as a tribute to Chopin, with Dannay merely a combination of the first two syllables of his birth name) and Manfred B. Lee (born Manford Lepofsky). They wanted a simple nom de plume and had the brilliant stroke of inspiration to employ Ellery Queen both as their byline and as the name of their protagonist, reckoning that readers might forget one or the other but not both.

Dannay was a copywriter and art director for an advertising agency while Lee was writing publicity and advertising material for a motion picture company when they were attracted by a $7,500 prize offered by *McClure's* magazine in 1928; they were twenty-three years old.

They were informed that their submission, *The Roman Hat Mystery*, had won the contest but, before the book could be published or the prize money handed over, *McClure's* went bankrupt. Its assets were assumed by *Smart Set* magazine, which gave the prize to a different novel that it thought would have greater appeal to women. Frederick A. Stokes decided to publish *The Roman Hat*

Mystery anyway, thus beginning one of the most successful mystery series in the history of the genre. Almost immediately, the cousins' plan to brand the author and character under the same name paid off, and the Ellery Queen name gained an iconic status.

Although Dannay and Lee were lifelong collaborators on their novels and short stories, they had very different personalities and frequently disagreed, often vehemently, in what Lee once described as "a marriage made in hell." Dannay was a quiet, scholarly introvert, noted as a perfectionist. Lee was impulsive and assertive, given to explosiveness and earthy language. They remained steadfast in their refusal to divulge their working methodology, claiming that over their many years together they had tried every possible combination of their skills and talent to produce the best work they could. However, upon close examination of their letters and conversations with their friends and family, it eventually became clear that, in almost all instances, it was Dannay who created the extraordinary plots and Lee who brought them to life.

Each resented the other's ability, with Dannay once writing that he was aware that Lee regarded him as nothing more than "a clever contriver." Dannay's ingenious plots, fiendishly detailed with strict adherence to the notion of playing fair with readers, remain unrivalled by any American mystery author. Yet he did not have the literary skill to make characters plausible, settings visual, or dialogue resonant. Lee, on the other hand, with his dreams of writing important fiction, had no ability to invent stories, although he could improve his cousin's creations to make the characters come to life and the plots suspenseful and compelling.

The combined skills of the collaborators produced the memorable Ellery Queen figure, though in the early books he was clearly based on the best-selling Philo Vance character created by S.S. Van Dine. The Vance books had taken the country by storm in the 1920s, so it was no great leap of imagination for Dannay and

Lee to model their detective after him. In all candor, both Vance and the early Queen character were insufferable, showing off their supercilious attitude and pedantry at every possible opportunity.

When Queen makes his debut in *The Roman Hat Mystery*, he is ostensibly an author, though he spends precious little time working at his career. He appears to have unlimited time to collect books and help his father, Inspector Richard Queen, solve cases. Although close to his father, the arrogant young man is often condescending to him as he loves to show off his erudition. As the series progresses (and as the appetite for Philo Vance diminished), Ellery becomes a far more realistic and likable character.

Most of the detective's less attractive traits are evident in *The Chinese Orange Mystery* (1934), one of the earliest of Queen's adventures, yet it shows off his strengths, too, as he is able to mentally juggle all the clues, motives, and personalities in a complex murder case and arrive, with unassailable logic, at the only possible solution.

In one of the most extraordinary beginnings of any detective novels of its era—or of any era, for that matter—an utterly ordinary, unmemorable, characterless man steps off a hotel elevator to visit the office of Donald Kirk, a wealthy young publisher, socialite, and stamp collector. The secretary tells the guest that Kirk is not in at the moment but leads him to an opulent waiting room where, alone, the man sits down to wait for his return. Several people drop by to see Kirk but leave without waiting. Later in the day, Kirk shows up with Ellery Queen and, when they walk into the waiting room, they are confronted by a nearly unimaginable sight.

Everything in the magnificent room has been turned upside down, inside out, and backwards. The pictures and the clock now face the wall, the rug has been turned upside down, the floor lamps stand on their shades. Every movable object in the room has been moved to reflect an *Alice-in-Wonderland*-like scene.

The very ordinary nobody is lying on the rug, wearing clothes that are on backward. His shirt, trousers, coat, even his shoes, have been reversed, and two decorative African spears have been pushed up his trouser legs, poking out at the waist under the inside-out suit jacket, the points of the spears stuck through the lapels. Worse, the man's head has been battered with a fireplace poker, splattering his brains across the floor. It's up to Ellery Queen to use all his observational and deductive reasoning skills to navigate one of the most bizarre murder scenes and extraordinary cases of his career.

The success of the novels got them Hollywood offers and they went to write for Columbia, Paramount, and MGM, though they never received any screen credits. The popular medium of radio also called to them and they wrote all the scripts for the successful *Aventures of Ellery Queen* radio series for nine years, from 1939 to 1948. In an innovative approach, the show interrupted the narration so that the actor voicing the Ellery character could ask that night's guests—well-known personalities acting as armchair detectives—to solve the case based on all the clues given so far (a similar approach is seen in the early Queen novels, which pause to alert the reader when the investigation has reached its conclusion). The listeners' theories almost invariably in vain, the program would then proceed, revealing the correct solution. The Queen character was also translated into a comic strip character and several television series starring Richard Hart, Lee Bowman, Hugh Marlowe, George Nader, Lee Philips, and, finally, Jim Hutton. *The Chinese Orange Mystery* served as the inspiration for the uninspired, low-budget motion picture, *The Mandarin Mystery* (1937), made by Republic Pictures. Directed by Ralph Staub, it starred (if that's the right word) Eddie Quillan, Charlotte Henry, Rita Le Roy, Wade Boteler, and Franklin Pangborn.

While Manfred B. Lee had no particular affection for mystery fiction, always hoping to become the Shakespeare of the twentieth century, Dannay had been interested in detective stories since his boyhood. He wanted to produce a magazine of quality mystery stories in all sub-genres and founded *Mystery* in 1933, but it failed after four issues when the publisher went bankrupt. However, after Dannay's long convalescence from a 1940 automobile accident that nearly took his life, he created *Ellery Queen's Mystery Magazine*; the first issue appeared in 1941 and remains the leading mystery fiction magazine in the world to the present day.

—OTTO PENZLER

Table of Contents

	FOREWORD	5
1.	THE IDYLL OF MISS DIVERSEY	9
2.	STRANGE INTERLUDE	22
3.	THE TOPSY-TURVY MURDER	35
4.	MR. NOBODY FROM NOWHERE	47
5.	ORANGES AND SPECULATIONS	56
6.	DINNER FOR EIGHT	70
7.	TANGERINE	79
8.	TOPSY-TURVY LAND	92
9.	FOOCHOW ERROR	109
10.	THE QUEER THIEF	123
11.	UNKNOWN QUANTITIES	137
12.	A GIFT OF GEMS	149
13.	BOUDOIR SCENE	169
14.	THE MAN FROM PARIS	177
15.	THE TRAP	195
	CHALLENGE TO THE READER	212
16.	THE EXPERIMENT	213
17.	LOOKING BACKWARD	223

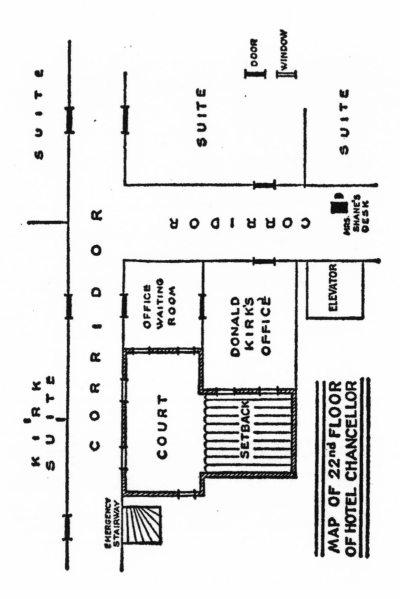

MAP OF 22nd FLOOR
OF HOTEL CHANCELLOR

Cast of Characters

In the order of their appearance

Miss Diversey: who nursed a sick man—and a hope

Dr. Hugh Kirk: septuagenarian scholar, who was often buried—in a book

Mrs. Shane: the Hotel Chancellor's floor clerk

James Osborne: Donald Kirk's *secret*ary

"Mr. Nobody from Nowhere"

Hubbell: a gentleman's gentleman—but no gentleman

Glenn Macgowan: who proved that a friend in need is a friend in deed

Irene Llewes: who played her part in the taming of the shrewd

Jo Temple: whose knowledge of Chinese helped Ellery get oriented

Donald Kirk: publisher of books and collector of gems, stamps—and trouble

Ellery Queen: who collared the criminal—and his victim

Marcella Kirk: who fainted or feinted when she saw the corpse

Nye: the hotel manager

Brummer: the hotel detective

Inspector Richard Queen: of the Homicide Squad

Dr. Prouty: Assistant Medical Examiner

Sergeant Velie: of the Homicide Squad

Felix Berne: the man who came late to dinner

Foreword

I AM NATURALLY prejudiced in favor of my friend Mr. Ellery Queen. Friendship aborts the critical faculties; especially friendship which has been invited to partake of fame. And yet, ever since those ancient days when I was first persuading Ellery to whip his notes into fiction form—through all the exciting novels that followed that first adventure—I cannot recall being more genuinely impressed than I was as I read the manuscript of *The Chinese Orange Mystery*.

It might well have been subtitled: The Crime That Was Backwards. With a further addendum: The Most Remarkable Murder-Case of Modern Times. But, as I say, I am prejudiced and perhaps that is a modest overstatement. The point is that if the crime itself was extraordinary, the mentality that went to work upon it was gigantic. Even now, knowing the answer, I sometimes disbelieve. And yet it was all so simple, indeed so inevitable. . . . The trouble is, as Ellery likes to point out, that all puzzles are irritatingly cryptic until you know the answer, and then you wonder why you were baffled so long. But I cannot quite subscribe to that; it took genius to solve the crime that was backwards, and I will stick to that opinion tho' Hell freeze over and I lose my friend—which is a potent possibility.

Sometimes, too, I feel secretly glad that I had nothing to do with that case. Ellery, who is in many ways a thinking machine, is no respecter of friendships when logic points an accusing finger. And it might very well have been that had I been in some way involved—if even as, let us say, Donald Kirk's attorney—Ellery might have caused good Sergeant Velie to clap the cuffs on my poor wrists. For it is remarkable that when I was at college I achieved a definitely fleeting fame in two athletic fields: I was my class backstroke swimming champion, and I rowed stroke-oar on the crew.

How these innocent facts would have made me a potential—no, no, a very active—suspect in the murder with which these pages are concerned I shall leave you to discover—unquestionably with pleasure—for yourself.

—J. J. McC.
New York

"The detection—or rather the solution—of crime calls for a combination of scientist and seer in the completest development of the detective. The genius for prophesying from events is a very special endowment of Nature and has been granted in its highest form only to a favored few. . . .

"I might paraphrase that interesting observation in Schlegel's Athenæum which goes:

'Der Historiker ist ein rückwärts gekehrter Prophet?'

by pointing out that: 'The detective is a prophet looking backwards.' Or Carlyle's more subtle observation about history by agreeing that: The process of detection (as opposed to History) is 'a distillation of rumor.'"

—Excerpt from an Anonymous Article in Esoterica Americana, Attributed by Some to Matsoyuma Tahuki, the Noted Japanese Authority on the Occident.

1. THE IDYLL OF MISS DIVERSEY

MISS DIVERSEY fled Dr. Kirk's study followed by a blistering mouthful of ogrish growls. She stood still in the corridor outside the old gentleman's door, her cheeks burning and one of her square washed-out hands pressed to the outraged starch of her bosom. She could hear the angry septuagenarian scuttling about the study in his wheel chair like a Galapagos turtle, muttering anathemas upon her white-capped head in a fantastic potpourri of ancient Hebrew, classic Greek, French, and English.

"The old fossil," thought Miss Diversey fiercely. "It's—it's like living with a human encyclopedia!"

Dr. Kirk made Jovian thunder from behind the door: "And don't come back, do you hear me?" He thundered other things, too, in the argot of strange tongues which filled his scholar's brain; things which, had Miss Diversey been possessed of the dubious advantages of higher culture, would have made her very indignant indeed.

"Slush," she said defiantly, glaring at the door. There was no reply; at least, no reply of a satisfactory nature. There's nothing, she thought with dismal consternation, you can say to a ghostly chuckle and the slam of a dusty book dug out of somebody's grave. He *was* the most exasperating old— She almost said it. For a moment, in fact, it trembled upon the brink of utterance. But her better nature triumphed and she closed her pale lips sternly. Let him dress himself if he wanted to. She had always hated dressing old people, anyway. . . . She stood irresolute for a moment; and then, her color still high, clumped down the corridor with the firm unhurried steps of the professional nurse.

The twenty-second floor of the Hotel Chancellor was pervaded, by inflexible regulation, with the silent peace of the cloister. The quiet soothed Miss Diversey's ruffled soul. There were two compensations, she thought, to playing nurse to a creaking, decrepit, malicious old devil afflicted—thank heaven there was justice!—with chronic rheumatism and gout. One was the handsome salary young Donald Kirk paid her for the difficult task of taking care of his father; the other was that the Kirk *ménage* was situated in a respectable hotel in the heart of New York City. The money and the geography, she thought with morbid satisfaction, made up for a lot of disadvantages. Macy's, Gimbel's, the other department stores were only minutes away, movies and theatres and all sorts of exciting things at one's doorstep. . . . Yes, she would stick it out. Life was hard, but it had its compensations.

Not that they weren't a trying lot at times. Lord knows she had crawled to the whims of plenty of nasty people in her day. And that old Dr. Kirk *was* nasty; there was no pleasing him. You'd think a body would be pleasant and human and grateful *sometimes*; give a person a "please" here or a "thank you" there. But not old Beelzebub. A tyrant, if ever there was one. He had eyes that gave a person the shivers; and his white hair stood on end as if it were trying to get as far away from him as it possibly could. He wouldn't eat when you wanted him to. He refused massages and threw shoes about. He would totter around the suite when Dr. Angini said he mustn't walk and refuse to budge when Dr. Angini said he must exercise. About the only good thing about him was that when his purple old nose was buried in a book he was quiet.

And then there was Marcella. Marcella! Snippy little fluff *she* was;

in fifty years she'd be the feminine counterpart of her father. Oh, she had her good points, reflected Miss Diversey grudgingly; but then so have criminals. Adding her up, good and bad, you wouldn't have much. Of course, conceded Miss Diversey, who had a strong sense of justice, she couldn't really be as worthless as all that; not with that nice tall pink-cheeked Mr. Macgowan so crazy about her. It certainly did take all kinds of people to make a world! Now, Miss Diversey was sure that if Mr. Macgowan had not happened to be Mr. Donald Kirk's best friend there never would have been an engagement between Mr. Macgowan and Mr. Kirk's young sister. That's what comes of having a brother *and* pots of money, thought Miss Diversey darkly. You go out and snare just about the best catch—Miss Diversey read the society-gossip columns critically—in the social whirl. Well, maybe when they were married he'd find out. They generally do, thought Miss Diversey, who possessed among other admirable qualities a decided strain of cynicism. The stories she could tell about these society people! . . . As for Donald Kirk, he was all right in his way; but his way was not Miss Diversey's way. He was a snob. That is, he treated people like Miss Diversey with a certain good-humored, absent tolerance.

It did seem, reflected Miss Diversey as she trudged down the corridor, that the easiest way to bury the woman part of a person was to become a trained nurse. Here she was, thirty-two—no, one must be honest with oneself; it was closer to thirty-three—and what were her prospects? That is to say, her romantic prospects? Nothing, simply nothing. The men she met in the travails of her profession were roughly of two kinds, she thought bitterly: those who paid no attention to her at all, and those who paid far too much. In the first category were doctors and male relatives of rich patients; in the second were internes and male employees of rich patients. The first class didn't recognize her as a woman at all, just a machine; Donald Kirk belonged to *that* class. The second kind wanted to—to take her apart with their grubby fingers to see what made her tick. That groveling little Hubbell, now, she thought with a curl of her lip—Mr. Kirk's butler and valet and Lord knows what else. When he was with his betters he was the soul of self-effacement and rectitude; but still and all she'd had to slap that pasty face of his only this morning. Patients, of course, didn't count. You could hardly get goo-goo about a person when you fetched bedpans and that sort of thing. Now, Mr. Osborne was different. . . .

A gentle vagueness settled upon Miss Diversey's hard features; almost a girlish smile. Thoughts of Mr. Osborne were—there was no denying it—pleasant. First of all, he was a gentleman; none of Hubbell's low tricks for *him*. Come to think of it, he was in a third class, sort of in a class by himself. Not rich, and yet not a servant. As Mr. Kirk's confidential assistant he was in between. Like one of the family and yet not like one of the family, as you might say; he worked on a salary like herself. That made it—somehow—very, very satisfying to Miss Diversey. . . . She wondered if she really hadn't overstepped the bounds of propriety weeks and weeks ago, when she'd only just met Mr. Osborne. How *had* the talk drifted around to—she blushed faintly—marriage? Oh, nothing personal, of course; she'd merely said that *she* would never marry a man who couldn't provide a good—a more than good—living. Oh, no. She'd seen too many marriages break up because of money; that is, lack of it. And Mr. Osborne had seemed so distressed, as if she'd hurt him; now, could that mean anything? Surely he wasn't thinking . . .

Miss Diversey took a firm grip on her errant thoughts. Her amble had brought her to a door on the opposite side of the corridor from the Kirk suite. It was the last door on the wall, the door nearest the other corridor that led from the elevators to the Kirk apartment. A plain door, really an undistinguished member of the family of doors; and yet sight of it brought a slight flush to Miss Diversey's cheeks, a flush subtly different from the angry red response to Dr. Kirk's brimstone blasphemies. She tried the handle; it gave.

It wouldn't hurt to peep in, she thought. If there were some one waiting in the anteroom it would mean that he—that Mr. Osborne was probably very busy. If the anteroom was empty, surely there wouldn't be any harm in . . . under the circumstances . . . The old fossil couldn't talk to *her* that way! . . . A person was human, wasn't she?

She opened the door. The anteroom was—happy chance—empty. Directly opposite her was the only other door of the room, and it was closed. On the other side lay . . . She sighed and turned to go. But then she brightened and hurried in. A bowl of fresh fruit on the reading table against the wall between the windows beckoned. It was nice of Mr. Kirk to be so thoughtful of other people, even strangers; and the Lord knew enough of *them* came to see him and sat in the little anteroom, with its nice English oak furniture and its books and lamps and rug and flowers and things.

She pecked among the fruits, making up her mind. One of those huge sugar-pears, now? Hothouse, most likely. But no, it was too close to dinner. Possibly an apple. . . . Ah, tangerines! Now that she came to think of it, tangerines were her favorites. Better than oranges, because they were easier to peel. And they came apart so nicely!

She stripped the rind from the tangerine with the industry of a squirrel and proceeded to chew the damp, sweet morsels of orange with her strong teeth. The pips she spat daintily into the palm of her hand.

When she had finished she looked about, decided the room and the table were too trim and neat and clean to be defiled with pips and orange-peel, and cheerfully hurled the handful of remains out one of the windows into the court made by the setback of the building four stories below. On passing the table, she hesitated. Another? There were two very alluring fat tangerines left in the bowl. . . . But she shook her head sternly and went out by the corridor door, shutting it behind her.

Feeling a little better, she sauntered around the bend into the main corridor. What to do? The old devil would kick her out if she went back now, and she didn't feel much like going to her own room. . . . She brightened once more. A stout middle-aged woman dressed in black, with severe gray hair, was sitting at a desk farther up the corridor, directly opposite the elevators. It was Mrs. Shane, clerk on duty on the twenty-second floor.

Miss Diversey shut her eyes when she passed a door on her right; the door which—she blushed again—opened into the office of Mr. Donald Kirk, the office adjoining the anteroom. It was in this office that the gallant Mr. Osborne was to be f— She sighed and passed on.

"Hullo, Mrs. Shane," she said cheerily to the stout woman. "How's the back this afternoon?"

Mrs. Shane grinned. She peered with caution up and down the corridor, kept an eye cocked on the elevators facing her, and said: "Why, it's Miss Diversey! I declare, Miss Diversey, I never see you any more! Is the old scoundrel keepin' you that busy?"

"Damn his soul," said Miss Diversey without rancor. "He's Satan himself, Mrs. Shane. Just now he chased me out of his room. Imagine!" Mrs. Shane clucked with horror. "Mr. Kirk's partner came back from Europe or some place today—that's Mr. Berne—and Mr. Kirk is giving a dinner-party for him. Naturally, he would have to go. So what do you think? He has to dress for dinner, so—"

"Dress?" echoed Mrs. Shane blankly. "Is he nekkid?"

Miss Diversey laughed. "I mean a tuxedo and things. Well _he_ can't dress himself. He can hardly stand on his feet, with his joints all twisted up with rheumatiz. Why, he's seventy-five if he's a day! But what do you think? He wouldn't let me dress him. *Chased* me out!"

"Imagine," said Mrs. Shane. "Men-folks are funny that way. I remember once my Danny—God rest his soul—was taken bad with lumbago and I had to—" She stopped abruptly and stiffened as the elevator evacuated a passenger. The lady, however, was not on the alert for possible defections of hotel employees. She exuded a faint odor of alcohol as she staggered by the desk bound up the corridor toward the other side of the floor. "See that hussy?" hissed Mrs. Shane, leaning forward. Miss Diversey nodded. "The things I could tell you about her, dearie! Why, my girls who clean up on this floor told me the *awfullest* things they've found in her room. Only last week they picked up from her floor a—"

"I've got to go," said Miss Diversey hastily. "Uh—is Mr. Kirk's office—I mean, has Mr. Kirk—?"

Mrs. Shane relaxed to fix Miss Diversey with a shrewd suspicious eye. "You mean is Mr. *Osborne* alone?"

Miss Diversey colored. "I didn't ask that—"

"I know, honey. He is that. There's been not a soul near that blessed office for an hour or more."

"You're sure?" breathed Miss Diversey, beginning to poke her square-tipped fingers in the reddish hair beneath her cap.

"Of course I'm sure! I haven't stirred from this spot all the afternoon, and nobody could 'a' gone into that office without me seeing him."

"Well," said Miss Diversey carelessly. "I think, since I'm here, I'll stop in for a minute. I've nothing to do, anyway. It gets so boring, Mrs. Shane. And then I do feel sorry for poor Mr. Osborne, cooped up in that office all day with not a living soul to talk to."

"Oh, I wouldn't say that," said Mrs. Shane with demoniac subtlety. "Only this morning there was a perfeckly *stunning* young lady. Something to do with Mr. Kirk's book publishing—an author, I do think. She was in there with Mr. Osborne for the longest time—"

"Well, and why shouldn't she be?" murmured Miss Diversey. "I'm sure *I* don't care, Mrs. Shane. And anyway it's his work, isn't it? Besides, Mr. Osborne isn't the kind . . . Well, so long."

"So long," said Mrs. Shane warmly.

Miss Diversey strolled back the way she had come, her strides growing smaller and smaller as she approached the enchanted area before the closed door of Donald Kirk's office. Finally, and by some miracle of chance precisely opposite the door, she came to a stop. Her cheeks tingling, she darted a glance over her shoulder at Mrs. Shane. That worthy dame, basking in the glow of acting a stout middle-aged Eros, was grinning broadly. So Miss Diversey smiled rather foolishly and put off all further pretense and knocked on the door.

James Osborne called: "Come in," in an absent tone and did not raise his pale face as Miss Diversey slipped with high-beating heart into the office. He was seated on a swivel-chair before a desk, working with silent concentration over a curious loose-leaf album with thick leaves faintly quadrilled and holding tiny rectangles of colored paper. He was a faded-looking man of forty-five, with nondescript sandy hair grizzled at the temples, a sharp beaten nose, and eyes imbedded in tired wrinkles. He worked over the bits of colored papers with unwavering attention, handling them with a small nickel tongs and the dexterity of long practice.

Miss Diversey coughed.

Osborne swung about, startled. "Why, Miss Diversey!" he exclaimed, dropping the tongs and scrambling to his feet. "Come in, come in. I'm dreadfully sorry—I was so absorbed . . ." A redness had come over his flat lined cheeks.

"You go right back to work," directed Miss Diversey. "I thought I'd look in, but since you're busy—"

"No. No, no, Miss Diversey, really. Sit down. I haven't seen you for two days. I suppose Dr. Kirk has been keeping you busy?"

Miss Diversey sat down, arranging her starched skirts primly. "Oh, we're used to that, Mr. Osborne. He's a little fussy, but he's really a grand old man."

"I quite agree. Quite," said Osborne. "A great scholar, Miss Diversey. He's contributed a good deal, you know, to philology in his day. A great scholar."

Miss Diversey murmured something. Osborne stood in an eager, sloped attitude. The room was very quiet and warm. It was more like a den than an office, fitted out by some sensitive hand. Soft glass curtains and brown velvet drapes shrouded the windows overlooking the setback court. Donald Kirk's desk was in a corner, heaped with books and albums. They both felt suddenly a sense of being alone with each other.

"Working on those old stamps again, I see," said Miss Diversey in a strained voice.

"Yes. Yes, indeed."

"Whatever you men see in collecting postage stamps! Don't you feel silly sometimes, Mr. Osborne? Grown men! Why, I've always thought only boys went in for that sort of thing."

"Oh, really no," protested Osborne. "Most laymen think that about philately. And yet it absorbs the attention of millions of people all over the world. It's a universal hobby, Miss Diversey. Do you know there's one stamp in existence which is catalogued at fifty thousand dollars?"

Miss Diversey's eyes grew round. "No!"

"I mean it. A bit of paper so messy you wouldn't give it another look. I've seen photographs of it." Osborne's faded eyes glowed. "From British Guiana. It's the only one of its kind in the world, you know. It's in the collection of the late Arthur Hind, of Rochester. King George needs it to complete his collection of British colonies—"

"You mean," gasped Miss Diversey, "King George is a *stamp-collector*?"

"Yes, indeed. Many great men are. Mr. Roosevelt, the Agha Khan—"

"Imagine that!"

"Now, you take Mr. Kirk. Donald Kirk, I mean. Now, he has one of the finest collections of Chinese stamps in the world. Specializes, you know. Mr. Macgowan collects locals—local posts, you know; stamps which were issued by states or communities for local postage before there was a national postage system."

Miss Diversey sighed. "It's certainly very interesting. Mr. Kirk collects other things, too, doesn't he?"

"Oh, yes. Precious stones. I haven't much to do with that, you see. He keeps that collection in a bank-vault. I devote most of my time to keeping the stamp collection in apple-pie order, and doing confidential work for Mr. Kirk in connection with The Mandarin Press."

"Isn't that interesting, now!"

"Isn't it."

"It's certainly very interesting," said Miss Diversey again. How on earth, she thought fiercely, did we ever get to talk about *these* things? "I read a book once published by The Mandarin."

"Did you, really?"

"*Death of a Rebel*, by some outlandish name."

"Oh! Merejinski. He was one of Felix Berne's discoveries—a Russian. He's always scouting around in Europe, you know, looking for foreign authors—Mr. Berne, I mean. Well." Osborne fell silent.

"Well," said Miss Diversey. And she fell silent.

Osborne fingered his chin. Miss Diversey fingered her hair.

"Well," said Miss Diversey a little nervously. "They do publish the artiest books, don't they?"

"Indeed they do!" cried Osborne. "I don't doubt Mr. Berne's come back with a trunkful of new manuscripts. He always does."

"Does he, now." Miss Diversey sighed; it was getting worse, much worse. Osborne regarded her crisp cleanness with admiring eyes—admiring and respectful. Then Miss Diversey brightened. "I don't suppose Mr. Berne knows about Miss Temple, does he?"

"Eh?" Osborne started. "Oh, Miss Temple. Well, I suppose Mr. Kirk's written him about her new book. Very nice, Miss Temple is."

"Do you think so? I think so, too." Miss Diversey's broad shoulders quivered. "Well!"

"You're not going so soon?" asked Osborne in a dashed voice.

"Well, really," murmured Miss Diversey, rising, "I must. Dr. Kirk's probably in a fit by now. All that exertion! Well . . . It's been very pleasant talking to you, Mr. Osborne." She moved toward the door.

Osborne swallowed. "Uh—Miss Diversey." He took a timid step toward her and, in alarm, she retreated, breathing very fast.

"Why, Mr. Osborne! What—what—?"

"Could you—would you—I mean, are you—"

"What, Mr. Osborne?" murmured Miss Diversey archly.

"Are you doing anything tonight?"

"Oh," said Miss Diversey. "Why, I guess not, Mr. Osborne."

"Then would you—go to the movies with me tonight?"

"Oh," said Miss Diversey again. "I'd love to."

"The new Barrymore picture's playing at Radio City," said Osborne eagerly. "I hear it's very good. It got four stars."

"John or Lionel?" demanded Miss Diversey, frowning.

Osborne looked surprised. "John."

"Well, I should say I'd love to!" exclaimed Miss Diversey. "I've always said John's my favorite. I like Lionel, too, but John . . ." She raised her eyes ceiling-ward in a sort of ecstasy.

"I don't know," muttered Osborne. "It seems to me in his last few pictures he's looked rather old. Time will tell, you know, Miss Diversey."

"Why, *Mr.* Osborne!" said Miss Diversey. "I do believe you're jealous!"

"Jealous? Me? Pshaw—"

"Well, I think he's simply divine," said Miss Diversey with cunning. "And it's wonderful of you to take me to see him, Mr. Osborne. I know I'll have the most thrilling time."

"Thank you," said Osborne glumly. "I meant to ask you . . . Well, that's fine, that's fine, Miss Diversey. It's about a quarter to six now—"

"Five-forty-three," said Miss Diversey mechanically, consulting her wrist-watch with professional swiftness. "Shall we say," her voice lowered and became intimate, "a quarter to eight?"

"That's fine," breathed Osborne. Their eyes touched, and both quickly looked away. Miss Diversey felt a sudden surge of warmth beneath the starched apron. Her blunt fingers began to search her hair mechanically.

Mr. Ellery Queen was wont to point out in confidentially retrospective moments that not the least remarkable feature of the affair was the subtle manner in which the dead man's very lack of existence impinged upon the unexciting little lives of little people. At one moment all was commonplace. Miss Diversey trifled with herself and Mr. Osborne's heart in Kirk's hide-away office. Donald Kirk was off somewhere. Jo Temple was dressing in a new black gown in one of the guest-rooms of the Kirk suite. Dr. Kirk's thorny nose was buried in a Fourteenth Century rabbinical manuscript. Hubbell was in Kirk's room laying out his master's evening kit.

Glenn Macgowan was striding fast up Broadway. Felix Berne was kissing a foreign-looking woman in his bachelor apartment in the East Sixties. Irene Llewes was regarding her very admirable nude figure in her bedroom mirror in the Chancellor.

And Mrs. Shane, who a few moments before had played Cupid, was suddenly called upon to play a new role—Prologue in The Tragedy of the Chinese Orange.

2. STRANGE INTERLUDE

AT PRECISELY 5:44 by Mrs. Shane's watch one of the elevator-doors opposite her station opened and a stoutish little man with a bland middle-aged face stepped out. There was nothing about him that excited the eye with a sensation of interest or pleasure. He was just a middle-aged creature grown to flesh, dressed in undistinguished clothing, wearing a greenish-black felt hat, a shiny black topcoat, and a woolen scarf bundled around his fat neck against the brisk Fall weather. He had pudgy hairless hands and he was carrying ordinary gray capeskin gloves. From the crown of his cheap hat to the soles of his black bull-dog shoes he was—nothing, the Invisible Man, one of the millions of mediocrities who make up the every-day wonderless world.

"Yes?" said Mrs. Shane rather sharply, measuring him accurately with a glance as she noticed his hesitancy. This was no guest of the Chancellor, with its $10-a-day rooms.

"Could you direct me to the private office of Mr. Donald Kirk?" asked the stout man timidly. His voice was soft and sugary, not unpleasant.

"Oh," said Mrs. Shane. That explained everything. Donald Kirk's office on the twenty-second floor was the port-of-call of many strange gentlemen. Kirk had instituted this office in the Chancellor to provide a quiet meeting-place for jewelry and phil-atelic dealers, and to conduct purely confidential publishing business which he did not care to air in the comparatively public surroundings of the Mandarin Press offices. As a result, Mrs. Shane was not unaccustomed to being accosted by queer people. So she snapped: "Room 2210, right there across the corridor," and went back to her perusal of a nudist magazine cleverly concealed in the half-open top drawer of her desk.

The stout man said: "Thank you," in his sweet voice and trudged obliquely across the corridor to the door on which Miss Diversey had rapped a few moments earlier. He made a pudgy fist and knocked on the panel.

There was an interval of silence from the room; and then Osborne's voice, curiously choked, said: "Come in."

The stout man beamed and opened the door. Osborne was standing by his desk, blinking and pale, while Miss Diversey stood near the door with flaming cheeks. Her right hand burned where male skin had touched it an instant before.

"Mr. Kirk?" inquired the stranger mildly.

"Mr. Kirk is out," said Osborne with some difficulty. "What can I—"

"I believe I'll go now," said Miss Diversey in a rather cracked tone.

"Oh, please!" said the visitor. "I assure you I can wait. Please don't let me interrupt—" He eyed her uniform brightly.

"I was going anyway," murmured Miss Diversey; whereupon she fled, holding her cheek. The door banged shut.

Osborne sighed and lowered his head. "Well . . . What can I do for you?"

"To tell you the truth," said the stranger, removing his hat and revealing a pinkish skull fringed with gray hair, "I was really looking for a Mr. Kirk, Mr. Donald Kirk. I want to see him very badly."

"I'm Mr. Kirk's assistant, James Osborne. What did you want to see Mr. Kirk about?"

The stranger hesitated.

"Does your business relate to publishing?"

He puckered his lips a little stubbornly. "My business is confidential, you see, Mr. Osborne."

Osborne's eyes grew steely. "I assure you I'm intrusted with all of Mr. Kirk's confidential business. It won't be violating any confidence—"

The stout man's colorless eyes fixed themselves upon the album of postage stamps on Osborne's desk. He said suddenly: "What's that, stamps?"

"Yes. Won't you please—"

The stout man shook his head. "No, I'll wait. Do you expect Mr. Kirk soon?"

"I can't say exactly. He should be back in a short time."

"Thank you, thank you. If I may—" He started toward one of the armchairs.

"If you'll wait in here, please," said Osborne. He went to the second of the two doors, opening into the office, and thrust it open, disclosing a room now dark in the closing dusk. He switched on a light above a bookcase just inside to the right, revealing the room from which Miss Diversey had filched the tangerine.

"Make yourself comfortable," said Osborne to the stout little man. "There are cigarettes and cigars in that humidor on the table; candy, magazines, fruit. I'll let you know the moment Mr. Kirk comes in."

"Thank you," murmured the stranger. "Very kind of you, I'm sure. This is pleasant," and he sat down, still bundled up to the neck, in a chair near the table. "Quite like a club," he said, nodding in a pleased way. "*Very* nice. And all those books, too." Three walls of the room were covered with open bookshelves, interrupted only by the doors on opposite walls and an artificial fireplace on the third, above which hung two crossed African spears behind a battered *Impi* war-shield. The fourth wall, broken up by two windows, held the reading table. Deep chairs stood before the bookcases like sentinels.

"Yes, isn't it," said Osborne in a dry voice, and he went back to the office, shutting the door behind him just as the stout little man sighed comfortably and reached for a magazine.

Osborne picked up the telephone on his employer's desk and called the Kirk suite. "Hello! Hubbell." He spoke irritably. "Mr. Kirk in?"

Hubbell's whining English voice said: "No, sir."

"When do you expect him back? There's some one waiting for him here."

"Well, sir, Mr. Kirk just 'phoned saying that he'd be late for the dinner-party and to have his clothes laid out." Hubbell's voice grew shrill. "That's Mr. Kirk all over! Always doing the unexpected, if I may say so, sir. Now here he tells me he'll be in at a quarter to seven and to set a place for 'an unexpected guest,' a Mr. King or Queen or somebody, and—"

"Well, set it, for heaven's sake," said Osborne, and hung up. He sat down, his eyes far away.

At twenty-five minutes past six the office-door opened and Glenn Macgowan hurried in. He was in dinner clothes, and he carried a hat and topcoat. He was smoking a slender cigar rather furiously and his crystal eyes were troubled.

"Still stamps, eh?" he said in his deep voice, flinging his towering length into a chair. "Old Faithful Ozzie. Where's Don?"

Osborne, intent on his album, looked up with a start. "Oh, Mr. Macgowan! Why, I don't know, sir. He hasn't shown up here."

"Damn." The big man chewed an immaculate fingernail. "He's

as unpredictable as next year's Derby winner. I once bet him a thousand dollars he couldn't get to an appointment on time and, by George, I won! Seen Marcella?"

"No, sir. She rarely comes in here, you see, and I—"

"Look here, Ozzie." Macgowan smoked nervously. There was a bigness about him that overflowed the chair. Above his broad shoulders he had a lean face and a high pale forehead. "I've got to see Don right away. Are you sure—?"

Osborne was astonished. "But won't you see him this evening at dinner, sir?"

"Yes, yes, but I've got to see him before dinner. Sure you don't know where he is?" said Macgowan impatiently.

"I'm sorry, sir. He left early and didn't say where he was going."

Macgowan frowned. "Let's have a paper and pencil." He scribbled hastily on the sheet Osborne hurried to provide, folded the paper, thrust it into an envelope, which he sealed, and tossed the envelope on Kirk's desk. "You'll see that he gets it before dinner tonight, Ozzie. It's important—and personal."

"Surely." Osborne tucked the envelope into one of his pockets. "By the way, sir, there's something I'd like to show you, if you have a moment."

Macgowan paused at the door. "I'm in a hurry, old chap."

"I'm sure you'll want to see this, Mr. Macgowan." Osborne went to a wall-safe and pulled out a large leather-bound, ledger-like volume. He carried it to his desk and opened it; it was full of mounted postage stamps.

"What's this, something new?" asked Macgowan, with sudden interest.

"Well, here's one item that's new, sir." Osborne pointed out a stamp and handed Macgowan a small magnifying glass from a litter of philatelic tools on the desk.

"Nanking issue of the dragon, eh?" muttered Macgowan, putting the glass to the green-and-rose stamp. "Something wrong with the surcharge, isn't there? By Jove, the bottom character's omitted!"

"That's right, sir," said Osborne with a vigorous nod. "That vertical surcharge ought to read *Chung Hua Ming Kuo*—if that's the way they pronounce it—'Middle Flowery People's Kingdom.' But on this stamp the last character was somehow dropped out, and the 'Kingdom' part's not there. Trouble with Chinese rarities, especially the surcharges, is that you've got to have a good working knowledge of the ideographs to be able to spot an error. This one's comparatively easy; *I* don't know Chinese from Greek. But old Dr. Kirk read this for me. Interesting, eh, sir?"

"Damnably. Where did Don pick this up?"

"Auction. About three weeks ago. Delivery was held up for some reason until yesterday. I think they were checking up its authenticity."

"He has all the luck, darn him," grumbled Macgowan, setting down the glass. "I haven't run across a really interesting local rarity in weeks." He shrugged and then said in an oddly quiet voice: "Did this Nanking set Don back much, Ozzie?"

Something tightened Osborne's lips, and his eyes grew cold. "I really couldn't say, sir."

Macgowan stared at him, and then suddenly slapped his thin back. "All right, all right, you loyal old coot. Don't forget that note. You tell Don I dropped in early purposely. I'll be back in time for dinner. Want to go downstairs and make a few calls."

"Yes, Mr. Macgowan," said Osborne with a smile, and returned to his desk.

It was extraordinary how events ranged themselves that evening. Everything seemed to fit, like a woman's new gloves. There was a smoothness, an inevitability, about things. And they all swirled about the head of poor Osborne, a colorless midge working at his job.

And all the time the door to the anteroom was closed, and nothing but silence came from there.

It was exactly 6:35, for example, when the office-door opened again and brought Osborne's head up sharply. A tall magnificent woman was consciously framed in the doorway, a smile on her red lips. Osborne climbed to his feet, more than half-annoyed.

"Oh," said the woman, and the smile vanished. It was as if she had put it on for the ceremony of making an entrance. "Mr. Kirk isn't here?"

"No, Miss Llewes."

"Isn't that disgusting!" She leaned against the open door thoughtfully, her green eyes studying the room. She was dressed in something tight and shimmering. Her bare arms protruded from beneath a short ermine wrap. There was a deep cleft between her breasts which tightened and loosened with her slow breathing. "I did want to talk to him."

"I'm sorry, Miss Llewes," said Osborne. To him there was something infinitely more substantial, if less delectable, in Miss Diversey. This woman was as unreal as a Garbo seen upon the silver screen. One might look, but not touch.

"Well . . . Thank you." She had an unreal voice, too; low and faintly hoarse, with an undercurrent of warmth. Osborne blinked and stared, fascinated, into her green eyes. She gave him a slow smile and vanished.

The two women met outside the office-door under the vigilant gaze of Mrs. Shane, who knew, saw, and heard all. Irene Llewes's ermine brushed the arm of the tiny woman in the black evening gown who had just come from the Kirk suite. The two women halted, frozen still by the same instantaneous surge of dislike. Mrs. Shane looked on with gleaming eyes.

They stared at each other for perhaps fifteen seconds unmoving; the tall woman, slightly inclined; the small woman, eyes raised steadily. Neither said a word. Then Miss Llewes passed on toward the transverse corridor, a glitter of the most mocking triumph in her green eyes. She walked as if it were a sensual pleasure—slowly, with a faint trace of hip-sway.

Jo Temple stared after her, her small fists clenched. There was a challenge very boldly flaunted by the undulation of Miss Llewes's hips.

"You know I can't match that, you cunning devil," said Miss Temple in a silent breath. "You and your sex appeal . . . hussy!"

Then she shrugged, smiling, and hurried into the office.

Osborne looked up again from his work, definitely annoyed. He rose and said: "Mr. Kirk hasn't come in yet. Miss Temple," in a tone of resignation.

"Why, Mr. Osborne!" murmured Jo. "You're positively clairvoyant. How did you know I wanted Donald?"

An unwilling grin came to Osborne's lips. "Well, you're the fourth in a short time, Miss Temple. This seems to be Mr. Kirk's busy day—and he's ducking it."

"And do you think Mr. Kirk would duck me, too?" she murmured, dimpling.

"I'm sure he wouldn't, Miss Temple."

"Now you're merely being polite. Oh, dear! I did so want to speak to him before . . . Bother! Well, thanks, Mr. Osborne. I suppose it can't be helped."

"I'm sorry. If there's anything I can do—"

"Really, it's nothing at all." She smiled and went out.

And just as Osborne sat down with a sigh of relief, the telephone rang.

He snatched it ferociously and barked: "Well?"

"Donald? Felix. Sorry I—"

"Oh," said Osborne. "This is Osborne, Mr. Berne. How are you, sir. Welcome home. Did you have a nice crossing?"

Berne said dryly: "Lovely." There was a faintly foreign something in his voice. "Isn't Kirk there?"

"I expect him any minute now, Mr. Berne."

"Well, tell him I'll be late for dinner, Osborne. Unavoidably detained."

"Yes, sir," said Osborne submissively. And then he shouted in an excess of repressed passion: "Well, why the devil don't you call the apartment?" But he had already hung up.

And then, at 6:45 to the minute, Donald Kirk came striding out of the elevators accompanied by a tall young man in evening clothes who wore *pince-nez* glasses.

There was nothing about Kirk to suggest the young millionaire man-about-town, owner of The Mandarin Press, socially one of New York's most desirable young bachelors. He was dressed in a dowdy tweed suit; his topcoat was unpressed; there was an ink-smudge on one of his thin nostrils; his shoulders drooped; and his hat was a shapeless felt crushed into one of his topcoat pockets. He looked harassed as no young millionaire is popularly supposed to look, and he was smoking a pipe which made Mrs. Shane sniff with disdain.

"Evening, Mrs. Shane. Come along, Queen. Lucky I bumped into you downstairs. Mind if I step into my office for a moment? Be with you in a jiffy."

"Not at all," drawled Mr. Ellery Queen. "I'm just a cog in the machine. Yours to command. What's it all about, anyway, Kirk, old fellow?"

But Kirk was dashing into the office. Ellery sauntered after and leaned against the jamb.

Osborne's frown changed magically to a smile. "Mr. Kirk! Thank heaven you've come back. I'm almost crazy. It's been the busiest afternoon—"

"Detained, Ozzie." Kirk dashed to his desk, shuffled through a heap of opened letters. "Anything important? Oh, excuse me. Queen, meet Jimmy Osborne, my right hand. Mr. Ellery Queen, Ozzie."

"How do you do, Mr. Queen. . . . Well, I don't know, Mr. Kirk. Only a few minutes ago Miss Llewes stopped in—"

"Irene?" The papers slipped from Kirk's fingers. "And what did she want, Ozzie?" he asked slowly.

Osborne shrugged. "She didn't say. Nothing special. Then Miss Temple was in, too."

"Oh, she was?"

"Yes. She just said she'd like to talk to you before dinner."

Kirk frowned. "All right, Ozzie. Anything else? Be with you in a second, Queen."

"Take your time."

Osborne scratched his sandy head. "Oh, yes! Mr. Macgowan was in about twenty minutes or so ago."

"Glenn?" Kirk seemed genuinely surprised. "You mean he dropped in early for dinner, I suppose."

"No, sir. He said he wanted to see you about something urgent. In fact, he left a note for you with me." Osborne dug the envelope out of his pocket.

"'Scuse me, Queen. I can't imagine—" Kirk tore open the envelope and pulled the paper out. He unfolded it quickly and devoured the message with his eyes. And as he read the most extraordinary expression came over his face. It disappeared as swiftly as it had come. He frowned and crushed the paper into a ball, stuffing it into his lefthand jacket pocket.

"Anything wrong, Kirk?" drawled Ellery.

"Eh? Oh, no, no. Just something—" He did not finish. "All right, Ozzie. Close up shop and go home."

"Yes, sir. I almost forgot. Mr. Berne telephoned a few minutes ago and said he'd be a little late. Detained, he said."

"Late for his own party," said Kirk with a wry grin. "That's Felix all over. All right, Ozzie. Come along, Queen. Sorry to have kept you waiting."

They were in the corridor when they were stopped by an exclamation from Osborne. Kirk poked his head back. "What's the matter, for goodness' sake?"

Osborne looked embarrassed. "I'm frightfully sorry. Just slipped my mind. There's a man been waiting in the anteroom there for the Lord knows how long, Mr. Kirk. Came about an hour ago, in fact. He wouldn't tell me who he was or what he wanted, so I stuck him in there to wait."

"Who is he?" asked Kirk impatiently. Ellery strolled back into the room with his friend.

Osborne threw up his hands. "Don't know. Never saw him before. He's certainly never been in this office on business. Tight as they make them. Very confidential matter, he said."

"What's his name? Damn it all, I can't stop to chin now. Who is he?"

"He didn't say."

Kirk gnawed his sunburned upper lip for a moment. Then he sighed. "Well, I'll get rid of him in a moment. Sorry, Queen, old man. Why don't you go into the apartment?"

Ellery grinned. "No hurry. Besides, I'm hopelessly shy. I'll wait."

"There's always somebody wanting to see me," grumbled Kirk, going to the office-door which led to the anteroom, in the wide crack at the bottom of which a line of light was visible. "If it isn't about books, it's about stamps, and if it isn't about stamps, it's about gems. . . . What's this, Ozzie? Door locked?" He looked around impatiently; the door did not budge.

"Locked?" said Osborne blankly. "That can't be, Mr. Kirk."

"Well, it is. The fool, whoever he is, must have bolted it from the other side."

Osborne hurried forward and tried the door. "That's funny," he muttered. "You know yourself, Mr. Kirk, I never keep that door bolted. Why, there isn't even a key to it. Just the bolt on the anteroom side. . . . Why in the world should he have bolted it, I wonder?"

"Anything valuable in there, Kirk?" drawled Ellery, coming forward.

Kirk started. "Valuable? You think—"

"It sounds remarkably like a case of common burglary."

"Burglary!" cried Osborne. "But there's nothing in there that's valu—"

"Let's have a peep." Ellery flung his topcoat, hat, and stick on a nearby chair and knelt before the door on a paper-thin Indian mat. He closed one eye and peered through the unobstructed keyhole. Then he rose, very quickly. "Is this the only door into that room?"

"No, sir. There's another from the other corridor, the one around the corner opposite Mr. Kirk's suite. Is there anything wrong?"

"I don't know yet," said Ellery with a frown. "Certainly there's something deucedly odd. . . . Come along, Kirk. This will bear investigation."

The three men hastened out of the office, to the astonishment of Mrs. Shane, and darted down the corridor. They turned the corner and ran to the left, stopping at the first door across the hall from the Kirk suite, the door Miss Diversey had used more than an hour earlier.

Ellery grasped the knob and turned. It moved, and he pushed; the door was unlocked. It swung inward slowly.

Ellery stood still, impaled by shock. Over his shoulder the faces of Donald Kirk and James Osborne worked spasmodically.

Then Kirk said in a flat shrinking voice: "Good God, Queen."

The room looked as if some giant hand had plucked it bodily from the building, shaken it like a dice-cup, and flung it back. At first glance it seemed in a state of utter confusion. All the furniture had been moved. There was something wrong with the pictures on the wall. The rug looked odd. The chairs, the table, everything. . . .

The goggling human eyes could not encompass more than a certain degree of destruction in one transfixed glimpse. There was primarily an impression of ruthless havoc, of furious dismantlement. But the impression was ephemeral; it could not withstand the single dreadful reality.

Their eyes were dragged to something lying across the room on the floor before the bolted door leading to the office. It was the stiff body of the stout middle-aged man, his bald skull no longer pink but white spattered with carmine, streaks of caked jelly radiating from a blackish depression at the top. He was lying face down, his short fat arms crumpled under him. Two unbelievable iron things, like horns, stuck out from under his coat at the back of his neck.

3. THE TOPSY-TURVY MURDER

"Dead?" whispered Kirk.

Ellery stirred. "Well, what do you think?" he said harshly and took a forward step. Then he stopped, and his eyes flashed from one incredible part of the room to another as if they could not believe what they saw.

"Why, it's murder," said Osborne in a queer interrogatory voice. Ellery could hear the man swallowing rapidly and unconsciously behind him.

"A man doesn't wallop himself over the head with a poker, Osborne," said Ellery, unmoving. They all looked at it without expression; a heavy brass poker, apparently from the rack of firetools before the ornamental fireplace, lay on the rug a few feet from the body. It was daubed with the same red jelly that smeared the stout little man's skull.

Then Ellery stepped forward, walking lightly as if he were afraid to disturb even the molecules of the air in the room. He knelt by the prone figure. There was so much to see, so much more to assimilate mentally. . . . He shut his eyes to the astounding condition of the still little man's clothes and felt beneath the body for the heart. No quiver of arterial life responded to his fingertips. He withdrew his own chilled hand and touched the skin of the man's bland pale face. It was cold with the unearthly cold of death.

There was a suspicion of purple on the face. . . . Ellery touched the dead chin with his fingers and tilted the head. Yes, there was a purplish patch of bruise on the left cheek and the left side of the nose and mouth. He had fallen like a stone to receive the hard kiss of the floor on that side of his face.

Ellery rose and silently retreated to his former position inside the doorway. "It's a question of perspective," he said to himself, never taking his eyes from the dead man. "You can't see much close up. I wonder—" A fresh surge of astonishment flooded his brain. In all the years that he had seen dead men in the fixed surroundings of violence he had never witnessed anything so remarkable as this dead man and the things that had been done to him and to his last resting-place. There was something uncanny about the whole thing, uncanny and horrifying. The sane mind shrank from acceptance. It was unholy, blasphemous. . . .

How long they stood there, the three of them, none of them knew. The corridor at their backs was very quiet. Only occasionally they heard the clang of the elevator-door and the cheerful voice of Mrs. Shane. From the street twenty-two stories below came the whispering sounds of traffic, wafted past the blowing curtains of one of the windows. For a weird moment the thought struck them simultaneously that the little man was not dead but merely taking a humorous rest on the floor, having selected his odd position and the extraordinary disruption of his surroundings out of some inscrutable whim. The thought was born of the benevolent smile on the dead man's fat lips, for his face was turned toward them. Then the impression faded, and Ellery cleared his throat noisily, as if to grasp something real, if only a sound.

"Kirk, have you ever seen this fellow before?"

The tall young man's breath whistled through his nostrils behind Ellery's back. "Queen, I swear I've never seen him before. You've got to believe me!" He clutched Ellery's arm with a muscular convulsiveness. "Queen! It's a ghastly mistake, I tell you. Strangers are always coming to see me. I never saw—"

"Tch," murmured Ellery, "get a stranglehold on your nerves, Kirk." Without turning he patted Kirk's rigid fingers. "Osborne."

Osborne said with difficulty: "I can vouch for that, Mr. Queen. He's never been here before. He was a total stranger to us. Mr. Kirk doesn't know—"

"Yes, yes, Osborne. With all the other appalling things about this crime, I can well believe . . ." He tore his eyes from the prone figure and swung about, a businesslike note springing into his voice, "Osborne, go back to your office and 'phone down for the physician, the manager, and the house detective. Then call the police. Get Centre Street; speak to Inspector Richard Queen. Tell him I'm on the scene and to hurry over at once."

"Yes, sir," quavered Osborne, and slipped away.

"Now, close that door, Kirk. We don't want any one to see—"

"Don," said a girlish voice from the corridor. Both men swung about instantly, blocking her line of vision. She was staring in at them—a girl as tall as Kirk, with a slender immature figure and great hazel eyes. "Don, what's the trouble? I saw Ozzie running. . . . What's in there? What's happened?"

Kirk said in a quick hoarse voice: "Nothing, nothing at all, 'Cella," and jumped out into the hall and placed his hands on his sister's half-bare shoulders. "Just an accident. Go back to the apartment—"

Then she saw the dead man lying on the floor in the anteroom. The color washed out of her face and her eyes rolled over like a dying doe's. She screamed once, piercingly, and tumbled to the floor as limply as a rag-doll.

At once, as if her scream had been a signal, bedlam howled about them. Doors across the corridor flew open and spewed forth people with glaring eyes and moving mouths. Miss Diversey, her cap askew, came padding down the hall. Behind her rolled the tall, hollow-boned, emaciated figure of Dr. Hugh Kirk, his wheelchair trundling swiftly; he was collarless and coatless, and his stiff-bosomed shirt lay open above his gray-haired chest. The tiny black-gowned woman, Miss Temple, came flying out of nowhere to drop on her knees beside the unconscious girl. Mrs. Shane puffed around the corner screeching questions. A bellboy sped past her, looking about wildly. A small bony British-looking man in butler's panoply stared pasty-faced out of one of the Kirk doors as the others milled about the fallen girl, blundering into one another.

In the confusion Ellery, who had not stirred from the doorway, sighed and retreated, closing the door of the anteroom behind him. The sounds became live echoes. He stood guard with his back to the door, just looking at the dead man and the furniture and back at the dead man again. He made no move to touch anything.

The house doctor, a broad squat cold-eyed man, got to his feet with amazement written all over his stony face. Nye, the manager, an elegant creature in a cutaway with a gardenia in his lapel as depressed-looking as himself, was biting his lips beside Ellery at the door. Brummer, the burly house detective, scraped his blue jaws rather pathetically at the open window.

"Well, Doctor?" said Ellery abruptly.

The man started. "Oh, yes. You want to know, I suppose, how long he's been dead. I should say he died at about six—a little over an hour ago."

"From the effects of the blow on his head?"

"Unquestionably. The poker shattered the skull, causing instant death."

"Ah," said Ellery. "That's a most vital point, Doctor—"

"Generally is," said the doctor with a grim smile.

"Ha, ha. There's no doubt in your mind about death having been instantaneous?"

"My dear sir!"

"I beg your pardon, but we must be sure. And the bruise on his face?"

"Caused by his fall, Mr. Queen. He was dead when he struck the floor." Ellery's eyes flickered, and the physician moved toward the door. "I'll be glad, of course, to repeat my opinion to your Medical Examiner—"

"Scarcely necessary. By the way, there couldn't be a different cause of death, I suppose?"

"Nonsense," said the squat man with asperity. "I can't say without a physical examination and autopsy what other signs of violence exist, but death occurred from the effects of the cranial blow, take my word for it. All the external indications—" Something gleamed in his cold eyes. "See here, you mean that the blow on the skull may have been inflicted after death from a different cause?"

"Some such idiotic notion," muttered Ellery, "was in my mind."

"Then get it out of your mind." The physician hesitated, struggling with an ingrained professional reticence. Then he shrugged. "I'm not a detective, Mr. Queen, and this sort of thing is decidedly out of my line. But if you're looking for something odd, may I point out the condition of this man's clothing?"

"Clothing? Yes, yes, point it out, by all means. I can't say, at this stage of the game, that I should disdain the viewpoint of even a layman."

The doctor eyed him sharply. "Of course," he said in a steel-barbed rasp, "with all your experience—I've heard of you, Queen—I suppose the condition of this man's clothing and its possible significance is childishly clear. But to my infantile mind it seems rather remarkable that—*he's got all his clothes on backwards*!"

"Backwards?" said Nye with a groan. "Oh, good Lord."

"Didn't you notice, Mr. Nye?" rumbled Brummer, scowling. "Damnedest thing *I* ever saw."

"Please, gentlemen," murmured Ellery. "Specifically, Doctor?"

"His coat is on as if he'd got into it the wrong way, as if somebody held it open facing him and he wriggled into the sleeves and then buttoned himself up the back."

"Masterly! Although not necessarily an exclusive diagnosis. Go on, sir."

Brummer said peevishly: "Why in hell should a man put his coat on backwards? It's nuts."

"A strong word, Brummer, but inept. 'Improbable' would be more to the point. Did you ever try to put *your* coat on backwards?"

"I don't see—" began the detective belligerently.

"Apparently not. I should explain that the improbability lies not in the donning of the coat, but in the buttoning."

"How d'ye figure that?"

"Do you think you could put your coat on backwards and button it up yourself, with the buttons studding the vertebrae along your spinal column? And the inverted, wrongly placed sleeves hampering the elevating possibilities of your arms?"

"I got you. Sure I could."

"Well, perhaps so," sighed Ellery. "Proceed, Doctor. Pardon the aside."

"You'll have to excuse me," said the doctor abruptly. "I merely wished to call your attention—"

"But I assure you, Doctor—"

"If the police want me," continued the cold-eyed man with a

faint emphasis on the third word, "I shall be in my office. Good evening!" And he stumped past Ellery out of the room.

"A clear case of the frustration psychosis," said Ellery. "Fool!"

The door clicked behind the physician in a dismal silence. They regarded the corpse with varying expressions—Nye glassily, Brummer gloomily, and Ellery with a furious frown. The pervading impression of unreality persisted. Not only was the dead man's coat on backwards, but his trousers were inverted and buttoned up behind as well. As were his white madras shirt and vest. His narrow stiff collar similarly was turned about, clamped with a shiny gold collar-button at the nape. His undergarments apparently exhibited the same baffling inversion. Of all his clothing only his shoes remained in the orthodox position.

His topcoat, hat, gloves, and woolen scarf lay on a chair near the table in a tumbled heap. Ellery sauntered to the chair and picked up the scarf. On one edge in the middle of the scarf were several bloodstains. A tiny stain, hardened to a crust, also existed at the back of the topcoat collar. Ellery dropped the garments with a frown and bent low, searching the floor. He could find nothing. No—yes, there was a splatter that might have been blood on the hardwood surface of the floor beyond the edge of the rug! Near the chair . . . He went quickly to the far side of the room and bent over the dead man. The floor about him was clean. Ellery rose and stood back, followed by the dull glances of the two men. The dead man lay parallel with the sill of the door, roughly between the two bookcases which flanked the doorway. The case to the left, as he faced the door, had been pulled from its original position flat against the wall so that its left side touched the hinges of the door and its right side swung out into the room, the shifted bookcase forming an acute angle with the door. The body lay half behind it. The case to the right had been moved farther to the right.

"What do *you* make of it, Brummer?" asked Ellery suddenly, turning around. There was no irony in his tone.

"I tell you it's nuts," exploded Brummer. "I never seen nothin' like it in all my born days, an' I pounded a beat, Mr. Queen, when your father was a Captain in his precinct days. Whoever pulled this ought to been put in the booby-hatch."

"Indeed?" said Ellery thoughtfully. "If not for one remarkable fact, Brummer, I should be tempted to agree. . . . And the gentleman's horns? You explain those, also, by the general irrationality of the murderer?"

"Horns?"

Ellery gestured toward the two iron points protruding from beneath the dead man's coat at his back. They were the broad flat pointed blades of African spears. As the man lay face down, the outline of the hafts bulged under his clothes. Apparently the spears had been thrust up his trousers at the back of the foot, one to each leg, rammed up and out at the waist, and pushed under the reversed coat at the man's back until they emerged from the V-shaped lapels. The butts of the spears were flush with the dead man's rubber heels. Each weapon was at least six feet in length, and the blades gleamed high above the bald bloody skull. The spears under the tightly buttoned trousers and coat gave the dead man a curious appearance: for all the world like a slain animal which had been trussed up and slung upon two poles.

Brummer spat out the window. "Cripe! Gives you the creeps. Spears. . . . Say, listen, Mr. Queen, you got to admit it's nuts."

"Please, Brummer," murmured Ellery with a wince, "spare us these repetitions. The spears, I confess, are difficult. And yet I've found that nothing in this world is incapable of explanation if only one is smart enough or lucky enough to think of it. Mr. Nye, are these *Impi* stickers the property of the hotel? I'd no idea our better hostelries went in for primitive decoration."

"Heavens, no, Mr. Queen," said the manager quickly. "They're Mr. Kirk's."

"Stupid of me. Of course." Ellery glanced at the wall above the fireplace. The African shield had been turned face to the wall. Four lines of lighter shade than the paint on the wall came out behind the inverted shield like the arms of an X. The spears had undoubtedly hung there, and the murderer had wrenched them from the wall.

"If I had any doubts about the nuttiness of this bird," growled Brummer doggedly, "I'd lose 'em when I took a look at the furniture, Mr. Queen. You can't get around that, can you? Only a lunatic would 'a' tossed all this fine expensive stuff around this way. Now, what the hell for, I ask you? Everything's cockeyed. There's no rhyme or reason to it, as the feller says."

"Brummer's right," said Nye with another groan. "This is the work of a madman."

Ellery regarded the house detective with honest admiration. "Brummer, you've placed that horny finger of yours on the precise point. Rhyme and reason. Exactly." He began to pace up and down. "That's exactly it. It stuck in my craw from the moment I walked onto this fantastic scene. Rhyme!" He snatched off his *pince-nez* and waved them about, as if he were trying to convince himself more than Brummer and Nye. "Rhyme! There's rhyme here that utterly defies analysis, that staggers the imagination. If there were no rhyme I should be pleased, very pleased. But rhyme—there's so much of it, it's so complete and so perfect, that I doubt whether there has ever been a more striking example of it in the whole history of logic!"

Nye looked bewildered. "Rhyme?" he echoed stupidly. "I don't see what you mean."

"You mean about the furniture, Mr. Queen?" asked Brummer, knitting his black brows painfully. "It just looks all—well, all messed up to me. Some nut went to a hell of a lot of trouble to wreck this room. I don't see—"

"Oh, heavens," exclaimed Ellery, "you're blind, both of you. What do you mean, Brummer, by 'messed up'?"

"You can see, can't you? Knocked around, shoved out of place."

"Is that all? Lord! You don't see anything broken, do you? Smashed? Demolished?"

Brummer coughed. "Well, no, sir."

"Of course you don't! Because this wasn't the work of a wrecker. It was the work of some one with a cold purpose, man, with a purpose worlds removed from mere stupid destruction. Don't you see that yet, Brummer?"

The detective looked miserable. "No, sir."

Ellery sighed and replaced his glasses upon his thin nose. "In a way," he muttered half to himself, "this becomes valuable exercise. Lord knows I need . . . Look here, Brummer, old fellow. Tell me what you see about the bookcases that strikes you as—ah— 'messed up.'"

"Bookcases?" The house detective regarded them doubtfully. They were sectional cases of unfinished oak; the odd thing about them was that they stood, for the most part neatly, arrayed on all three walls with their closed backs facing into the room. "Why, they're turned around to face the walls, Mr. Queen."

"Admirable, Brummer. Including," Ellery frowned in a puzzled way, "the two sections flanking the doorway to the office there; although I note with baffled interest that the section to the left of the door has been pulled in front of the door and turned on an acute angle into the room for a bit. And that the one to the right has been shoved off to the right. Well! How about the rug?"

"It's been turned over, Mr. Queen."

"Precisely. You're gazing at the back. And the pictures on the walls?"

Brummer's face was brick-red now, and his reply came in a sullen mutter. "What you drivin' at, anyway?"

"Any notion, Mr. Nye?" drawled Ellery.

The manager raised his padded shoulders. "I'm afraid I'm not very good at this sort of thing, Mr. Queen," he said in a soupy voice. "All I can concentrate on right now is the terrible scandal, the notoriety, the—the—"

"Hmm. Well, Brummer, since this has turned out to be a demonstration, let me expound the gospel of Rhyme." He took out a cigaret and lit it thoughtfully. "The bookcases have been turned around to face the wall. The pictures have been turned around to face the wall. The rug on the floor has been flipped over to lie face down. The table, which has a drawer—you can see that by the two cracks at the back—has been turned around to face the wall. That grandfather clock over there has been turned around to face the wall. These very comfortable chairs have been turned around so that the backs are forward and the seats face the wall. That floor-lamp of the bridge variety has been turned around so that the shade faces the wall. The large lamp and the two table lamps have been turned upside down to rest precariously upon their shades and to wave their nude bases in the air. Turned around, turned around!" He puffed a sharp billow of smoke at the detective. "Well, Brummer, what do these make *in toto*? Put them all together and they spell what?"

Brummer glared, baffled.

"Rhyme, Brummer, rhyme! Rhyme of the couplet variety. There's a monotonous regularity about this rhyme that simply astounds me. Don't you see that not only have the dead man's clothes been removed and replaced on his body backwards, but that *the furniture and everything else of a movable nature in this room have also been turned backwards*?"

The two men gaped at him.

"By God, Mr. Queen," cried Brummer, "you've hit it on the snoot!"

"By God, Mr. Brummer," said Ellery grimly, "there's rhyme here that will write detectival history when this case is solved—if it ever is. Everything is backwards! Everything. Not just one movable object, mind you, or two or three, but everything. There's your rhyme. But how," he muttered, beginning to stride about again, "how about the *reason*? Why *should* everything have been turned backwards? What is it intended to convey, if it's intended to convey anything at all? Why, Brummer; eh?"

"I don't know," said the detective in a hushed voice. "I don't know, Mr. Queen."

Ellery paused in his stride to stare at him. Nye slumped against the door in an attitude of complete befuddlement. "Nor do I, Brummer," said Ellery from behind clenched teeth, "yet."

4. MR. NOBODY FROM NOWHERE

INSPECTOR QUEEN was a little bird of a man—a gray-plumed and rather aged bird with a bird's uncanny unwinking eyes and a stiff gray mustache under a small beak that might have been chiselled out of horn. He possessed, too, something of the bird's capacity for freezing into stone when the occasion called for immobility, and a quick pattering gait like the hop of a bird when action was demanded. And at those times when he stepped out of character and did not growl, he even cheeped. Large red men had been known to quail at his gentlest chirp, however, since there was something formidable about the old gentleman's very birdliness, as it were; so that the detectives under his wing feared as well as loved him.

Now they feared far more than they loved, for his chirp had a harsh crackle in it that bespoke irritation. It was all very well for the due process of a murder investigation to be under way, with his men running over the room like a pack of sniffing dogs; but the annoying puzzle of the crime that was backwards kept staring him disagreeably in the face. He felt an unaccustomed futility.

He directed operations absently, from long habit; and all the while the fingerprint detail were spraying the room, the official photographer was snapping the body and the furniture and the door, Assistant Medical Examiner Prouty was kneeling beside the dead man, and the homicide men under Sergeant Velie were gathering names and statements, the old gentleman was wondering how on earth a mere cop could be expected to find plausible reasons for the shockingly implausible phenomena of this murder-case. He was too cautious to dismiss without reflection the topsy-turvy nature of the clues as purposeless vagaries of an insane mind. But what else was a man to think?

"What do *you* think, son?" he snapped to Ellery while his men filled the room with their clatter.

"I don't think anything yet," Ellery said impatiently. He was staring morosely at his cigaret as he leaned against the sill of the open window. "No, that's not honest. I'm thinking a host of things, most of them so abominably far-fetched that even I hesitate to go to work on them."

"Must be pretty far-fetched in that case," grunted the Inspector. "I'm going to forget all about this crazy backwards business. It's too much for my simple brain. I'll go to work the usual way—identity, connections, motive, alibis, availability, possible witnesses."

"Good luck," murmured Ellery. "That's sensible. But if you should collar the chap who did this amazing job right now I'd still want to know what the reason for the backwards folderol is."

"You and me and the Commissioner, too," said the Inspector grimly. "Ah, Thomas. What have you got from those people?"

Sergeant Velie loomed before them. "This thing," he announced in his cavernous voice, which held a note of wonder, "is the darbs."

"Well?"

"This bird Nye, the house manager, never saw the stiff before, *he* says. Nor any of the clerks or hops. He wasn't stayin' at the Chancellor here, that much is sure. One of the elevator-men remembered takin' him up in his car around a quarter to six, and this fat old dame Mrs. Shane on the floor here directed him to Kirk's office. He asked for Kirk by name—Donald Kirk, he said."

"Kirk's always receiving strangers," said Ellery absently. "He uses these two rooms as an auxiliary office. He's a collector of postage stamps and precious stones, dad."

"One of *them*," sniffed the Inspector. "Publisher, isn't he?"

"The Mandarin Press was founded by his father—that howling old buzzard with chronic rheumatism—but the old man's been retired for years and Kirk and Felix Berne, who was taken into partnership by Dr. Kirk toward the end of his regime, run the Press now. Don handles all the really private matters connected with The Mandarin right here."

"Sweet layout! Books, stamps, and bawbies. Well, Thomas what are you waiting for?"

"Well," said the gigantic Sergeant hastily, "Mrs. Shane told the fat little duck where to go and he went. Miss Diversey, Dr. Kirk's nurse, was in the office with Osborne, Kirk's assistant. She heard the little guy ask for Kirk, then she lammed. He wouldn't tell Osborne what he wanted or anything, so Osborne showed him in here through the communicatin' door there and left him, closin' the door. And that's the end of the little fat guy."

"You know the rest, dad," said Ellery with a gloomy nod. "We found the door bolted when we tried it from the office side. Bolted from inside this room, as you can see."

The Inspector eyed the only other door, the one to the corridor, and then looked over Ellery's shoulder. "Nothing doing on the windows," he muttered. "Only a human fly could climb up here from that setback, and human flies aren't murderin' anybody this season. Not even a ledge out there. So it's the corridor-door. Did you take a good look at that bolt, Thomas?"

"Sure. It's well oiled and doesn't make any noise at all when you shove it over. No wonder Osborne didn't hear it goin' into place. He's a kind of studious guy, anyway, an' he says he was workin' on Kirk's stamps, so he didn't hear anything."

"You'd think," snapped the Inspector, "he'd hear all this furniture being shoved around!"

"Pshaw, dad," said Ellery wearily, "you know Osborne's type as well as I do. If he was occupied doing something during the murder-period, you may be sure he was deaf, dumb, and blind. He's as loyal to Kirk as a woman in love, and he's fanatically devoted to Kirk's interests."

"All right, all right, so it's this hall-door," said the Inspector. "What did you find out about the emergency stairway, Thomas?"

"It's at the end of the hall outside here, Inspector. Way down the corridor across from the rear of the Kirk apartment. Fact, the door to the stairway is right opposite old Kirk's bedroom. Anybody could have come up or down the stairs, popped into the hall, sneaked down past the Kirk rooms to this door, pulled the job, and made a getaway the same way."

"And Mrs. Shane near the elevators couldn't see any one in that case, hey? The cross-hall's out of her line of vision except where the two meet?"

"That's right. She said anyway she didn't see anybody in this part of the floor after the dead guy came up, except that nurse, that Miss Temple" the Sergeant consulted a notebook, "a woman by the name of Irene Llewes—both guests here—and a Mr. Glenn Macgowan, Mr. Kirk's pal. They all went into the office, chinned with Osborne, and went out again. Macgowan took the elevator down. The Llewes woman went off toward the Kirk apartment; she didn't go in, though, so she probably took those stairs down—her rooms are on the floor below. Miss Temple went back to the Kirk apartment—she's a guest of Kirk's. So did the nurse. Seems this Miss Diversey'd stopped in this anteroom before she went to the office; said it was neat as a pin. Well, that's all, Inspector. Nobody else. So it looks like whoever pulled this job used those stairs, and never even showed up around the corner so this Shane dame could see him."

"That is," said the Inspector nastily, "*if* whoever pulled this job doesn't belong in the Kirk apartment."

"That's the way I figure it, too," rumbled the Sergeant with a scowl. "And I figure the killer bolted that office-door to keep Osborne or whoever else might be in there from interruptin' him while he was doin' his hocus-pocus with the furniture in here."

"And locked the corridor-door, too, I s'pose, for the same reason," nodded the Inspector, "although we'll probably never know. When he was through he went out that way, leaving the door closed but unlocked, the way it was found. Didn't bother to unbolt that door to the office. Maybe he figured it would give him more time for the getaway. Well!" He sighed. "Anything else?"

Ellery puffed at his sixth cigaret. He was listening very intently for all his air of abstraction. His eyes he kept riveted on the kneeling figure of Dr. Prouty, the Assistant Medical Examiner, busy with the dead man.

"Yes, sir. Osborne and Mrs. Shane told me about the others comin' in and out. Mrs. Shane also backed up Osborne when he said that from the time the little guy came until Mr. Kirk and Mr. Queen arrived he—that's Ozzie, they call him—didn't leave the office even once. So—"

"Yes, yes," murmured Ellery. "It's quite obvious that the murderer had to come in and leave the anteroom through that corridor-door." There was something impatient in his tone. "Now how about the man's identity, Velie? Surely there's something there? I scarcely touched the man's clothing."

"Ha," said Sergeant Velie in his volcanic basso, "there's something else that's screwy about this crime, Mr. Queen."

"Eh?" said Ellery, staring.

"What's this, Thomas?"

"No identification."

"What!"

"Nothin' in the pockets, Mr. Queen. Not a scrap of anything. Just some lint, like the stuff that always accumulates in a guy's pockets. They're goin' to analyze but it won't do 'em any good. No tobacco spillings—he evidently didn't smoke. Just nothin'."

"Rifled, by George," murmured Ellery. "Odd! I wonder—"

"I'm going to have a look at those duds," growled the Inspector, lunging forward. "The labels—"

Sergeant Velie's girder-like arm stopped him. "No use, Inspector," he said sympathetically. "There ain't any." The Inspector glared. "I'm tellin' you! They've all been cut out."

"Well, I'll be damned!"

Ellery said thoughtfully: "Odder still. I'm beginning to feel a vast respect for our friend the basher. Thorough, isn't he? Velie, do you mean to say that there's nothing, nothing at all? How about the underwear?"

"Plain two-piece. No lead there. Labels gone."

"Shoes?"

"All the numbers are scratched out and inked in with some of that indelible ink from the desk there—India ink."

"Amazing! Collar?"

"Same. Couldn't possibly tell the laundry-marks. Same on the shirt, too." Velie's gargantuan shoulders twitched. "It's the darbs, like I was telling you, Mr. Queen. Never saw anything like it."

"Every effort, unquestionably, to keep the victim's identity untraceable," muttered Ellery. "And *there's* a sticker. Why, in the name of an illogical God? Rips out the labels, inks out identifiable marks on laundry and shoes, removes all contents of the man's pockets—"

"If there were any," grunted the old gentleman.

"Amended. All the clothing is cheap and seems new. Might be a lead there. . . . Ho! What's this?"

They looked at him, startled. He had snatched off his glasses and was staring incredulously at the dead man. "His necktie—it's gone!"

"Oh, that," shrugged Velie. "Sure. We saw that. Didn't you?"

"No. I hadn't noticed it before. That should be important, vitally important!"

"Sure looks it," said the Inspector, frowning. "With the necktie missing, then the fool or genius or maniac or whatever he is that pulled this job took it away with him. Now why the devil did he do that?"

"You can search me," said the Sergeant blankly. "I think it's just screwy, the whole thing. Gimme a good clean simple mob kill!"

"No, no," said Ellery in an irritable tone, "that's not the tack at all, Velie. It's not crazy; it's clever. It has meaning. Why did he take the tie away? There's a question." He mumbled furiously to himself. "Obviously, because even with its label torn out—to reduce it to its most advantageous terms—it must still have been identifiable! Traceable."

"But how could that be?" snorted the Inspector. "That doesn't make sense. How could you trace a cheap tie?"

"Maybe it was made out of a special kind of goods," suggested the Sergeant hopefully, "that would be easy to trace back."

"Special kind? That would make it an expensive one." The Inspector shook his head. "You couldn't imagine that fat little grampus with his cheap get-up wearing an expensive tie. No, it's not that." He threw up his hands. "Well, I don't know what to make of it. It's got me sunk. . . . Well, Hesse?"

A detective grunted something and the old gentleman pattered off. When the Inspector returned he was excited.

"Say, he wasn't smashed near the door at all!" he exclaimed. "We've found blood on the floor near that chair." He thumbed the chair near the table against the wall. "He must have been struck down near the chair."

"Ah, so you've seen that, have you?" drawled Ellery. "Interesting, I must say. Then what the deuce is he doing near the office-door behind that shifted bookcase?"

"The devil!" snarled the old gentleman. "This is getting crazier by the second. Let's see what Doc Prouty has to say."

Dr. Prouty was rising and brushing off his knees. His cloth hat was perched at a rakish angle on his bald head, and faint perspiration gleamed on his forehead. The Inspector sprang over to engage him in furious conversation. Sergeant Velie drifted off to talk to a detective stationed at the corridor-door.

Ellery straightened from the sill, his brow puckered like the skin of a gnome. He stood still for a long time. Then he rapped his right temple with a baffled fist and sauntered toward his father and the doctor. Midway he stopped, very suddenly. Something bright had caught his eye. Scattered pieces of brightness on the table. . . . He went to the table. The bowl of fruit, like everything else on the unpolished wood, had been turned upside down. Beside the bowl lay the ragged fragments of the rind of a tangerine, and a few dry pips. Vaguely he recalled seeing them before. . . . He lifted away the overturned bowl and studied the exposed fruits. Pears, apples, grapes. . . .

Without turning he said: "Sergeant." Velie came lumbering back. "Didn't you say that the nurse, Miss Diversey, had testified to entering this room a few minutes before the arrival of the—the devil! the dead man?"

"Why, sure."

"Fetch her like a good chap. No noise about it want to ask her something."

"Sure, Mr. Queen."

Ellery waited quietly. When Sergeant Velie returned a moment later he had in tow the tall nurse, her face quite pale. She kept her eyes averted from the corpse.

"Here she is, Mr. Queen."

"Ah, Miss Diversey." Ellery turned. "You were in this room, I understand, at about five-thirty this evening?"

"Yes, sir," she said nervously.

"Did you notice this fruit-bowl, by any chance?"

Something startled leaped into her eyes. "Fruit? Why—yes, sir. In fact, I—I helped myself to a piece."

"Splendid!" smiled Ellery. "That's better luck than I could have hoped for. And did you notice the tangerines particularly?"

"Tangerines?" She was frightened now. "I—I ate one."

"Oh." Disappointment showed plainly on his face. "Then these fragments of rind are from the tangerine you ate?" He indicated the peelings.

Miss Diversey stared at them. "Oh, no, sir. I threw mine, pits and all, out that open window there."

"Ah!" Disappointment vanished to be replaced by eagerness. "Did you notice how many tangerines were left after you had taken one?"

"Yes, sir. Two."

"That's all, Miss Diversey," murmured Ellery. "You've been most helpful. All right, Sergeant."

Velie grinned vaguely and led the nurse away.

Ellery turned back to stare with remarkable interest at the cluster of whole fruits on the table. There was only one tangerine.

5. ORANGES AND SPECULATIONS

DR. PROUTY was saying in a blast of words that shot past the foul black cigar between his teeth: "Well, that's all I can tell you, Inspector. Can't add a damn' thing to what this house doctor told you," when Ellery stalked up to them and said over the Assistant Medical Examiner's shoulder: "Dad, get some quiet here, will you?"

The old man stared at him. "What's buzzing in your bonnet now?" He raised his voice. "Keep still a minute, you men!"

Silence fell.

"Gentlemen," said Ellery in a low voice, "I'm going to ask you a ridiculous question. But I want it answered just the same. Has any one of you taken anything from that bowl of fruit on the table?"

The men gaped. No one replied. The Inspector scuttled to the table and glared down at the orange peelings and the dry pips. "Nobody swiped a tangerine?"

They shook their heads vigorously.

"That's all," murmured Ellery. He motioned his father and Dr. Prouty closer. "I've been able to establish that there were two tangerines in that bowl only a few minutes before the victim was shown into this room. Now there's only one. Curious, eh?"

Dr. Prouty took the dead cigar out of his mouth. "Curious? What the devil's curious about it, Queen?" Then his eyes glittered. "Oh! You mean poison?"

"Heavens, no. Nothing so *outré*. I'll accept your own good

56

word that our friend Mr. Nobody died of a particularly vicious swipe on the skull. But it *is* curious—considering certain other complementary facts."

"As for instance?"

Ellery shrugged. "We're not ready for theorizing yet. I suggest, however, that you keep those tangerine peelings in mind."

"But why, for cripe's sake?" snorted the Inspector. "You mean you think the murderer stopped for a little snack of orange after he got through cracking the little feller's head?"

"Possibly," muttered Ellery. "Although it's much more likely that the little feller stopped for a snack of orange just before the murderer went about the head-cracking business."

"Easy enough to test that," said Dr. Prouty, reaching for his bag. "I'll give you a quick autopsy. If he ate the orange I'll find it in his tummy—and a nice fat tummy it is, gentlemen! Nicest little tummy I've seen in ages. . . . Here's the order, Inspector. I suppose the Morgue bus'll be here as soon as the boys get through with their crap game." He handed the old man an official slip and loped from the room. In the corridor a sudden thought apparently struck him, for he shouted back: "I'll look for poison anyway, Queen!" and hurried off, chuckling.

Ellery strolled over to the corpse and stared down thoughtfully. The stout man's garments were in disarray after Dr. Prouty's cheerful examination. He had been turned over on his back and now lay staring peacefully up at the ceiling. One of the fingerprint men was straddling the body in the act of dusting the door to the office with grayish powder. "If you could only talk," sighed Ellery, "you unlucky little devil! Maybe you could throw some light on all this fantastic criminal exhibitionism. . . . Any prints, old chap?" he asked the fingerprint man.

"Don't look like it, Mr. Queen. There ought to be, though, if the bird that did the job pulled that bolt on the right side of this door. It's nice and oily, and oil makes swell prints. . . . Nope! All wiped off. Hell, we ain't got a thing."

"Nowhere else?"

"I don't know about Kelly there, but I didn't get a thing."

Kelly, working nearby, raised his Irish head and shook it sadly. "Nor me, Mr. Queen. I'd be a damn' sight better off seein' a movie."

Ellery nodded absently. He was roused from his reverie by the sound of Donald Kirk's voice from the doorway.

"I tell you I don't know him," Kirk was crying to the Inspector. Sergeant Velie, colossal Nemesis, tramped behind. "I told Mr. Queen that. I can swear to it. Absolutely a stranger—"

"Well," said the Inspector in a soft voice, "it won't hurt to have another squint at him, will it, Mr. Kirk? Take it easy. Nobody's hounding you. Just one good long look." He shoved the dishevelled young man gently forward.

"Queen!" Kirk lurched toward him. "For God's sake, Queen, I can't stand this persecution any longer. You *know* I never saw him. I told you so! I—"

"Now, now," murmured Ellery, "you've a bad case of nerves, Kirk. There's no need for panic, and no one, of course, is persecuting you. Stiffen up!"

Kirk made two fists and swallowed. "Right," he mumbled. Then he went slowly forward and with an effort looked down. The Inspector watched his face with bright inquisitive eyes. The dead man stared up, smiling his benignant smile. Kirk swallowed again and said in a steadier voice: "No."

"That's fine, that's fine," said the Inspector instantly. "There's only one other thing, Mr. Kirk. This man asked for you by name as if he knew you pretty well. How do you explain that?"

"I've explained all that to the Sergeant here," said Kirk in a weary tone, "until I'm sick of it. There are strangers coming to see me at this office all the time. I collect gems; I'm a specializing philatelist; and I receive a good many people on confidential matters relating to The Mandarin. I can explain this fellow's asking for me by name only on one of these counts."

"You think, then, he's probably a dealer or agent in jewelry or stamps?"

The broad shoulders shrugged. "It's a good possibility. Much better than the book angle. Generally my visitors on publishing business are authors or authors' representatives. This man is neither, so far as I know."

"Stamps and gems." The Inspector sucked the end of his mustache. "Well, that's something, anyway. Thomas!" The Sergeant tramped forward. "Play those leads. Get a quick print from the photographer of this bird's pan and see that it goes through all the stamp and jewelry places. Something tells me he's not going to be easy to identify." Velie lumbered off. "You know, Mr. Kirk," continued the Inspector, squinting at the tall young man, "his pockets have been emptied and all possible identifying marks and labels in his clothes scratched out or removed."

Kirk looked bewildered. "But why—"

"Somebody doesn't want us to know who the victim is. That's a new wrinkle to me in a homicide. Generally the killer makes every effort to keep his own identity a secret. Here's a killer that goes the tribe one better. . . . Well, gentlemen, I don't think there's anything more for us to do here. Mr. Kirk, let's amble over to your rooms and have a little chin-chin with your family."

"Anything you say." Kirk's tone was spiritless. "Although I assure you, Inspector, there can't be any connection between this and any one in my—It's impossible."

"Impossible, Mr. Kirk? That's a strong word. Which reminds me. We'll defer that visit a couple of minutes." The Inspector raised his voice. "Piggott!" One of the detectives bounded forward. "Get a sheet or something from one of the chambermaids and cover up the stiff. Everything but his face."

The detective disappeared.

Kirk whitened. "You're not going to—"

"Why not?" said the Inspector with a disarming smile. "Murder's a hard business, Mr. Kirk, and investigating it's even harder. It's the one business where you come to grips with the real facts of life. And death. Not like collecting stamps or diamonds at all. . . . Ah, Piggy. Good boy. Artistic now; just the pan. Good! Thomas, get everybody from the Kirk apartment in here."

They came in slowly, a silent nervous group. The least perturbed among them seemed Dr. Kirk. The fierce old man was fully dressed now; his white shirt-front glittered angrily from the wheel chair being pushed by a subdued Miss Diversey. His gauntness was amazing; he was like a bony shell filled with fury.

"What's this mumbo-jumbo about a murder?" he was roaring, waving his long skinny arms. "Positively indecent, Donald! Why do you permit us to be dragged into this?"

"Don't make a row, father," said Kirk wearily. "These gentlemen are the police."

Dr. Kirk's white mustache lifted in a snarl. "Police! As if any one with two eyes and ears couldn't tell. Ears particularly. You can always tell a policeman by his indefatigable mangling of the simplest past participles." He turned on the Inspector a pair of iceberg eyes. "You're in charge here?"

"I am," snapped the Inspector. Under his breath he muttered: "And I'll mangle *your* past participles!" Aloud he continued with a savage smile: "And I'll thank you, sir, to quit raising a rumpus."

"Rumpus? Rumpus? Obscene word. Who's raising a rumpus,

may I ask?" growled Dr. Kirk. "What do you want of us? Quickly, please."

"Father," said Marcella Kirk with a frown. She seemed shaken by her experience; her oval face was brilliantly pale.

"Be quiet, Marcella. Well, sir?"

Ellery, Kirk, and Detective Piggott were standing side by side, like a trio of tightly ranked soldiers, before the office-door, concealing the dead man. The fingerprint men, the photographers, had vanished. Except for Sergeant Velie, Detective Piggott and one other officer the men from headquarters who had thronged the room were gone, most of them dispatched by the Sergeant on various investigatory errands. In the corridor outside, in charge of two uniformed men, stood a group of people—Nye, Brummer, Mrs. Shane, a few others—surrounded by clamoring newspapermen.

Sergeant Velie shut the door in their faces.

The Inspector looked his audience over carefully. Marcella Kirk stood beside her father's wheelchair with a restraining hand on his shoulder. Miss Diversey drooped behind. The black-gowned little woman, Miss Temple was eying Donald Kirk with the queerest attention; he seemed unconscious of her scrutiny and stared directly before him. Glenn Macgowan, grimacing with distaste, lounged beside Marcella. And, by herself, in the shimmering tight gown, her eyes quite fathomless, stood Irene Llewes; and she, too, was studying Donald Kirk's face. Behind them all were the valet-butler Hubbell and Osborne, who was trying hard not to look at Miss Diversey.

The Inspector took out his worn snuff-box and thrust a pinch up each slender nostril. He sneezed three times, amiably, and put the box away. "Now, ladies and gentlemen," he began in a genial tone, "a murder's been committed in this room. The body is lying behind Mr. Kirk, Mr. Queen, and Detective Piggott." Their eyes wavered and shrank. "Dr. Kirk, you indicated a moment ago that you wanted no fuss. Nor do we. I'm inviting the man or woman who killed that poor little chap to step forward."

Some one gasped, and Ellery from his vantage-point searched their faces swiftly. But they all looked petrified. Dr. Kirk, his hair standing on end, half-rose in his chair and gasped: "Do you mean—are you insinuating that some one here—Why, this is infamous!"

"Sure is," smiled the Inspector. "That's the hell of murders, Dr. Kirk. Well?"

Their shocked eyes fell.

The Inspector sighed. "All right, then. Step aside, boys." Silently Kirk, Ellery, and Piggott obeyed.

For an instant they glared with fascinated horror at the serene dead face smiling up at them. Then they began to stir. Marcella Kirk swallowed convulsively and swayed, looking ill. Macgowan placed his big brown hand on her bare arm, and she stiffened. Miss Temple shivered suddenly and turned her head away; she did not look at Donald Kirk any longer. Only Irene Llewes seemed unmoved; except for her pallor she might have been staring at a fallen waxworks figure.

"All right, Piggott, cover him up," said the Inspector briskly. The detective stooped and the weird smiling face vanished. "Well, ladies and gentlemen, has any one anything to tell me?" No one replied. "Dr. Kirk!" snapped the old gentleman. The septuagenarian's head came up with a jerk. "Who is this man?"

Dr. Kirk made a face. "I haven't the faintest idea."

"Miss Kirk?"

Marcella gulped. "N-nor I. It's ghastly!"

"Miss Llewes?"

The woman shrugged her magnificent shoulders. "Nor I."

"Mr. Macgowan?"

"I'm sorry, Inspector. I've never seen that face before."

"By the way, Mr. Macgowan, some one told me you're a collector of postage stamps yourself; eh?"

Macgowan looked interested. "Quite so. Why?"

"Have you ever seen this man around the stamp places? Think hard; it may come back to you."

"Never. But what has that—"

The Inspector waved his delicate fingers. "You, there," he said sharply. "The buttling man. What's your name?"

Hubbell was startled. His pasty face became the color of wet sand. "H-Hubbell; sir."

"How long have you worked for Mr. Kirk?"

"Not v-very long, sir."

Donald Kirk sighed. "He's been in my employ a little over a year."

"Please. Hubbell, did you ever see this dead man before?"

"No, sir! No, sir!"

"You're positive?"

"Oh, yes, sir!"

"Hmm. I've got the statements of the rest." The Inspector nursed his chin thoughtfully. "I suppose you all realize what my position is. Here I have a murdered man on my hands who's apparently a total stranger to the lot of you. Yet he came up here and asked for Mr. Kirk, who says he doesn't know him from Adam. Now somebody knew he was in this room and killed him here. The door there to the corridor wasn't locked and anybody could have walked in here, found him, and done the job. The person who did it may even have known he was coming here, and planned the whole thing ahead of time. But murders like this aren't usually committed against strangers. There's a connection between this man and his murderer. . . . I hope you see what I'm driving at."

"Now look here, Inspector," said Glenn Macgowan suddenly in

his deep voice. "It seems to me you're taking our possible part in this affair too seriously."

"And how is that, Mr. Macgowan?" murmured Ellery.

"Why, anybody had access to this room by way of the emergency stairs and this empty corridor. The murderer may be any one of the seven million people in New York! Why one of us?"

"Hmm," said Ellery. "That's always a staggering possibility, of course. On the other hand, has it occurred to you, if we're to take Mr. Kirk's word for it that he never saw the man before, that the murderer—*one of this group*—suggested to the man that he come to see Kirk, with the deliberate intention of involving Kirk?"

The tall young publisher was staring wildly at Ellery. "But, Queen—by God, that can't be true!"

"Any enemies, old chap?" said Ellery.

Kirk's eyes fell. "Enemies? Not that I know of."

"Nonsense," said Dr. Kirk abruptly. "That's piffle, Donald. You've no enemies—not enough brains to make 'em—so who in the world would want to involve you in a murder?"

"No one," said Kirk dully.

"Well!" smiled the Inspector. "You're easily eliminated, Mr. Kirk, if there's any doubt. Where were you at six this evening?"

Kirk said very slowly: "Out."

"Oh," said the Inspector. "I see. Out where?"

Kirk was silent.

"Donald!" roared Dr. Kirk. "Where were you, boy? Don't stand there like a lump!"

There was the most terrifying hush. It was shattered by Macgowan, who took a quick step forward and said in an urgent voice: "Don, old boy. Where were you? It won't go any further—"

"Donald," cried Marcella. "Please, Don! Why don't you—"

"I was out walking all afternoon," said Kirk from stiff lips.

"With anybody?" murmured the Inspector.

"No."

"Where'd you go?"

"Oh—Broadway. Fifth Avenue, the Park."

"As a matter of fact," said Ellery softly in the silence that followed, "I bumped into Kirk in the lobby downstairs. Quite evidently came in from out of doors; eh, Kirk?"

"Of course: Surely."

"I see," said the Inspector, and fumbled for his snuffbox again. Miss Temple turned her head far aside. "All right, ladies and gentlemen," continued the old gentleman in the quietest voice imaginable. "That's all for tonight. Please don't leave town until you hear from me, any of you."

The Inspector nodded to Sergeant Velie, and the Sergeant silently opened the door. They filed out like prisoners, to be swallowed instantly by the reporters.

Ellery was the last to leave. As he passed his father their eyes met. The old man's were inscrutable. Ellery shook his head and went on. In the corridor, smoking indolently, stood two white-uniformed men. They were flicking their ashes into a huge crate-like basket on the floor, regarding the shouting newspapermen with amusement.

"We really," said Marcella Kirk in a small voice when they had escaped the clutches of the press and were assembled in safety in the salon of the Kirk suite, "we really should be having dinner, I suppose."

Old Dr. Kirk roused himself. "Yes, yes, by all means," he said heavily. "A splendid idea, my dear. I'm ravenous. We mustn't—" He stopped short in the middle of the sentence, quite unconsciously. His saturnine face was etched in lines of troubled thought.

"I, too," said Glenn Macgowan quickly with a forced laugh. He gripped Marcella's hand. "I think we've had enough of horrors for one night; eh, darling?"

She smiled up at him, murmured an apology, and hurried out.

Ellery stood in a corner by himself, feeling almost guilty. It was quite as if they considered him a prying interloper, a spy. Dr. Kirk in particular shot venomous glares his way. He felt distinctly uncomfortable. And yet something warned him to stay. There was that one puzzling matter. . . .

Donald Kirk had sunk into a chair, his head on his breast; occasionally he passed his hand with a sort of dazed desperation through his hair. Dr. Kirk, wheeling his chair furiously about the room talking to his guests, shifted his glance from time to time to his son with something pained and uneasy in his icy old eyes. Miss Temple sat very quietly, even smiling a little. Only Irene Llewes made no effort to dissemble. It was as if she, too, felt herself an intruder; and as if, like Ellery, she had her own reasons for remaining where she was not wanted.

Ellery sucked a tortured fingernail and awaited his opportunity. Then, when he thought the moment had come, he crossed the room and sat down in a Queen Anne chair beside Donald Kirk.

The young man looked up with a start. "Uh—Queen. Sorry I'm such rotten company. I don't—"

"Nonsense, Kirk." Ellery lit a cigaret. "I'm going to be honest with you, old fellow. There's something in the wind—the wind blowing your way. Don't have to be an Einstein to arrive at that conclusion. Something's bothering you, dreadfully. You weren't out walking all afternoon, despite the fact that I met you in the lobby; I have a notion your appearance in the lobby was for the benefit of the public." Kirk drew in his breath sharply. "You lied, Kirk, and you know you lied. Why don't you tell the truth and clear yourself? I think you know me well enough to feel assured of my discretion."

Kirk bit his lip and stared sullenly down at his hands.

Ellery studied him for a moment and then sank back, smoking. "Very well," he murmured. "It's apparently something personal. . . . By the way, Kirk, to get back to more mundane things. You were fearfully mysterious with me late this afternoon. Called me up and asked me to climb into my dinner-clothes, amble up here, keep my eyes open—particularly to keep my eyes open. . . ."

The young man shifted in the chair. "Oh, yes," he said tonelessly. "I did, didn't I?"

Ellery flicked ashes into a receiver without taking his eyes off Kirk. "Would you mind elucidating, old man? We'd met casually—scarcely were friendly enough to warrant a sudden dinner invitation with strangers out of the blue—"

"Why?" Kirk wet dry lips. "Why, no special reason, Queen. Just—just a little joke of mine."

"Joke? I'm afraid I don't see the point. Joke to ask me to keep my eyes open?"

"That was just my subtle way of insuring your coming. Matter of fact," continued Kirk in a rapid low voice, laughing hollowly, "I had a deep and dirty reason for getting you up here. Wanted you to meet Felix Berne, my partner. I was afraid you'd refuse if I asked you point-blank—"

Ellery laughed. "So that's it. A professional approach?"

Kirk grinned eagerly. "Yes, yes, that's it. We don't as a rule publish your sort of thing—"

"You're thinking of a different word, I'll wager," chuckled Ellery. "Kirk, I'm astonished. Piracy, by George! I thought publishers had some conception of ethics. Don't tell me you're really thinking of publishing a detective story?"

"Something like that. Times aren't very good in the business, you know. Detective stories enjoy consistently good sales—"

"Don't believe all you hear," said Ellery sadly. "Well, well. I must say I'm bowled over. The great Mandarin Press. What will Harry

Hansen and Lewis Gannett say? And Alec? Even though he does love a good juicy homicide filled with Greeks and one-syllable Anglo-Saxon words? Dear, dear. . . . I don't think my present publisher will care for the idea."

"It was just a thought," muttered Kirk.

"Oh, no doubt," murmured Ellery.

Glenn Macgowan was glancing over at Kirk with a curious uneasiness. Kirk seemed aware of Macgowan's interest and shut his eyes. "I wonder," he mumbled after a time, "where Felix is."

"Berne? Good Lord! I'd forgotten all about him." And then, without warning, Ellery leaned forward and jabbed Kirk's knees. There was a spasmodic jerk and the young man's eyes flew open, bloodshot and frightened. "Kirk," said Ellery softly, "*let me see that note Macgowan left with Osborne for you.*"

"No," said Kirk.

"Kirk, give me that note!"

"No. You've no right asking me. It's—it's personal. Macgowan's my intended brother-in-law. He's virtually one of the family. I can't divulge—"

"Are you being deliberately incoherent," said Ellery, still softly, "or do you mean to imply that his note referred not to you but to some one connected with both of you? To be specific—your sister Marcella?"

Kirk groaned. "For God's sake, no! I didn't mean that. I didn't mean to lie about it. I won't lie. But I won't tell you, Queen. I can't. I'm in—"

The door from the dining-room opened and tall Marcella appeared, followed by pale Hubbell wheeling a portable bar. A tray covered with frosty glasses was on the bar. . . . Kirk muttered an apology and scrambled to his feet. "I need a couple of those," he choked. Hubbell served the ladies.

"That's the first sensible thing you've said this evening, my son," exclaimed Dr. Kirk, wheeling his chair rapidly to the bar. "Hubbell, let me have one of those detestable concoctions!"

"Father," said Marcella, gliding forward. "Dr. Angini said—"

"Hang Dr. Angini!"

The cocktails inspired a slight gaiety. The old man, his thin cheeks flushed, was cynically delightful. He attached himself openly to Miss Llewes, and she was laughing in her low throaty voice. Ellery, looking up from his cocktail, caught a curious expression of distaste on Marcella's face; even Macgowan seemed disgusted. Kirk alone was oblivious; he saw, knew nothing, downing his fourth cocktail without pausing for breath. He had quite forgotten that he was still wearing street clothes—the dowdy tweeds that hung their folds in shame before the black-and-white neatness of the three other men.

Hubbell had disappeared.

And then the door opened and Inspector Queen's slender figure appeared behind a dark stocky man in evening clothes of foreign cut. The newcomer had wicked black eyes and a thin mouth that lay still below a mouse-colored mustache.

"Excuse me," said the Inspector, looking curiously about at the drinking company. "This *is* Mr. Felix Berne, isn't it?"

The dark man said angrily: "I've been telling you! Kirk! Tell this idiot who I am!"

The Inspector's shrewd eyes swept from Kirk to Ellery, caught something in Ellery's disapproving stare, blinked; and the next moment he vanished as suddenly as he had appeared, leaving Berne standing there with his bitter mouth open.

"Welcome home, Felix," said Kirk wearily. "Miss Temple, may I present—"

"Dinner is served," said a colorless British voice, and they turned to find Hubbell standing stiffly in the doorway to the dining-room.

6. DINNER FOR EIGHT

ELLERY FOUND himself seated at the long oval table between Kirk, at his right, and Miss Temple. Diagonally across from him sat Berne, a scowl on his intelligent face. Marcella and Macgowan were neighbors; and Miss Llewes and Dr. Kirk, who sat at the head of the table. Of the eight only Miss Llewes and Dr. Kirk were gay. The old gentleman's angular torso, assisted into the chair by Miss Diversey who had then vanished, genuflected toward his companion with all the rusty vigor of an ancient cavalier. His frosty eyes were no longer frosty; they sparkled with a youthful warmth, bathed in curious lights.

The woman, decided Ellery, was an enigma. She laughed throatily, showing brilliant white teeth; she murmured behind her hand to the old man; she accepted his chuckling sallies with a nonchalant grace that spoke long practice . . . and yet there was something essentially mirthless in her expression and her eyes never lost their wary gleam. Why was she there? That she was a semi-permanent resident of the Chancellor Ellery had learned; she had checked in from nowhere two months before. From the conversation he was able, too, to deduce that before her arrival at the Chancellor she had been unknown to the Kirks; and Berne apparently was meeting her for the first time. She was not native New York, of that he felt certain; there was a Continental air about her, and she spoke glibly of Cannes and Vienna and Cap d'Antibes and the Blue Grotto and Fiesole.

He contented himself with watching her enamelled face and Kirk's. The young man was horribly uneasy. He could scarcely keep his eyes off his father.

And at Ellery's left tiny Miss Temple ate quietly, her long black lashes concealing her eyes.

For a long time no one mentioned the murder. For the most part the dinner was uncompanionable.

Before dinner Felix Berne had made a superficial excuse—an unembroidered apology. He had "been detained"; he was "sorry." He had landed that very morning, it appeared, and "personal affairs" had occupied him "all day." Toward Miss Temple he was neither cold nor cordial: she had been a discovery of Donald Kirk's. Never having met her before and not having read her manuscript, he seemed cynically content to place the burden of critical proof upon his partner's shoulders.

But over the soup Berne suddenly burst into bitter speech. "I don't know why every one's so silent about that ghastly business across the corridor. Why the mystery, Donald? I was stopped at the elevators on this floor by some stupid flatfoot and subjected to the most humiliating cross-examination."

All conversation abruptly ceased. The warm light fled Dr. Kirk's eyes; Miss Llewes became rigid; Jo Temple's lashes curled up; Macgowan frowned; Marcella bit her lip; Donald Kirk became very pale; and Ellery felt his muscles tense.

"Why talk about it?" muttered Kirk. "It's spoiled the evening already, Felix. I'm sorry if—"

Berne's black eyes flicked around the table. "There's something more to this than meets the eye. Why did that irritating little Inspector insist on dragging me into that anteroom of yours and uncovering a basket and showing me the beatific face of a dead man?"

"He did—that?" faltered Marcella.

Ellery said lightly: "That irritating little Inspector, Mr. Berne, happens to be my father. I shouldn't condemn him, you know, for doing his duty. He's trying to identify the body."

The black eyes gleamed with interest. "Ah! I beg your pardon, Mr. Queen. I hadn't caught your father's name. Identify the body? Then the man's unknown as yet?"

"Nobody knows who he is," growled Dr. Kirk with a grumpy look, squirming in his chair, "and what's more nobody cares. At least *I* do not. Come, come, Felix! This is scarcely post-*hors d'oeuvres* conversation."

"I really can't agree with you, Doctor," murmured Miss Llewes. "I find it thrilling."

"You," Ellery heard the tiny woman at his left breathe, "would." But no one else heard.

"I daresay Miss Llewes and I," said Berne with a grim smile, "have the Continental attitude toward such things—a lack of squeamishness. Eh, Miss Llewes? Under the circumstances, Mr. Queen, I'm really sorry I wasn't able to render more assistance. The man was a stranger to me."

"Well," grinned Ellery, "you have company."

There was an interval of silence. Hotel waiters removed the soup plates.

Then Berne said quietly: "I take it you've a—professional interest in this case, Mr. Queen?"

"More or less. I generally dawdle about the fringes, Mr. Berne. I find homicides quite stimulating."

"A curious taste," snapped Dr. Kirk.

"Nor can I say, Mr. Queen," murmured Miss Temple, "that I share your tastes in stimulation, either." She shivered a little. "I still retain an Occidental aversion to death. My friends the Chinese would appreciate your attitude."

Ellery regarded her with a slow dawning of interest. "Your friends the Chinese? Ah, yes. Stupid of me. I'd quite forgotten. You've lived in China most of your life, haven't you?"

"Yes. My father was in the American diplomatic service."

"It's quite true about the Chinese. There's a strain of fatalism in the Oriental make-up that breeds first resignation to human death and then, as a natural development, contempt for human life."

"Nonsense," said Dr. Kirk in a shrill temper, "supreme non-sense! If you were a philologist, Mr. Queen, you would realize that the ideographic origin of—"

"Here, here," murmured Felix Berne, "no lectures, Doctor. We're digressing. I understand the man asked for you, Donald." Kirk started. "Odd."

"Isn't it?" said Kirk nervously. "But, Felix, I assure you—"

"Look here," said Glenn Macgowan from the other end of the table in a harsh voice, "we're making a mountain out of a molehill. Mr. Queen, I understand that you're something of a logician in your attack on crime problems."

"Something," smiled Ellery, "is *the mot juste.*"

"Then surely it's obvious," snapped Macgowan, "that since this man is unknown to any of us, his murder really can't concern any of us? The fact that he was killed on the premises was sheer coin-cidence, even accident."

Hubbell, bending over Marcella's glass with a swathed bottle of sauterne, spilled a few drops of wine on the cloth.

"Oh, dear," sighed Marcella. "Even poor Hubbell's been af-flicted."

The man turned scarlet and effaced himself.

"You mean, of course, Mr. Macgowan," said Miss Temple softly, "that, as you said before, some one followed him here and took advantage of his isolation in a perfectly strange room to—murder him?"

"Why not?" cried Macgowan. "Why look for complications when there's a simple explanation?"

"But, my dear Macgowan," murmured Ellery sadly, "we haven't a simple crime."

Macgowan muttered: "But I don't see—"

"I mean that the killer went in for embroidery." They were very silent now. "He removed the dead man's outer garments and re-clothed him so that his garments clothed the body in the reverse of the normal position. Backwards, you see. He turned every piece of furniture in the room which normally faced *into* the room so that it faced the wall. Backwards again. All movable objects suffered the same inexplicable fate—the lamps, the bowl of fruit—" he paused—"the bowl of fruit," he repeated, "the rug, the pictures, the *Impi* shield on the wall, the humidor. . . . You see, it wasn't merely a question of killing a man. It was a question of killing a man in specific surroundings under specific circumstances. That's why I challenge your theory, Mr. Macgowan."

There was another silence while the fish plates were removed.

Then Berne, who was staring at him with fixed attention, said: "Backwards?" in a surprised voice. "I did notice that things were upset, and his clothes—"

"Twaddle," growled Dr. Kirk. "Young man, you're being in-trigued by an obvious attempt at pure mystification. I can perceive no sensible motive for the criminal's having turned everything backwards except that of creating confusion for the sake of confu-sion. He was making it harder for the police. He was attempting to foster the illusion of a subtle crime to obscure its very *naïveté*. Or else he was a maniac."

"I'm not so sure of that, Doctor," said Miss Temple in her soft voice. "There's something about this—Mr. Queen, what do you think about it? I'm convinced you have some theory to account for this extraordinary crime."

"Generally, yes." Ellery mused, unsmiling, his eyes on the cloth. "Specifically, no. I should say, Doctor, that you'd hit the essential truth about this affair if not for one fact. But that fact, unfortunately, invalidates your argument."

"What's that, Mr. Queen?" asked Marcella breathlessly.

Ellery waved his hand. "Oh, it's nothing sensational, Miss Kirk. It's merely that there is in this crime, far from confusion—as your father maintains—actual *pattern*."

"Pattern?" frowned Macgowan.

"Unquestionably. Had one thing, or two, or three, or even four been turned backwards, I should agree to a certain feeling of confusion. But when *everything* movable has been turned backwards, when *everything* is confused—so to speak—then the confusion takes on meaning *per se*. It becomes a pattern of confusion; no longer, then, confusion at all. Here everything has been confused *in the identical way*. Everything movable has been turned backwards. Don't you see what that suggests?"

Berne said slowly: "Rot, Queen, rot. I don't believe it."

"I have the feeling," Ellery smiled, "that Miss Temple also sees what I mean, Mr. Berne—and perhaps even agrees with me. Eh, Miss Temple?"

"It may be the Chinese part of me again," the tiny woman said with a charming shrug. "You mean, Mr. Queen, that there's something about the crime, or some one connected with the crime, that possesses *a backward significance*? That some one turned everything backwards *to point to* something backwards about some one, if I make myself clear?"

"Jo—Miss Temple," cried Donald Kirk, "you can't believe that. It's—why, it's as far-fetched as anything I've ever heard!"

She glanced briefly at him and he fell back, silent. "It *is* esoteric," she murmured, "but then in China you come to accept queer, queer things."

"In China," grinned Ellery, "you apparently improve even a fine natural intelligence. That's precisely what I do mean, Miss Temple."

Berne chuckled. "This has been worth that foul crossing from Havre. My dear Miss Temple, if your book on China is half so esoteric, I'm afraid we're in for a merry time with the reviewers."

"Felix," said Kirk. "That's not kind."

"Miss Temple," said Miss Llewes in a velvety murmur, "evidently knows what she's talking about. Really brilliant! I don't see how in the world you ever grasped that, Miss Temple."

The tiny woman was pale; one of her small hands on the stem of her wine-glass was trembling.

And Berne said again, in the same cool casual voice: "I thought, Donald, you'd found a new Pearl Buck, but it begins to look as if you've unearthed merely a feminine Sherlock Holmes."

"Damn it!" growled Kirk, stumbling to his feet. "That's the rottenest thing I've ever heard you say, Felix. Take that back—"

"Heroics, Donald?" said Berne, raising his eyebrows.

"Donald!" roared Dr. Kirk. The tall dishevelled young man sank back in his chair, quivering. "Enough of that, Felix! I'm sure you will want to apologize to Miss Temple." There was an iron note in his rumbling voice.

Berne, who had not stirred, murmured: "No offense intended, Miss Temple." But his black eyes glittered strangely.

Ellery coughed. "Uh—my fault entirely. Really my fault." He fingered his wine-glass, studying its clear ruby contents.

"But for heaven's sake," said Marcella in a shrill voice, "*I* can't bear this much longer myself. I *must* know. Jo, you said . . . Mr.

Queen, who could have done such a thing? Left all those backward signs? The murderer? That poor little dead man?"

"Now, Marcella," began Macgowan.

"Not the victim," cooed Miss Llewes. "He died instantly, my dear, or so I've heard."

"Nor the murderer," said Kirk harshly. "No man would be fool enough to leave a clue pointing to himself. Unless he left the clue to point to some one else, some one he—he wanted to frame for the crime. That's a possibility, by God! I'll wager that's it!"

Dr. Kirk was scowling ferociously.

"Or," murmured Miss Temple in a hurried breathless voice, "all that may have been done by some one who came in after the crime, had seen or divined who did it, and took that very complicated way of leaving a trail to the criminal for the police."

"Score again, Miss Temple," said Ellery quickly. "You've the analytical mind *par excellence.*"

"Or," drawled Felix Berne, "the murderer was the Mad Hatter, and he did the whole thing to incriminate the Walrus and the Carpenter. Or might it have been the Cheshire Cat?"

"You will please," thundered Dr. Kirk, his eyes blazing, "stop this nonsensical speculation at once. At once, do you hear? Mr. Queen, I hold you accountable. Strictly accountable! If it is your intention, sir, to hold an inquiry—obviously you're suspicious of all of us—I should appreciate your doing it under official circumstances, and not when you are a guest at my table. Otherwise, I shall be obliged to ask you to leave!"

"Father!" whispered Marcella in a sick voice.

"Father, for heaven's sake—"

Ellery said quietly: "I assure you, Dr. Kirk, I had no such intention. However, since my presence seems undesirable, I'm sure you will excuse me. I'm sorry, Kirk."

"Queen," muttered Kirk miserably, "I—"

Ellery pushed back his chair and rose. In the act of rising he tipped over his wine-glass, and the red liquid splashed over Donald Kirk's tweeds.

"Clumsy of me," murmured Ellery, seizing a napkin with his left hand and dabbing at the stains. "And such excellent port, too. . . ."

"It's nothing, nothing. Don't—"

"Well, good evening," said Ellery pleasantly, and strode from the room leaving a thick and heavy silence behind him.

7. TANGERINE

Mr. ELLERY Queen deposited his ash stick upon his father's desk and applied a match to his third cigaret of the morning. The Inspector's old nose was buried in a heap of correspondence and reports.

"Trouble with you," said Ellery, sinking into the only comfortable chair in the room, "is that you get up so confoundedly early. Djuna told me this morning when I strolled in to breakfast that you hadn't even stopped for a spot of coffee." The Inspector grunted without looking up. Ellery raised his lean arms and stretched, yawning driblets of smoke. "The fact is that *I* had my usual marvelous night's repose. Didn't even hear you crawl out of bed."

"Stop it," growled the Inspector. "When you get so damn' chatty this hour of the morning I know there's something bothering you. Turn off the gas for a couple of minutes and let me run through these reports in peace."

Ellery chuckled and sank back; then he lost his chuckle and stared out through the iron bars. There was nothing especially inspiring about the sky over Centre Street this morning; and he shivered a little. He closed his eyes.

The Inspector's deskman ran in and out and the old gentleman rasped questions over his communicator. Once the telephone rang and the Inspector's voice became a thing of beauty. It was the Commissioner, demanding information. Two minutes later the telephone rang again: the Deputy Chief Inspector. Honey dripped from Inspector Queen's lips; yes, there was progress of a sort; there might be something in the Kirk lead; no, Dr. Prouty had not yet submitted his autopsy report; yes—no—yes. . . .

He flung the receiver down and snarled: "Well?"

"Well—what?" said Ellery drowsily over his cigaret.

"What's the answer? You looked darned pleased with yourself at one stage of the game last night. Any ideas? You always have 'em."

"This time," murmured Ellery, "they exist in abundance. But they're all so incredible I think I'll keep them to myself."

"The original clam." The old gentleman flipped the heaped papers before him with a scowl. "Nothing. Just nothing. I can't make up my mind to believe it."

"Believe what?"

"That an insignificant little squirt like that could just walk into a New York hotel out of thin air."

"No trace?"

"Not even smoke. The boys worked like beavers all night. Of course, it's still pretty early. But from the looks of things . . . I don't like it." He jabbed snuff up his nostrils viciously.

"Fingerprints?"

"I'm having his prints checked with the files this morning. He might be an out-of-town hood, but I doubt it. Not the type."

"There was 'Red' Ryder," said Ellery dreamily. "As I recall the gentleman, he dressed in the finest Bond Street, spoke with an Oxonian accent, and looked like a don. And yet he never saw even the purlieus of Leicester Square. Mott Street, I believe."

"And besides," continued the Inspector, unheeding, "this thing has all the earmarks of a nut kill. Not a mob job at all. Backwards!" He snorted. "When I get my hands on the bird that did this, I'll backwards him to hell and back again. . . . What happened last night, Mr. Queen?"

"Eh?"

"At the dinner. Society, hey? I saw you lapping up the booze," said the old gentleman bitterly. "Turnin' drunk in your father's old age. Well?"

Ellery sighed. "I was evicted."

"What!"

"Dr. Kirk kicked me out. I was abusing his hospitality, it seems, by causing the dinnertable conversation to flow through homicidal and detective channels. That's not done in polite society, it appears. Never so chagrined in my life."

"Why, the doddering old punk, I'll wring his neck!"

"You'll do nothing of the kind," said Ellery sharply. "The dinner did me heaps of good—as did the cocktail—and I learned several things."

"Oh." The Inspector's rage subsided magically. "What?"

"That Miss Jo Temple, who hails from China and points east, is a most astute—even remarkable—young woman. Intelligent. Pleasure to talk with her. I think," he said thoughtfully, "intense cultivation is called for."

The Inspector stared. "What's up your sleeve this time?"

"Tush! Nothing at all. Also that Dr. Kirk—obscene as it may seem—has sinister designs upon the luscious person of Miss Irene Llewes; who in her turn may be designated as the Enigma."

"Talk sense."

"He cultivated *her* last night." Ellery puffed a billow at the ceiling. "Not that I'm accusing the old codger of philandering. That's just the appearance of things. I'm convinced there's a bee of altogether different stripe buzzing about the old gentleman's bonnet. He's not half so grumpily witless as he seems. . . . He seeks surcease with the Llewes wench. Why? A sensational query. I think he suspects something."

"Gah!" said the Inspector in disgust. "When you chatter this way I could strangle you with my bare hands. Listen. What about young Kirk? And this slick-looking article, Berne?"

"Kirk," said Ellery carefully, "is a problem. You know, he asked me to have dinner with his party last night—asked me by 'phone yesterday afternoon. Very mysterious; counselled me to keep my eyes open. After the discovery of the murder he said it had been a joke; hadn't meant anything by it at all. Except some preposterous bilge about getting me up there to meet Berne with an eye to changing publishers. Joke, eh? I think," said Ellery with a shake of his head, "not."

"Hmm. You want to handle him, or shall I put the screws on? He acted damn' funny about his movements yesterday afternoon."

"Lord, no! When will you learn, good Polonius, that you can't get anything out of really intelligent people with *thuggee* methods? Leave that harassed young publisher to me. . . . Berne is difficult. Smart as a whip. From all I've heard about him he combines three major characteristics: an uncanny nose for arty best-sellers, an inhuman facility at contract bridge, and a weakness for beautiful women. Dangerous combination. Don't know what to make of him at all. He was suspiciously late last night for his own party. I'd try to trace his movements yesterday if I were you."

"I'm doing that with the whole bunch. Especially Kirk. There's something slightly stinking there. Well!" The Inspector sighed. "I've started the ball rolling on the stiff all along the line. His clothes are being checked. He's been mugged from a dozen different angles and his photo's going out today over the regular network, complete with physical description. As I said, the boys are working on his movements before he showed at the Chancellor—Missing Persons are helping. Doc Prouty's due soon with the autopsy report. But so far—nothing."

"Aren't you being impatient? There are no fingerprints, I suppose."

"Nothing to amount to anything. Oh, they found a mess of Kirk's and Osborne's and this nurse's around; but that's as it should be. The point is that the door and the poker, the two important places, were wiped clean. Or else the killer wore gloves. Damn the movies!"

Ellery snuggled down in his chair to gaze dreamily at the ceiling. "The more I think about this case," he murmured, "the more fascinated I become. And the more puzzled."

"It's got its points," said the Inspector dryly, "only they're all crazy. The way I look at it, it's a pure question of identification. The very fact that the killer took such pains to conceal his victim's identity indicates that, if we only could find out who the little coot was, we'd be on a hot trail toward the killer. So I'm not worrying."

"Shrewd," said Ellery with an admiring grin.

"We'll find out who this bird is ourselves, or else he'll be identified by some anxious relative. We let the boys snap their cameras all over the place last night after you left, and his smiling pan is in the papers and on the street this morning. Wouldn't be surprised if somebody 'phoned in about him any minute. When that happens, we're on Easy Street."

"Headed, I suppose you mean, for the last round-up. A conclusion and a confidence," drawled Ellery, "in neither of which I can concur." He put his head between his hands and stared at the ceiling. "All that backwards rigmarole . . . remarkable, dad, simply remarkable. I don't think you realize just how remarkable it is."

"I realize how cock-eyed it is," growled the Inspector. "Well, I suppose you're all set to spring the big surprise. Who did it? I don't take any stock in your 'puzzled' cracks."

"No, no, I meant that, dad. I haven't the faintest notion who did it, or for what reason. Not the faintest even in the general sense. Any one of three classes of persons may have turned everything topsy-turvy. The murderer, his possible accomplice, or some cautious blunderer onto the scene of the crime. Of course, the victim's out—he died instantly. I could make out a case against any of the three having done all that hocus-pocus. Yet one of them must have."

"Say," said the Inspector suddenly, sitting erect. "How the devil do we know the fat little bird didn't turn everything topsy-turvy *himself*? He could have done it before he was murdered!"

"And what," said Ellery, rising and going to the window, "became of his necktie?"

"Might have thrown it out the window, or else the killer did. . . . But no, that's wrong," muttered the Inspector. "We searched the setback below the windows and didn't find anything. Couldn't have burned it, either. Fireplace is phony, for one thing; and for another there were no ashes."

"Burning," said Ellery without turning, "is conceivable, for the ashes might have been carried off. But you're wrong on a different count. He was struck on the back of the head. When he was found his coat was on backwards. His topcoat and scarf were off—lying on a chair. There are bloodstains on the collar of the topcoat. That means that when he was struck he was wearing the topcoat. Unless you assume the preposterous theory that his clothes under the topcoat were on backwards at the time he walked into the Chancellor, then you must concede that his murderer turned the clothes around on his body after he was struck and after the stains splashed the collar of his topcoat. If it was the murderer who turned the clothes backwards, then surely it was the murderer who turned all the other things backwards, too."

"So what?"

"Pshaw, nothing at all. I'm in deepest muck. And what do you say to those iron spears stuck up his clothing, eh?"

"Oh, that," said the Inspector vaguely. "That's simply another proof that it's all nutty, the whole business. *Couldn't* be a sensible reason for that."

Ellery scowled out the window without replying.

"Well, you worry about those things. We'll work along the orthodox lines. I tell you this other tripe doesn't mean a damn."

"Everything means something," cried Ellery, wheeling. "I'll wager you a good dinner to a thimbleful of bootleg that when we've solved this case we'll find that the backwards business is at its root." The Inspector looked skeptical. "One thing is certain. Everything was turned backwards to indicate something backwards about something or somebody connected with the dead man. Therefore I'm going to devote my feeble energies to discovering, if I can, everything which possesses a possible backwards interpretation, no matter how trivial or far-fetched it may appear on the surface."

"Good luck to you," grunted the Inspector. "I think you're batty even to bother."

"And as a matter of fact," said Ellery, flushing a little, "there are already several items connected with possible backwards interpretations. What d'ye know about that?"

The old gentleman's fingers paused in the act of raising the lid of his snuff-box. "There *are*?"

"There are. But you," said Ellery with a grim smile, "do your job and I'll do mine. And I do wonder who'll get there first!"

Sergeant Velie barged through the Inspector's door, his derby pushed far back on his leonine head. There was unusual excitement in his hard eyes.

"Inspector! Mornin', Mr. Queen. . . . Inspector, I got a hot lead!"

"Well, well, Thomas," said the Inspector quietly. "Found out who the stiff is, I'll bet."

Velie's face fell. "Nah. No such luck. It's about Kirk."

"Kirk! Which one?"

"The young 'un. Know what? He was spotted in the Chancellor at half-past four yesterday afternoon!"

"Seen? Where?"

"In one of the elevators. I dug up an elevator-boy who remembers takin' Kirk up around that time."

"To what floor, Velie?" asked Ellery slowly.

"He didn't remember that. But he was sure it wasn't the regular floor—the twenty-second. He'd 'a' remembered that, he said."

"Curious logic," remarked Ellery in a dry tone. "Walking along Broadway and Fifth Avenue, eh? That's all, Sergeant?"

"Isn't that enough?"

"Well, stick to him, Thomas," said the Inspector with an abstracted look. "We'll keep that under our hats. Don't want to scare him. But you check that bird's pedigree from the day he was weaned. Got the stamp and jewelry leads covered?"

"The boys are still out."

"Right."

When the door had shivered at Sergeant Velie's parting slam Ellery said with a frown: "And that reminds me. I'd quite forgotten. . . . Have a peep at this." He pulled a crumpled envelope from his pocket and tossed it to the Inspector.

The Inspector looked at him narrowly. Then he picked up the envelope and smoothed it flat. He slipped his thin fingers inside and extracted a sheet of paper. "Where'd you get this?"

"I stole it."

"Stole it!"

"Thereon hangs a tale." Ellery shrugged. "I'm rapidly sliding

downhill, pater, as far as my morals are concerned. Simply deplor-
able. . . . When Kirk and I arrived at the office at a quarter of seven
Osborne gave Kirk a note which Macgowan had left only minutes
before. I thought Kirk looked queer when he read it. He stuffed it
into his pocket and then we discovered the dead man."

"So, so?"

"Later, before dinner, I asked Kirk for the note and he refused to show it to me. Said it was something personal between
him and Macgowan, who's his best friend as well as his intended brother-in-law. Well, sir, in the height of the excitement at-
tending my eviction by the wrathy Dr. Kirk, I managed to spill
some excellent Oporto over young Mr. Kirk's clothes and with
ludicrous ease snaggled the envelope from his pocket. What d'ye
make of it?" The note said:

> I know now. You're dealing with a dangerous character. Go
> easy until I can talk to you aside. Don, watch your step.
>
> MAC.

It was a hurried pencil-scrawl.

The Inspector smiled wolfishly. "The plot, as they say in the
movies, thickens. Cripe! I wish he'd been a little more explicit.
Have to have those two lads on the carpet after all."

"Nothing of the kind," said Ellery quickly. "I tell you that will
spoil everything. Here!" He grabbed a memorandum pad and a
pencil and scribbled a name. The Inspector goggled. "Try this on
that carpet of yours."

"But who—"

"See if you can find a person of that name—the first name may
be wrong, remember—in the files. Might flash it to all police departments in the country. But I have a snooping suspicion that Scotland
Yard or the *Sûreté* may be the port-of-call. Cable right off."

"But who the deuce is it?" demanded the Inspector, reaching

for his buzzer. "Somebody in the case? It's a brand-new name to me—"

"You've been introduced," said Ellery grimly. And he sank back into the comfortable chair while the Inspector set the wheels moving.

Dr. Prouty's cigar preceded him like a black standard as he shambled through the doorway. He paused to eye the Queens critically.

"Good morning, dear children. What's this? Are my eyes deceiving me, or am I back at the Morgue again? Why the gloom?"

"Oh, Doc," said the Inspector eagerly. Ellery waved an absent hand. "What's the verdict?"

The Assistant Medical Examiner seated himself with a sigh and stretched his gawky legs. "Death by violence at the hands of person or persons unknown."

"Gah-h-h!" snarled the Inspector. "Quit kidding. This is serious. Did you find anything?"

"Not a solitary thing. Not one little single solitary thing."

"Well, well?"

"He has," drawled Dr. Prouty, "a small hairy protuberance, known vulgarly as a mole, two inches below and to the right of his navel. An item of identification, I daresay, useless for your purposes unless you discover a loving—er—wife. His corporeal remains represent genus *homo*, sex male. Age approximately fifty-five—perhaps sixty; he's well-preserved—with a weight in life of one-fifty-three, a height of five feet four and one-half inches, and I should say an immoderate appetite, since he's got a belly like a bloated frog. Blue-gray eyes, dark blond hair turned gray—what there is of it—"

"Appetite," muttered Ellery.

"Eh? I hadn't finished. No scars or surgical incisions. Very shiny and whole, his dermis, like an egg. Corns on his toes, though." Dr. Prouty sucked thoughtfully on his dead cigar. "He died, unquestionably, as a direct result of a strong blow on his skull. He never knew what hit him. And Queen, my lad, I'm happy to report that despite all the fearsome tests capable of demonstration in my well-known laboratory alembics, there's not a trace of poison in his system."

"You and your alembics!" shouted the Inspector. "What's got into you, Doc? Everybody's crazy today. Can't you talk like a human being? Is that all?"

"We now," continued Dr. Prouty imperturbably, "return to the aforementioned appetite which seems to have caught the fancy of young Mr. Queen there. Despite the visible evidences of gluttony, our friend the corpse ate very lightly yesterday. He evacuated early as well. In his stomach and œsophagus was to be found nothing but—and here we come to you, my dear Queen—the half-digested remains of an orange."

"Ah," said Ellery with a queer sigh. "I was waiting for that. Tangerine?"

"How the devil should I know? You can't make such fine distinctions, young man, when you're messing about the contents of a strong digestive system after the gastric juices have had their innings and the peristaltic action . . . Here, here! I wander. But since you found the rind of a tangerine in the room, I should be inclined in my Holmesian way to guess in the affirmative. With which I pay my respects and bid you both a pleasant good morning. Goods to be held until called for? Very good—"

"Hold on, Doctor," murmured Ellery; the Inspector was apoplectic with suppressed wrath. "Would you say the tangerine had been eaten in that room?"

"From the comparative times involved? But certainly, *mon ami*. Ta-ta," and, chuckling, Dr. Prouty swung off with a jaunty stride.

"Ass!" hissed the Inspector springing to his feet and slamming the door behind the Assistant Medical Examiner. "Makes a cheap vaudeville-house out of my office. Don't know what's come over that man. He used to be—"

"Tut, tut. You're not especially yourself this morning, either, you know. Dr. Prouty, permit me to inform you, has just contributed one of the most brain-tickling developments of the case."

"Bah!"

"Bah yourself. I refer to the tangerine. We had to be sure that our little man ate it in that room. That room. . . . Everything about that room is important. And the tangerine—Of course you see the essential point."

"See? See? God Almighty!"

"What," asked Ellery abstractedly, "is a tangerine?"

The old gentleman stared with baleful eyes. "Asking me riddles now! An orange, you idiot."

"Precisely. And what kind of orange, please?"

"What ki—How should I know and what difference does it make, anyway?"

"But you do know," said Ellery earnestly. "You know. I know. Every one knows. And I'm beginning to believe the murderer knows, as well. . . . A tangerine is known familiarly as a *Chinese orange*!"

The Inspector deliberately circled his desk and raised his hands to the theoretical heavens. "My son," he said in a stern voice, "this is the last straw. This bird went into a strange room to wait for somebody. While he waited he spied a bowl of fruit on a table. He was hungry—Doc said so himself. So he picked himself out a nice juicy tangerine and ate it. Then somebody came in and bashed him one. What in the name of all that's sane and sensible is wrong with that?"

Ellery bit his lip. "I wish I knew. Chinese orange. . . . Oh, hell, I can't explain it. It's not the orange part of it—" He rose and reached for his coat.

"All right," said the Inspector, dropping his arms wearily. "I give up. Go the whole hog. Go puzzlin' your brains about Chinese oranges and Mexican tamales and alligator pears and Spanish onions and English muffins, for all I care! All I say is—can't a man eat an orange without some crackpot like you reading a mystery into it?"

"Not when it's a Chinese orange, honorable ancestor. Not," snapped Ellery suddenly with a surge of temper, "when there's a novelist from China in the cast and a collector of postage stamps who specializes in China and everything's backwards about the crime and . . ." He stopped suddenly, as if he felt that he had said too much. A look of remarkable intelligence came into his eye. He stood that way, stockstill for a moment, then he clapped his hat on, tapped his father's shoulder absently, and hurried out.

8. TOPSY-TURVY LAND

HUBBELL OPENED the door of the Kirk suite and seemed faintly startled at seeing Mr. Ellery Queen standing there, Homburg in hand, stick companionably raised, smiling, with an air of good-fellowship.

"Yes, sir?" whined Hubbell, without stirring.

"I'm a bounder," said Ellery cheerfully, thrusting the ferrule of his stick over the sill. "That is, I bound. Or perhaps I should say that I'm a rebounder, Hubbell. Yes, yes; I rebound after I'm thrown. Thrown out. May I—?"

Hubbell seemed distressed. "I'm very sorry, sir, but—"

"But what?"

"I'm sorry, sir, but there's no one at home."

"That same dear old trite observation." Ellery looked sad. "Hubbell, Hubbell, boil and bubble, or is it toil and trouble. . . . How *does* the witches' chant go? But the point is I'm not wanted, I take it?"

"I'm sorry, sir."

"Nonsense, man," murmured Ellery, pushing gently past the fellow, "that sort of ukase is evoked only against unwanted guests. I'm here in an official capacity, you see, so you can't keep me out. Dear, dear; life must be complicated for the great serving class." He stopped short on the threshold of the salon. "Don't tell me, Hubbell, that you spoke the truth!" The salon was empty.

Hubbell blinked. "Whom did you want to see, Mr. Queen?"

"I'm not particular, Hubbell. Miss Temple will do. I scarcely think I could conduct a reasonably amiable conversation with Dr. Kirk at the moment, you know. I'm fearfully sensitive about being kicked out of places. Miss Temple, old fellow. She's in, I trust?"

"I'll see, sir." And Hubbell said: "Your coat and stick, sir?"

"Official, I said," drawled Ellery, wandering about. "That means you keep your coat on. *And* your hat, if you're a second-grade detective. Excellent Matisse, that. If it is Matisse . . . Hubbell, for heaven's sake, stop gawping and fetch Miss Temple!"

The tiny woman came in very quickly. She was dressed in something cool and gentle.

"*Good* morning, Mr. Queen. Why so formal? You haven't brought your handcuffs, I trust? Take your coat off, do. Sit down." They shook hands gravely. Ellery sat down, but he did not take his coat off. Jo Temple continued in a swift breathlessness: "May I apologize, Mr. Queen, for that horrid scene last night? Dr. Kirk is—"

"Dr. Kirk is an old man," said Ellery with a wry smile, "and I'm a damned fool for being angry with his senilities. May I compliment you, Miss Temple, upon your choice of gown? It reminds me of a hydrangea or something, if that's what they have in China."

She laughed. "You mean the lotus blossom, I presume? Thank you, sir; that's the prettiest compliment I've had since I came West. Occidentals haven't much imagination when it comes to flattering women."

"I wouldn't know about that," said Ellery, "since I'm a misogynist anyway," and they grinned together. Then they both fell silent, and nothing could be heard except the stiff stalk of Hubbell across the foyer.

Jo folded her small hands in her lap and eyed Ellery steadily. "And what's on your mind, Mr. Queen?"

"China."

He said it so suddenly that she gave a slight start; and then she sank back with her lips compressed. "China, Mr. Queen? And why is China on that clever mind of yours?"

"Because it annoys me, Miss Temple. Annoys me dreadfully. I never thought a mere five-letter word could annoy me so much. I had nightmares about it all last night."

She continued to regard him with unwavering eyes as she reached out to an end-table and fetched a cigaret-box and opened it and offered him a cigaret. Neither said anything while the smoke curled cosily.

"So you couldn't sleep last night?" she said at last. "Odd, Mr. Queen. Neither could I. That poor little man kept haunting my pillow. He smiled at me for four solid hours out of the darkness." She shivered lightly. "Well, Mr. Queen?"

"From all I've heard," drawled Ellery, "to return to the original subject, China is a sadly *backward* country."

She sat up at that, frowning. "Come, come, Mr. Queen, let's stop this idiotic fencing. Just what do you mean by that?"

"I mean," said Ellery softly, "that I am thirsty for knowledge, Miss Temple, and that in this case you're obviously the fountainhead. Tell me something about China."

"China's being very rapidly modernized, if that's what you mean. It's gone a long way since the Boxer affair. Matter of economic necessity, in a way. With the Japanese forcing their way in—"

"But I didn't mean that, you know." Ellery sat up and crushed out his cigaret. "I meant 'backward' literally."

"Oh," she said, and fell silent. Then she sighed. "I suppose I might have known. It was more or less inevitable. Yes, what you imply is perfectly true. There are some really amazing—shall I call them coincidences?—to be drawn from the literal backwardness of China. I can't blame you for putting me on the rack, with this incomprehensible business of a backwards crime absorbing your attention."

"Good girl," murmured Ellery. "Then we understand each other. You realize, Miss Temple, that I don't know where I'm going. This is all probably sheerest drivel. It may mean nothing at all that makes sense. And then again—" He shrugged. "Social, religious, economic customs are purely a matter of perspective. From our Western point of view anything that, let's say, the Chinese do that is different from what we do—or opposite—may be construed, Occidentally, as being 'backwards.' Is that true?"

"I suppose so."

"For example, although I'm the veriest tyro in Oriental lore, I've heard somewhere that the Chinese—curious custom!—on meeting friends shake hands not with the friends but with themselves. Is *that* true?"

"Quite. It's an ancient custom and a good deal more sensible than ours. For, you see, the root-idea behind it is that when you shake hands with yourself you're sparing your friend possible suffering."

"How?" grinned Ellery. "Or should I say—come again?"

"You don't transmit disease so easily that way, you see,"

"Oh."

"Not that the old Chinese knew anything about germs, but having observed—" She sighed, and stopped, and sighed again. "See here, Mr. Queen, this is very interesting and all that, and I'm not averse to augmenting your fund of general information, but it's so silly, this search after phantom backwardnesses. Really, isn't it?"

"Do you know," murmured Ellery, "women are peculiar. There's an original observation! But it seemed to me that only yesterday you were taking this backwards: stuff quite seriously. And today you're calling it silly. Elucidate."

"Perhaps," she said cautiously, "I've reconsidered."

"Perhaps," said Ellery, "not. Well, well! We seem to have reached the well-known *impasse*. Indulge my silliness, Miss Temple, and tell me more. Tell me everything you know, everything you can conjure up at the moment, about Chinese customs or institutions which may be construed as 'backwards,' in the sense that they are diametrically opposed to customs or institutions here."

She stared at him for a long moment, seemed about to ask a question, changed her mind, closed her eyes, and put the cigaret to her tiny mouth. When she spoke it was in a soft murmur. "It's so hard to know where to begin. They differ at so many points, Mr. Queen. For instance, very often in building thatched huts you'll find that the Chinese peasantry—especially in the South—will set the roof on the framework and *build down*, instead of building up as you—as we do."

"Go on, please."

"I suppose, too, you've heard that the Chinese pay their doctors as long as they are well, and stop payment when they fall ill."

"An ingenious arrangement," drawled Ellery. "Yes, I've heard of that. And?"

"When they want to be cooled, they drink hot liquids."

"Marvelous! I begin to fancy your Chinese more and more. I've found, myself, that raising the internal temperature makes the external temperature much more bearable. Go on; you're doing splendidly."

"You're ragging me!" she cried suddenly. Then she shrugged and said: "I beg your pardon. Of course, you've heard of the Chinese custom of eating as loudly as possible during a meal at a strange house and belching with enthusiasm at the expiration of the meal?"

"To assure one's host, I take it, that one has appreciated the food?"

"That's it exactly. Then there's . . . Let me see." She put her finger on her perfect lower lip and mused. "Oh, yes! A Chinese will use a hot towel to cool himself—the same principle as the hot drink, you see—and a wet napkin to wipe himself dry of perspiration. It's infernally hot there, you know."

"Imagine!"

"Of course, they keep to the left side of the road, not the right—but that's not exclusively Oriental; so do most Europeans. Let's see, now. They place a low wall before their front doors as a barrier to evil spirits, since their demons can travel only in a straight line. So all approaches to front doors are winding paths around the wall, thus effectively keeping out the evil ones."

"How naïve!"

"How logical," she retorted. "I see you've the beastly Occidental patronizing air where Orientals are concerned. The white man's burden sort of thing—"

Ellery blushed. "*Touché*. Anything else?"

She frowned. "Oh, there must be thousands of things. . . . Well, the women wear trousers and the men wear robes which give the effect of skirts. Then Chinese students study aloud in classrooms—"

"For heaven's sake, why?"

She grinned. "So that the instructor may be sure they're really studying. Then, too, a Chinese is one year old when he's born, since it's taken for granted that life begins at conception, not at emergence from the womb. And, for that matter, a Chinese celebrates his birthday only at New Year's, no matter in what part of the year he may have been born."

"Good lord! That makes it simple, doesn't it?"

"Not so simple," she said grimly. "Because the Chinese New Year's Day is as variable as a fishwife's tongue. It's not constant, since it is figured on the basis of a rather capricious thirteen-month year. Then, too, my friends pay their bills only twice a year—at the fifth moon and at New Year's; which makes it very cosy for debtors, since they simply go into hiding when the time comes round and the poor creditor goes poking through the streets in broad daylight with a lighted lantern looking for his dun."

Ellery stared. "Why the lighted lantern?"

"Well, if it's the day after New Year's the very fact that the creditor carries a lighted lantern shows that it *isn't* the day after New Year's at all, you see, but still the night before! How do you like that?"

"Love it," chuckled Ellery. "I see I've been heinously backward myself. There's an idea that could be appropriated by the Western World with profit. How about the Chinese theatre? Anything backwards there?"

"Not really. Of course, there are no stage properties, Mr. Queen—sort of Elizabethan in that respect. Then, too, their music is all in one scale, and the minor at that; and all Chinese sing in falsetto; and they pick out their coffins and select their funeral attire before they die; and their barbers cut your hair and shave you not in shops but in the street; and the greatest revenge your enemy can wreak on your head is to kill himself on your doorstep—"

She stopped very abruptly, biting her lips. And she gave him a swift sharp look from under her remarkable lashes and then looked down at her hands.

"Indeed?" said Ellery gently. "That's most interesting, Miss Temple. Good of you to recall it. And what's the brilliant notion behind *that* little ceremony, may I ask?"

She murmured: "It bares to all the world the secret of your enemy's culpability, and marks him eternally with public shame."

"But you're—uh—dead?"

"But you're dead, yes."

"Remarkable philosophy." Ellery studied the ceiling thoughtfully. "Quite remarkable, in fact. Sort of Japanese *hara-kiri* with variations."

"But that couldn't have anything to do with this—with this murder, Mr. Queen," she said breathlessly.

"Eh? Oh, I daresay not. No, surely not." Ellery took off his *pince-nez* and began to scrub the shining lenses with his handkerchief. "And how about Chinese oranges, Miss Temple?"

"I beg your pardon?"

"Chinese oranges. You know—tangerines. Anything backwards in that connection?"

"Backwards? Well . . . But then they're not really tangerines, Mr. Queen. Oranges in China are much larger than tangerines, much more varied, much more delicious, than here." She sighed a little. "Goodness! You've never eaten an orange, really, until you've sunk your teeth into one of those big, luscious, juicy, sweet . . ." She sang out a word suddenly that made Ellery almost drop his glasses.

"What's that?" he said sharply.

She repeated the word in a sort of nasal sing-song. It did sound remarkably like "tanger—" something. "That's one of the dialect words for orange. There are—oh, scores, I guess. Each variety has a different name, and each name differs according to the section of China you're in. Those honey-oranges, now—"

But Ellery was not listening. He was massaging his lean jaw and gazing at the wall. "Tell me," he said with shocking abruptness. "Why did you step into Don Kirk's office yesterday, Miss Temple?"

For a moment she did not reply. Then she folded her hands again and smiled faintly. "You do jump about, don't you, Mr. Queen? Nothing serious, I assure you. I'd just happened to think about it, and I'm a very impulsive person, so I popped out after dressing for dinner to see Don—to see Mr. Kirk about it."

"About what?"

"Why, the Chinese artist."

"Chinese artist!" Ellery leaped to his feet. "Chinese artist! What Chinese artist?"

"Mr. Queen, whatever's the matter with you?"

He seized her tiny shoulder. "What Chinese artist, Miss Temple?"

She turned a little pale. "Yueng," she said in a small voice. "A friend of mine. He's been studying at Columbia University, as so many Chinese in this city do. He's the son of one of Canton's richest native importers. And he has a perfectly remarkable water-color genius. We'd been looking for someone to do the jacket illustration for my book—the one Mr. Kirk is publishing—and I just happened at that moment to think of Yueng. So I dashed in—"

"Yes, yes," said Ellery. "I see. And where is this Yueng, Miss Temple? Where can I locate him?"

"On the Pacific."

"Eh?"

"When I found that Donald—that Mr. Kirk wasn't in, I went back to the suite here and telephoned the University." She sighed. "But they told me he had suddenly decided to return to China a week and a half ago—I think his father died, and that would be an unspoken command, of course, to return. The Chinese take their fathers very seriously, you know. So I suppose poor Yueng's on the high seas now."

Ellery's face fell. "Well," he muttered, "there couldn't be anything in that direction, anyway. Although . . ." When he spoke again he was smiling. "By the way, didn't I hear you say yesterday that your father's in the American diplomatic service?"

"Was," she said quietly. "He died last year."

"Oh! I'm sorry. You were, I suppose, raised in a Western home?"

"Not at all. Father observed the Western customs for official purposes, but I had a Chinese nurse and I was brought up in almost a pure Chinese atmosphere. My mother died, you see, when

I was a child; and father was so busy . . ." She rose, and despite her tininess she gave an impression of height. "And is that all, Mr. Queen?"

Ellery picked up his hat. "You've really been very helpful, Miss Temple. My undying gratitude, and all that. I've learned—"

"That I'm the person involved in this affair," she said in a soft voice, "who expresses backwardness, as it were, more clearly than any one else?"

"Oh, but I didn't say that—"

"Because I've been brought up in a country in which backwardness, from the Western point of view, is the rule, Mr. Queen?"

Ellery flushed. "There are some things, Miss Temple, that are forced upon a man when he's investigating—"

"I suppose you realize what nonsense this all is?"

"I'm afraid," said Ellery ruefully, "that you don't like me today as much as you did yesterday, Miss Temple."

"Sensible woman," said a curt voice, and they both turned quickly to find Felix Berne surveying them coolly from the archway of the foyer. Donald Kirk was behind him.

Donald looked as if he had slept in his clothes. It was the same dowdy tweed, and it was fearfully crumpled, and his necktie was askew and his hair drooped over his eyes and his eyes were rimmed with red circles and he was badly in need of a shave. Berne's slight figure was immaculate, but there was a faint unsteadiness in the pose of his head.

"Hello," said Ellery, picking up his stick. "I was just going."

"Seems to be a habit with you," said Berne with a mirthless grin. He regarded Ellery with calm bitter eyes.

Ellery started to say something, then saw the look in Donald Kirk's eye and refrained.

"Shut up, will you, Felix," said Donald hoarsely, coming forward. "Glad I found you, Queen. Gives me the opportunity to apologize for father's rotten manners last light."

"Nonsense," said Ellery quickly. "Not another word. I daresay I got what I deserved."

"Each man to his own reward," drawled Berne. "One good feature about you, Queen, at any rate." He turned deliberately to Jo. "I stopped in, Miss Temple, to discuss the title of your book with you. It seems that Donald here has some obscene notion of aping the Buck titles and employing something like *Second Cousins* or *Half-Brothers* or *The Good Grandfather*. Now I—"

"Now I," said Jo evenly, "think that you're being despicable, Mr. Berne."

A brown tide began to spread under Berne's skin. "Look here, you—"

"You know perfectly well that Mr. Kirk had no such idea. And certainly it was furthest from my mind. You've been abominably uncivil since I met you, Mr. Berne. If it isn't possible for you to be reasonably a gentleman, I'll be forced to refuse to discuss my book with you at all!"

"Jo," cried Kirk. He glared at his partner. "I can't understand what in the name of God's come over you, Felix!"

"Damned impertinence," said Berne thickly.

"There's no compulsion on the part of The Mandarin Press, you know," continued Jo in the same even, unhurried voice, "to publish my book. I'm perfectly willing to tear up my contract, Mr. Berne. Is that what you want?"

The man stood absolutely still; only his chest rose, and the whites of his eyes showed blankly. There was something deadly and implacable in his glare; and when he spoke it was in a voice like congealed syrup. "What I want . . . If Donald chooses to publish any one barely out of diapers intellectually and with some half-baked manuscript that's a poor imitation of a great work, it's all right with me. That's why The Mandarin is so close to—" He stopped. Then he said with a spitting snarl: "I've looked over that magnificent opus of yours, Miss Temple, having wasted a perfectly good night's sleep to do it. And I think it stinks."

She turned her back on him and walked to the window. Ellery stood quietly watching. Kirk's brown hands opened and closed, and he took a step toward Berne and said in a thickened voice: "You'd better beat it, Felix. You're drunk. I'll settle with you at the office."

Berne licked his lips. Ellery said: "Just a moment, gentlemen, before the physical part of the drama begins. Berne, why were you late last night?"

The publisher did not take his eyes off his partner.

"I asked you, Berne," said Ellery, "why you were late last night."

The man turned his dark head slowly at that, regarding Ellery with an absent, almost insulting vacuity. "Go to hell," he said.

And it was at that moment, with Jo trembling with indignation at the window, Donald clenching his fists impotently, and Berne and Ellery measuring each other with their eyes, that a cracked old voice howled from somewhere in the bowels of the apartment: "Help! I've been robbed! Help!"

Ellery sped through the dining-room, past a startled Hubbell, through a pair of bedrooms into the study of Dr. Kirk. Jo and Donald ran at his heels. Berne had disappeared.

Dr. Kirk was hopping up and down in the center of his disarranged study, one hand on the back of his wheelchair to steady himself, the other clutching at his bristly white hair. He bellowed: "You! You Queen fellow! I've been robbed!"

"Of what?" panted Ellery, glancing swiftly about.

"Father!" cried Donald, springing to the old man's side. "Sit down; you'll exhaust yourself. What's the matter? What's been stolen? Who robbed you?"

"My books!" roared the septuagenarian, his face purple. "My books! Oh, if I find that thieving scoundrel . . ." He subsided suddenly with a groan in the wheelchair.

Miss Diversey, white-faced, stole into the study from the corridor, looking frightened. She flung one quick glance at her charge's face and flew to his side. He pushed her away with such force that she staggered and almost fell.

"Get away, you harpy," he screamed. "I'm sick of you, you and your exercises and your precious Dr. Angini. Damn all doctors and nurses! Well, Queen, well, well, well! Don't stand there gaping like an aborigine! Find the rascal who stole my books!"

"I'm not gaping," said Ellery with a sour smile, "I'm waiting for calmness and reason, my dear Doctor. If you'll turn off the violence, perhaps we can get a rational statement out of you. I assume by this time that some books of yours are missing. How do you know they've been stolen?"

"Detective," snorted the old gentleman. "Imbecile! See that shelf?" He pointed a long bent forefinger at one of the built-in shelves, more than half of which was empty.

"Oh, I've observed that and made the complex deduction that that was the abiding-place of your precious volumes. Suppose you stop being unintelligible, Doctor, and answer my question."

"How do I know they've been stolen?" groaned Dr. Kirk, swaying his craggy head from side to side like a python. "Oh, good Lord preserve us from idiots! They're gone, aren't they?"

"Not necessarily the same thing, Doctor. When did you miss them? When did you see them last?"

"An hour ago. Immediately after my breakfast. Then I went into my bedroom to dress and have this—this female Aesculapius," he glared at Miss Diversey, who was standing pale and subdued at the farthest wall, "pull and tug and slobber over me, and by the time I got back here a moment ago they were gone."

"Where were you, Miss Diversey?" said Ellery sharply.

The nurse said in a tearful voice: "He—he chased me out, sir. I went to the office—I mean, to talk to *some one* with a little human feeling . . ."

"I see. Doctor, didn't you hear anything going on in this room while you dressed next door?"

"Hear? Hear? No, nothing!"

"He's a little deaf," muttered Donald Kirk. "And rather sensitive about it."

"Stop that confounded whispering, Donald! Well, well, Queen?"

Ellery shrugged. "I've never laid claim to pretensions of clairvoyance, Dr. Kirk. Just what books have been taken?"

"My Pentateuchal commentaries!"

"Your *what*?"

"Ignoramus," growled the old gentleman. "Hebrew books, idiot, Hebrew books! I've devoted the last five years of my life to a research into the rabbinical writings on the theory that—"

"Hebrew books," said Ellery slowly. "You mean books written *in* Hebrew?"

"Well, of course, of course!"

"And nothing else?"

"No. Thank heaven they spared my Chinese manuscripts, the vandals. I should feel utterly lost—"

"Ah," said Ellery. "Chinese manuscripts? You're familiar with the language of the ideographs, of course. I remember now. Yes, yes, your philological fame has reached even these mortal ears, Doctor. Well, well. . . . Quite vanished, eh?" Ellery went to the shelf and looked down. But his eyes were not on the empty boards. They were drawn within themselves and shining with a distant light.

"I can't understand why any one should want to steal those books," said Donald with a weary shake of his head. "Lord, cataclysms come in pairs! What the devil do you make of it, Queen?"

Ellery turned slowly. "I make a good deal of it, old fellow, mostly fog. By the way, Doctor, these books of yours are valuable?"

"Bah! They're worthless to any one but a scholar."

"Very interesting. . . . You see, Kirk, there's one really remarkable thing about Hebrew books."

Dr. Kirk stared, interested despite himself. Jo Temple watched quietly the set of Ellery's lips—quietly and yet with a sort of controlled apprehension, as if she were afraid of what they might say.

"Remarkable?" said Kirk, bewildered.

"Quite. For Hebrew is an unorthodox language. Chirographically and typographically. *It is written backwards.*"

"Backwards?" gasped Miss Diversey. "Oh, sir, that's—"

"It is written," muttered Ellery, "backwards. It's read backwards. It's printed backwards. Everything about it is precisely the reverse of the Romance languages. Is that correct, Doctor?"

"Certainly it's correct!" snarled the old gentleman. "And why restrict its difference to the Romance? And why in the name of the seven bulls of Bashan should that startle you?"

"Well," said Ellery apologetically, "the crime was backwards, you see."

"Oh, heaven protect the lowly scholar," groaned Dr. Kirk. "And what the devil of it? I want my books back. You and your backwardnesses!" He paused, and a fiery gleam sprang into his dried-out eyes. "Look here, idiot, are you accusing *me* of that inconsequential little homicide?"

"I'm accusing no one," said Ellery. "But you can't deny that it's very odd under the circumstances."

"So's your hat," snarled Dr. Kirk. "Get my books back!"

Ellery sighed and grasped his stick firmly. "I'm sorry, Doctor, but at the moment I can see no way of restoring your volumes. You might telephone my father—Inspector Queen—at Police Headquarters and inform him of this latest development. . . . Miss Temple."

She started. "Yes, Mr. Queen?"

"I'm sure we'll be excused for a moment." They were stared at as Ellery drew the tiny woman out into the corridor and closed the door securely behind them. "Why didn't you mention it before, O Lotus Blossom?"

"Mention what, Mr. Queen?"

"I've just recalled it myself. Why didn't you mention the fact that one of the outstanding examples of backwardness in the whole Chinese gamut is—the Chinese language?"

"Language? Oh!" She smiled faintly. "You're such a suspicious person, Mr. Queen. I just didn't think of it. You mean of course that, aside from Hebrew, Chinese is probably the only language in the world which is printed backwards; and it's written from top to bottom instead of from side to side, besides. But what of it?"

"Nothing—except that," murmured Ellery, "you failed to mention it."

She stamped her foot. "Oh, you're as bad as the others! Is there something in the air here that makes people silly? Every one except Donald Kirk seems afflicted with a mild insanity; and even he—And suppose I didn't mention it? You can't say it has any significance here, anyway. You notice that the thief didn't steal Dr. Kirk's *Chinese* books!"

"That," said Ellery with a frown, "is what's bothering me. Why? An oversight with cosmic implications. Or perhaps I'm making a mountain out of the well-known molehill. At any rate, this thing needs the application of thought. . . . China, China, China! I'm beginning to wish I had a Charlie Chan on the scene to clarify these esoteric mysteries of Orientalism. I'm completely bewildered. Nothing makes sense, nothing at all. This is the world's most mystifying crime."

"I wish," said Jo with lowered eyes, "I could help you, indeed I do."

"Hmm," said Ellery. "Well, thank you, Miss Temple." He seized her hand and pumped it. "Things could always be worse. And perhaps they will be. For God knows what will turn out backwards tomorrow!"

9. FOOCHOW ERROR

DJUNA, THE Queens' boy-of-all-work, thrust his olive and hatchety young face into the bedroom the next morning. "Why, Mr. Ellery!" he exclaimed. "I didn't know you'd got up!"

His astonishment was based upon experience, and the current blasting of it. Mr. Ellery Queen—who neither toiled nor spun, except within the environs of his mind—was not the earliest riser in the world; and indeed his lean figure sprawled in innocent sleep upon the second of their twin beds caused the Inspector to erupt, like a patient volcano, each morning in a growling thunder of expostulation. But this morning there he was, his hair still ruffled from sleep, sitting up in pongee pajamas, *pince-nez* perched on the bridge of his thin nose, gravely reading a fat book at the unheard-of hour of ten o'clock.

"Wipe that smirk off your face, Djuna," he said absently, without looking up from the page. "Can't a man get up early one morning?"

Djuna frowned. "What you reading?"

"Somebody's massive tome on Chinese customs, you heathen. And I can't say it's much help." He flung it aside, yawning, and plopped back on the pillow with a luxurious sigh. "Might rustle me a yard of toast and a liter of coffee, Djun."

"You better get up," said Djuna grimly.

"And why had I better get up, young 'un?" murmured Ellery in a smothered voice from the depths of the pillow.

"'Cause some one's waiting here to see you."

Ellery bolted upright, the glasses dangling from his ear. "Well, of all the exasperating—! Why didn't you say so before, homunculus? Who is it? How long has he been waiting?" He scrambled out of bed and reached for his dressing-gown.

"It's a Mr. Macgowan, an' how'd you know it was a 'he'?" demanded Djuna with restrained admiration, lounging against the door.

"Macgowan? That's strange," muttered Ellery. "Oh, that! Very simple, number one boy. You see, there are only two sexes—not taking into account certain accidents of nature. So it was at the very least a fifty-fifty guess."

"G'on," said Djuna with a disbelieving grin, and vanished. Then he materialized again, sticking his gamin head back into the room, and said: "Got the coffee on the table," and vanished once more.

When Ellery emerged into the Queens' living-room he found tall Glenn Macgowan pacing restlessly up and down before the fire that crackled in the grate. He ceased his patrol abruptly. "Ah, Queen. I'm sorry. Had no idea I'd be routing you out of bed."

Ellery shook his big hand lazily. "Not at all. You did me a service; there's no telling when I'd have got up. Join me in some breakfast, Macgowan?"

"Had mine, thank you. But don't let me stop you. I can wait."

"I hope," chuckled Ellery, "you're cultivating what Bishop Heber was pleased to term 'Swift's Eighth Beatitude,' although it's really Popish in origin."

"I beg your pardon?" gasped Macgowan.

"Popish advisedly. I meant Pope. In a letter to John Gay he wrote: 'Blessed is he who expects nothing for he shall never be disappointed.' I don't feel in the donative mood this morning. . . . Well, well! I find I'm ravenous, now that I put my mind to it. We can talk while I'm refueling." Ellery sat down and reached for his orange-juice, leaving Macgowan with a partly open mouth. He observed that one bright young eye was fixed to the crack of the kitchen door—fixed very curiously upon his visitor. "Sure you won't join me?"

"Quite." Macgowan hesitated. "Er—do you always talk this way before breakfast, Queen?"

Ellery grinned as he gulped. "I'm sorry. It's a nasty habit."

Macgowan resumed his pacing. Then he stopped short jerkily and said: "Ah, Queen. Sorry about the other night. Dr. Kirk's unpredictable. I assure you Marcella and I—all of us—felt very bad about the whole dismal business. Of course, the old gentleman's exercising the prerogative of senility. He's a tyrant. And besides, he doesn't understand the necessities of official investigation—"

"Quite all right," said Ellery cheerfully, munching toast. And he said nothing more, seeming content to leave the conversation to his visitor.

"Well." Macgowan shook his head suddenly and sat down in an armchair by the fire. "I imagine you're wondering why I've come here this morning."

Ellery raised his cup. "Well, I'm human, I suppose. I can't say I was precisely prepared for it."

Macgowan laughed a little gloomily. "Of course, I did want to express my apologies personally. I feel like one of the Kirk family, now that Marcella and I . . . Look here, Queen."

Ellery sank back with a sigh, dabbing his lips with his napkin. He offered Macgowan a cigaret, which the big man refused, and took one himself. "There!" he said. "That's worlds better. Well, Macgowan? I'm looking."

They studied each other in silence for some time, quite without expression. Then Macgowan began to fumble in his inner breast-pocket. "Y'know, I can't quite make you out, Queen. I get the feeling that you know a good deal more than you pretend—"

"I'm like the grasshopper," murmured Ellery. "Protective coloration. Really, that's an air cultivated for purposes of my avocation, Macgowan." He squinted at his cigaret. "I assume you have the murder in mind?"

"Yes."

"I know nothing. I know," said Ellery sadly, "rather less than nothing, when it comes to that. I might, however, ask you what *you* know." Macgowan started. "I hadn't got round to you, you see. But you do know something, and I think it would be wise for you to let me share your knowledge. I'm the repository for more secrets than you could throw at a dead cat, if that's the polite custom. I'm unofficial—blessed state, you understand. I tell what I think should be told and keep all the rest to myself."

Macgowan stroked his long jaw nervously. "I don't know what you mean. I holding something back? Really—"

Ellery eyed him calmly. Then he put the cigaret back into his mouth and smoked with a thoughtful air. "Dear, dear. I must be losing my grip. Well, Macgowan, what's on your mind—or rather in your hand?"

Macgowan unfolded his big fist and Ellery saw in the broad palm a small leather object, like a card-case. "This," he said.

"One case, leather or leatherette. Unfortunately I haven't X-ray eyes. Let's have it, please."

But without taking his eyes off the case in his hand and without raising his hand Macgowan said: "I've just purchased—what's in this case. Something valuable. It's pure coincidence, of course, but I believe in anticipating trouble—trouble that might lead me into some embarrassment, though I assure you I'm perfectly innocent of any . . ." Ellery watched the man unblinkingly. He was extraordinarily nervous. "There's nothing in it for me to conceal, but if I neglected to mention it, some one of the police, I fancy, might find out. That would be awkward, perhaps unpleasant. So—"

"Obviously inspection is called for," murmured Ellery. "What *are* you talking about, Macgowan?"

Macgowan handed him the leather case.

Ellery turned it over in his fingers curiously, with that deliberate detachment which years of examination of strange objects had bred in him. It was made of a plain morocco, black, and apparently operated on a simple spring-catch arrangement. He pressed the small button and the lid flew back. Inside the case, imbedded in a hollow of satin, lay a rectangular envelope of stiff milky glassine. And in the envelope, incased in a pochette, lay a postage stamp.

Silently Macgowan produced a stamp-tongs of nickel and offered it to Ellery. Ellery opened the envelope and with the tongs, rather clumsily, extracted the pochette. The stamp showed clearly through the cellophane. It was an oversize stamp, wider than deep, and perforated evenly along its four edges. The border was an ochre-yellow in color, and the bottom was designed as a sort of Chinese flower-garland. In the two lower corners appeared the denomination of the stamp: $1. In squat ochre letters running across the top of the border was the word: *Foochow*, capitalized.

But inside the border, where even to Ellery's untrained eye it was evident that there should have been a pictorial design of some kind in another color, there was—nothing. Merely the blank white paper of the stamp.

"That's funny, isn't it?" murmured Ellery. "I'm not a philatelist, but I can't remember ever having seen or heard of a stamp that was blank in the center of the design. What's the idea, anyway, Macgowan?"

"Hold it up to the light," said Macgowan quietly.

Ellery flung him a sharp glance and obeyed. And instantly he saw, through the thin paper, a very charming little scene in black. In the foreground there was what appeared to be a long ceremonial canoe of some kind, filled with natives; and in the background a harbor scene; obviously, from the legend at the top, a view of the harbor of Foochow.

"Amazing," he said. "Perfectly amazing." And something glittered in his eye as he flung Macgowan another sharp glance.

Macgowan said in the same quiet voice: "Turn the stamp over."

Ellery did so. And there, incredible as it seemed, was the harbor scene in its black printing-ink, impressed upon the back of the stamp. There was a gloss of dried gum over it, cracked and streaky.

"Backwards?" he said slowly. "Of course. Backwards."

Macgowan took the tongs with the pochette between its tines and replaced the pochette in the envelope. "Queer, isn't it?" he said in a smothered voice. "The only error of its kind to my knowledge in the whole field of philately. It's the sort of rarity collectors dream about."

"Backwards?" said Ellery again, as if he were asking himself a question the answer to which was too pat to be true. He leaned back in his chair and smoked with half-closed eyes. "Well, well! This *has* been a fruitful visit, Macgowan. How on earth does such an error occur?"

Macgowan snapped the lid of the case shut and replaced the case almost carelessly in his breast-pocket.

"Well, this is a two-color stamp, as you saw. What we term a bicolor. Ochre and black in this instance. That means that the sheet of stamps—they come in sheets, of course—aren't printed separately; the sheets of stamps had to be run through the presses twice."

Ellery nodded. "Once for the ochre, once for the black. Obviously."

"Well, you can deduce what happened in this strange case. Something went wrong after the ochre impression had been made and dried. Instead of placing the sheets face up in the press, a careless printer permitted them to get in *face down*. Consequently the black impression came out on the back of the stamps, not the face."

"But, Lord, there must be some sort of government inspection! Our own postal authorities are strict, aren't they? I still don't understand how this stamp managed to get into circulation. I always thought that when errors of this sort occurred the sheets were summarily destroyed."

"So they are in most cases, but occasionally a sheet or two gets out—either as a clerk's mistake, or else they're stolen by some official for the sole purpose of exploiting them philatelically. For example, the sheet of twenty-four-cent U.S. airmail inverts which is so well-known simply slipped by the inspectors. This Foochow . . ." Macgowan shook his head. "There's no telling what actually happened. But here's the stamp."

"I see," said Ellery; and for a space only the brisk sounds of Djuna washing the breakfast dishes in the kitchen broke the silence. "So you've come to me, Macgowan, to tell me about your purchase of it. Afraid of its backwardness?"

"I'm afraid of nothing," said Macgowan stiffly; and Ellery, studying those level eyes and the set of that long jaw, could well believe. "At the same time, I'm a canny Scot, Queen, and I'm not going to be caught with my pants down in something . . ." He did not finish. When he spoke again it was in a lighter tone. "This Foochow stamp is what we call a 'local'—that is, the city of Foochow, one of the Treaty Ports, used to issue its own postage stamps for local postage purposes. I'm a specialist in locals, you see; don't collect anything else. Locals from anywhere—U.S., Sweden, Switzerland. . . ."

"Tell me," murmured Ellery. "Is this something new? You've run across something whose existence has never been suspected?"

"No, no. Among experts it's been known for years that such a printer's error occurred during the issuance of these stamps, but it's always been assumed that the misprinted sheets were destroyed by the Foochow postal authorities. This is the first copy I've ever seen."

"And how did you come by it, may I ask?"

"It's a rather peculiar story," said Macgowan with a frown. "Ever hear of a man named Varjian?"

"Varjian. Armenian? Can't say I have."

"Yes, he's Armenian; a great many of these fellows are. Well, Varjian is one of the best-known stamp-dealers in New York. This morning, quite early, he telephoned me at home and asked me to come down to his office at once, saying that he had something to show me in which he was sure I'd be interested. Well, I've been on a fruitless rampage this week—hadn't picked up a thing of interest, you see; and then the murder had left a bad taste in my mouth . . . I felt I owed myself a little spree." Macgowan shrugged. "I knew Varjian wouldn't call me unless he had something good. He's always on the lookout for locals for me; there aren't many collectors who go in for that sort of thing and consequently locals are scarce." He settled back and folded his hands on his broad chest.

"He's done this before, I suppose?"

"Oh, yes. Well, Varjian showed me the Foochow. The copy, he said, had either slipped by inspection in a full sheet or had been smuggled out of the printer's by some one who recognized the enormous value of such an extraordinary rarity. It's lain dog-go somewhere for years, unquestionably—of course it's an old stamp; it was issued in the Treaty Port heyday in the province of Fukien—and here all of a sudden it turns up. Varjian offered it for sale."

"Go on," said Ellery. "Aside from the coincidental fact of the stamp's distinctive error, which I'll admit is a disturbing note, I don't see anything queer in this business—yet."

"Well." Macgowan rubbed his nose. "I don't know. You see—"

"Is it authentic? Not a forgery, or anything like that? It seems to me it would be easy enough to forge such a stamp."

"Lord, no," said Macgowan with a smile. "It's unquestionably genuine. There are always certain minute and identifiable characteristics of the plates from which stamps are printed; and I satisfied myself that the Foochow showed those characteristics, which are virtually impossible to forge. And then Varjian guaranteed it; and he's an expert. The paper, the design, sometimes the perforations . . . oh, quite all right, I assure you. It's nothing like that."

"Then what," demanded Ellery, "is bothering you?"

"The source of the stamp."

"Source?"

Macgowan rose and turned to the fire. "There's something very queer in the wind. I naturally wanted to know where Varjian had picked up the Foochow. Often the ownership of a rare item is as important in establishing its authenticity as the more usual internal evidence. And Varjian wouldn't say!"

"Ah," said Ellery thoughtfully.

"You see? He was absolutely close-mouthed about where he'd got it. Said he couldn't tell me."

"Did you gather the impression that he really didn't know, or rather that he knew but wouldn't tell?"

"He knew, all right. I got the feeling that he was acting as agent for some one. And that's what I don't like."

"Why?"

Macgowan turned, and his bulk was black against the crisp little fire. "I don't really know why," he said slowly, "but I just don't like it. There's something smelly somewhere—"

"Do you think," murmured Ellery, "that it's stolen property? Is that what's bothering you?"

"No, no. Varjian is honest, and I have his word for it that the stamp wasn't stolen—I asked him point-blank. He was quite of-fended, in fact. I'm sure he spoke the truth there. He asked me why I wanted to know the source of the stamp; I'd never been so 'partic-ular' before, he said. His actual words! That in itself was a peculiar statement, coming from him; downright insulting, really. But then I suppose he resented the implication that he was handling ques-tionable merchandise. . . . He'd called me first of all, he explained, because I was the biggest collector of locals he knew."

"I wish I could see some sense in it," said Ellery moodily. Then he looked up at the big man with a grin. "But I can't."

"I suppose I'm running true to form," muttered Macgowan, shrugging. "Overcautious. But you can see my position. Here was something—well, backwards popping up out of nowhere on the heels of a damned murder that . . ." He knit his brows. "And then there was something else queer about the business."

"You seem to have put in an uncomfortable morning," laughed Ellery. "Or are you always so cautious? Well, what was it?"

"You'd have to know Varjian to appreciate it. He's straight as a die, as I've said—but he *is* Armenian, with the usual bargaining instincts of his race. You have to know how to buy from Varjian. He always asks prices which are exorbitant and he must be dealt with shrewdly. I can't recall the time when I haven't had to beat down his initial asking-price. And yet," said Macgowan slowly, "this time he set a price and absolutely refused to budge from it. And I had to pay what he demanded."

"Well," drawled Ellery, "that's different. If what you say is true, there's no question in my mind that the man acted as agent for some one who had stipulated in advance the selling-price of the stamp; plus, I suppose, a commission."

"You really think so?"

"Positive of it."

"Well," said the big man with a sigh, "I guess I'm being an old woman about this business. But I felt that I had to tell some one about it. I'm all clear?"

"As far as I'm concerned, you are," said Ellery genially. And then he rose and crushed his cigaret in an ashtray. "By the way, would you mind introducing me to this Varjian, Macgowan? It mightn't hurt to check up a bit."

"Then you *do* think . . ."

Ellery shrugged. "There's only one thing about it I don't like—the fact that it's coincidental. And I detest coincidences."

The establishment of Avdo Varjian, Ellery found, was a small shop on East Forty-first Street with dusty windows cluttered with cards of postage stamps. They went in and found themselves in a narrow store with a battered counter covered with glass, under which were similar cards each bearing priced stamps. There was a vast old-fashioned iron safe at the rear.

Varjian was a tall thin dark man with sharp features and beautiful black eyes under long lashes. There was something quick and authoritative about his gestures, and his fingers were as deft and sensitive as an artist's. He was busy over the counter with an old shabby man who was consulting a torn notebook and calling for stamps by number, when they came in; and he shot Macgowan a keen glance and said: "Ah, Mr. Macgowan. Something wrong?" Then he looked at Ellery out of the corner of his eyes and looked away again.

"Oh, no," said Macgowan stiffly. "I just dropped back to introduce a friend of mine. We'll wait if you're busy."

"Yes," said Varjian, and turned back to the shabby old man.

Ellery watched him tentatively as the man served his customer. He handled his tongs as if they were alive. It was a pleasure to see him strip the little slips of adhesive hinge from the backs of stamps, he worked so surely. He was a character, Ellery recognized, and in his proper setting he might have been a figure out of a continentalized Dickens. The store, the man, the stamps exuded a musty flavor, like the nostalgic odor of the Old Curiosity Shop to a sighing bookworm. Ellery became fascinated as he watched the little bits of colored paper being tucked into a pocketed card. Macgowan sauntered about looking at the cheap display cards without seeing them.

Then the shabby old man took four twenty-dollar bills out of a wallet which might have held a Crusader's bread and cheese, and received some small bills and silver in exchange, and went out of the shop with his card tucked away in his clothes and a faraway smiling expression in his eyes.

"Yes, Mr. Macgowan?" said Varjian softly, before the echoes of the old-fashioned hanging doorbell had died away.

"Oh." Macgowan was rather pale. "Meet Mr. Ellery Queen."

Varjian turned the remarkable lamps of his black eyes upon Ellery. "Mr. Ellery Queen? So. You are a collector, Mr. Queen?"

"Not of postage stamps," said Ellery in a dreamy voice.

"Ah. Coins, perhaps?"

"No, indeed. I'm a collector, Mr. Varjian, of odd facts."

Lids obscured three-quarters of the glittering pupils. "Odd facts?" Varjian smiled. "I'm afraid, Mr. Queen, I don't understand."

"Well," said Ellery jovially, "there are odd facts and then there are odd facts, you see. This morning I'm on the trail of a *very* odd fact. I wager it will become the choicest item in my collection."

Varjian showed milkwhite teeth. "Your friend, Mr. Macgowan, is joking with me."

Macgowan flushed. "I—"

"I was never more serious," said Ellery sharply, leaning across the counter and staring into the man's brilliant eyes. "Look here, Varjian, for whom were you acting when you sold Mr. Macgowan that Foochow stamp this morning?"

Varjian returned the stare for slow seconds, and then he relaxed and sighed. "So," he said reproachfully. "I would not have believed it of you, Mr. Macgowan. I thought we had agreed it was to be a confidential sale."

"You'll have to tell Mr. Queen," said Macgowan harshly, still flushed.

"And why," asked the Armenian in a soft voice, "should I tell anything to this Mr. Queen of yours, Mr. Macgowan?"

"Because," drawled Ellery, "I am investigating a murder, *Monsieur* Varjian, and I have reason to believe that the Foochow is tied up in it somewhere."

The man sucked in his breath, alarm flooding into his eyes. "A murder," he choked. "Surely, you are—What murder?"

"You're procrastinating," said Ellery. "Don't you read the newspapers? The murder of an unidentified man on the twenty-second floor of the Hotel Chancellor."

"Chancellor." Varjian bit his dark lip. "But I didn't know . . . I do not read the papers." He felt for a chair behind the counter and sat down. "Yes," he muttered, "I acted as agent in the sale. I was asked not to reveal the person—for whom I acted."

Macgowan placed his fists on the counter. He shouted: "Varjian, who the hell was it?"

"Now, now," said Ellery. "There's no need for violence, Macgowan. I'm sure Mr. Varjian is ready to talk. Aren't you?"

"I will tell you," said the Armenian dully. "I will also tell you why I telephoned to you the first of all, Mr. Macgowan. A murder . . ." He shivered. "My—this person told me," and he licked his lips, "to offer it to you first."

Macgowan's big jaw dropped. "You mean to say," he gasped, "that you sold me the Foochow this morning on specific instructions? You were to sell only to me?"

"Yes."

"Who was it, Varjian?" asked Ellery softly.

"I—" Varjian stopped. There was something extraordinarily appealing in his black eyes.

"Speak up, damn you!" thundered Macgowan, lunging swiftly forward. He caught the Armenian's coat in his big fist and shook the man until the dark head wobbled and went olive-gray.

"Cut it out, Macgowan," said Ellery in a curt voice. "Drop it, I say!"

Macgowan, breathing hoarsely, relinquished his grip with reluctance. Varjian gulped twice, staring with fright from one to the other.

"Well?" snarled Macgowan.

"You see," mumbled the Armenian, shifting his tortured eyes about, "this person is one of the greatest specializing collectors in the world on—"

"China," said Ellery queerly. "Good God, yes. Foochow—China."

"Yes. On China. You see—you see—"

"Who was it?" roared Macgowan in a terrible voice.

Varjian spread his hands in a pitiable gesture of resignation. "I am sorry to have to . . . It was your friend Mr. Donald Kirk."

10. THE QUEER THIEF

MACGOWAN SEEMED utterly crushed. For most of the journey by taxicab from Varjian's to the Hotel Chancellor he sat slumped against the cushions, silent and white. Ellery said nothing, but he was thinking with a furious frown.

"Kirk," he muttered at last. "Hmm. Some things pass comprehension. In most cases one is able to apply at least a normal knowledge of human psychology to the activities of the cast. People—all people—do things from an inner urge. All you have to do is keep your eyes open and gauge the psychological possibilities of the puppets around you. But Kirk . . . Incredible!"

"I can't understand it," said Macgowan in a low dreary tone. "There must be some mistake, Queen. For Donald to do anything like that . . . to me! It's—it's unthinkable. It's not like him. Deliberately to involve me. I'm his best friend, Queen, perhaps the only real friend he has in the world. I'm to marry his sister, and he loves her. Even if he was angry with me, if he had something against me . . . he knows that to hurt me would hurt her, too—terribly. I can't understand it, that's all."

"There's nothing for it but to wait," said Ellery absently. "It *is* strange. By the way, Macgowan, how is it you didn't know he had that Foochow in his collection? I thought you birds hung together."

"Oh, Donald's always been rather uncommunicative about his

stuff, particularly with me. You see, in a sense we're rivals; it's not the only instance of friends sharing everything except their mutual hobbies. We go everywhere together, for instance—or we did, before I became engaged to Marcella—but to stamp-auctions and to stamp-dealers. . . . Naturally, since I'm a collector myself I've never intruded on his secrets. Once in a while he, or Osborne, shows me a choice item. But I never saw that one before. A local rarity like this—" He stopped short so suddenly that Ellery looked at him with sharp wonder.

"Yes? You were going to say—"

"Eh? Oh, nothing."

"Nothing my aunt's foot, as dear Reggie would say. What's so strange about Donald Kirk's owning a local rarity? It's Chinese, isn't it, and he's a specialist on China, isn't he?"

"Yes, but . . . Well, he's never had any before to my knowledge," mumbled Macgowan. "I'm sure he hasn't."

"But why shouldn't he have, man, if it's Chinese?"

"You don't understand," said Macgowan irritably. "Except in the case of U.S. collectors—that is, collectors of United States stamps—few specialists in any specific field go in for locals. They're not considered real philatelic objects. No, that's a clumsy explanation. Virtually every country in the world went through a period, before the passage of their respective national postage acts, of diversified local issues of stamps—cities, communes, towns issuing their own local stamps. Most American collectors don't consider these genuine philatelic objects. They want only stamps issued and used nationally—by a whole country. Kirk is like the rest; he's always collected nationally authorized issues of China exclusively. I'm one of those nuts who go in for the unusual—I collect only locals of all countries. Not interested in the orthodox issues. This Foochow is really a local—there were a number of Chinese Treaty Ports which issued their own stamps.

Then how," Macgowan's face darkened, "did Donald come to have this Foochow local?"

They were silent for a while as the taxi threaded its way among the pillars of Sixth Avenue.

Then Ellery drawled: "By the way, how valuable is the Foochow?"

"Valuable?" Macgowan repeated absently. "That depends. In all cases of rarities the price is a variable consideration, depending upon how much it has brought at its last sale. The famous British Guiana of 1856—the one-cent magenta listed by Scott's as Number 13—which is in the possession of the Arthur Hind estate is worth $32,500.00, as I remember it—I may be wrong in my recollection, but it cost Hind that or somewhere around that. It's catalogued at $50,000.00, which means nothing. It's worth $32,500.00 because that's approximately what Hind paid for it at the Ferrary auction in Paris. . . . This Foochow set me back a cool ten thousand."

"Ten thousand dollars!" Ellery whistled. "But you'd no idea what it had brought previously, since it's not been generally known before. So how could you—"

"That's the figure Varjian set, and stuck to, and that's the amount I made out my check for. It's worth the money, although it's a pretty stiff price. Since, as far as I know, it's the only one of its kind in existence—and especially considering the peculiar nature of the error—I could probably turn it over for a profit today if I put it up at auction."

"Then you weren't victimized, at any rate," murmured Ellery. "Kirk didn't try to soak you, if that's any consolation. . . . Here we are."

As they were removing their coats in the foyer of the Kirk suite, they heard Donald Kirk's voice from the salon. "Jo . . . I've something I want to tell you—ask you."

"Yes?" said Jo Temple's voice softly.

"I want you to know—" Kirk was speaking rapidly, eagerly, "that I really think your book is great, swell, Jo. Don't mind Felix. He's something of a boor, and he's an embittered cynic, and when he's drunk he's really not responsible for what he says. I didn't take your manuscript because it—because of *you* ..."

"Thank you, sir," said Jo, still very softly.

"I mean—it wasn't a question of the—well, the usual nasty implication. I really wanted the book—"

"And not me, Mr. Donald Kirk?"

"Jo!" Something apparently happened, for he continued after a moment in a strained voice. "Don't mind what Felix said. If it doesn't sell a thousand copies it will still be a swell book, Jo. If—"

"If it doesn't sell a thousand copies, Mr. Donald Kirk," she said demurely, "I shall return to China a wiser but sadder woman. I'm visualizing hundreds of thousands. . . . But what was it you were going to say?"

Macgowan looked uncomfortable, and Ellery shrugged. They both made as if to step noisily through the archway, and they both stopped.

For Kirk was saying in a queer breathless voice: "I've fallen in love with you, damn it! I never thought I could. I never thought any woman could make me lose my head—"

"Not even," she inquired in a cool voice that trembled strangely in its undertones, "Irene Llewes?"

There was a silence, and Ellery and Macgowan looked at each other, and then they cleared their throats loudly together and stepped into the salon.

Kirk was on his feet, his shoulders sagging. Jo sat in a strained attitude, the tension about her nostrils belying the faint smile on her lips. They both started, and Kirk said quickly: "Uh—hello, hello. I didn't know it was you. Come together, eh? Well. Sit down, Queen, sit down. Seen Marcella, Glenn?"

"Marcella," said Macgowan heavily. "No, I haven't. Good morning, Miss Temple."

"Good morning," she murmured without looking up. The white skin of her throat was no longer white, but scarlet.

"Marcella's out somewhere. Should be back soon. Always gadding about somewhere, 'Cella," chattered Kirk, moving about restlessly. "Well, well, Queen! Something new? Another inquisition?"

Ellery sat down and adjusted his *pince-nez* in a sober, judicial manner. "I've a rather serious question to ask you, Kirk."

Jo rose swiftly." "I think you men want to be alone. If you'll excuse me, please—"

"Question?" echoed Kirk. His face had gone gray.

"Miss Temple," said Ellery in a grave tone, "I think you had better remain."

Without a word she reseated herself.

"What kind of question?" asked Kirk, licking his lips. Macgowan was standing by one of the windows, staring motionlessly out, his broad back a silent baffled barrier.

"Why," said Ellery in a clear voice, "did you instruct a dealer named Avdo Varjian to sell your friend Glenn Macgowan a local stamp rarity of the city of Foochow?"

The tall young man sank into a chair and without looking at any of them said in a cracked voice: "Because I was a fool."

"Scarcely an informative reply," said Ellery dryly. And then his eyes narrowed, and he was shocked to observe the expression on Miss Temple's elfin face. Her pretty candid features were drawn up in a grimace of the most remarkable amazement; she looked quite as if she could not believe her ears. And she was staring at her host with enormous eyes.

"Glenn," said Kirk in a mutter.

Macgowan did not turn from the window. He said hoarsely: "Well?"

"I didn't think you'd find out. It wasn't important. There was the stamp, and I knew that you—Hell, Glenn, I'd rather have had you get it than any one else in the world. You know that."

Macgowan wheeled like a tired horse, his eyes stony. "And the fact that it's backwards didn't occur to you, I suppose," he said bitterly.

"*Tch, tch*" said Ellery mildly. "Let me handle this, Macgowan. Kirk! Your business affairs are your own concern, and what subtle little nuances may arise from the peculiar nature of the affair are probably none of my business. But the Foochow happens to be an inverted object, you see—something with that persistent and puzzling backwards significance again. And that is my business."

"Backwards," murmured Miss Temple, putting her hand to her mouth and staring at Donald Kirk still.

Ellery could have sworn he saw horror in Donald's eyes. Was it assumed? He glanced sharply at Macgowan. But the big man had turned back to the window again, and there was something angry and stubborn in the set of his shoulders.

"But I didn't—" began Kirk, and stopped dazedly.

"You see," drawled Ellery, "you have two things to explain, old chap: why you sold the Foochow stamp at this time and in such a surreptitious manner, and where you got it in the first place."

There was silence as Hubbell stamped across the foyer, darting one unguarded curious glance into the salon as he passed.

Then Kirk said: "I suppose it has to come out," dully, quite without hope. "And that's why I said I acted like a fool. I couldn't have expected—" He buried his face in his hands momentarily, and a wonderful softness came over Miss Temple's face as she watched his boyish despair. He looked up, haggard. "Glenn knows something of my condition. It isn't what you'd think, seeing this establishment, the way we live. This goes for you, too, Jo. Perhaps I should have told you . . . I'm in rather a tight spot financially at the moment, you see."

Miss Temple said nothing.

"Oh," said Ellery. Then he said cheerfully: "Well! That's scarcely an uncommon state of affairs these hectic days, Kirk. The Mandarin is shaky?"

"It's bad enough. Credits, collections, bookstores going out of business by the score. . . ." Donald shook his head. "We have a terrific amount of money outstanding. For a long time now I've been feeding the business cash, in a desperate attempt to save it. Berne's broke, of course; I don't know where he spends his money, but he never has any. Things can't go on this way; business must get better, and when it does we'll pull out all right, because we've got a solid list, thanks chiefly to Berne's genius for picking winners. But meanwhile—" He shook his shoulders in a curious bodily expression of despair.

"But the stamp," said Ellery gently.

"I've been forced to turn a few items from my collection recently into cash. That's how it came about that—"

Macgowan turned about and said in metallic tones: "I see all that, Donald, but what I still don't see is why you sold it under cover that way, putting me in the rotten position of seeming to have . . . Why didn't you come to me, Donald, for God's sake?"

"Again?" said the young man laconically.

Macgowan bit his lip. "There was no necessity of—saying that, Donald. I didn't mean to—"

"But there is." Kirk rose and faced them tensely. "For some time, Queen—since I've got to clear my conscience and get the record straight—I've been touching Glenn for money. Substantial loans, you understand. Father's no money of his own; he doesn't know . . . I haven't wanted to bother him about—well, about the mess I'm in. My own fortune has dwindled to the point where it's impossible for me to raise any more cash. The bulk of it is tied up in frozen assets. They're quite the most Arctic assets in the world, I suspect." He grinned without humor. "So—I've been borrowing from Glenn, who's been more than generous. There's nothing wrong in that, although I've wished a thousand times that I hadn't been forced to do it. Of course, Glenn has known about my fix all along. . . . But the drain's terribly severe, Queen—terribly. And suddenly I needed a lot of cash again—for various things." His eyes were half-closed. "The most valuable stamp in my collection was the Foochow, strangely enough. I felt that I couldn't offer it to Glenn openly for cash when I already owed him so much, and it was the cash I needed. So I used Varjian to sell it to Glenn under cover, since I really wanted him to have it if I couldn't. That's all."

He sat down very abruptly. Miss Temple was studying him with the strangest, serenest, softest interest.

Macgowan muttered: "I see it now, Don. I'm sorry about—But how about the fact," he cried, "that the Foochow illustrates one of those damned backwards significances of Queen's, Donald? Didn't it occur to you that by making me buy the stamp at this time you were laying me open to all sorts of nasty accusations?"

Donald raised red-rimmed eyes. "Glenn, I give you my word. . . . It never occurred to me. Not for an instant. Oh, Lord, Glenn, do you really think I'd have done that deliberately? Maliciously? You can't think that. Or you, Queen. It wasn't until you mentioned it that I realized . . ."

He slumped back, exhausted. Macgowan hesitated, his face a study in conflicting emotions, and then went to Kirk and thumped his shoulder and growled: "Forget it, Don. It's I who've been the fool. I've been a chump throughout. Forget it. You know if there's anything I can do—"

"Hmmm," said Ellery. "And now that that's settled, Kirk, how about the second of my queries?"

"Second?" asked Kirk, blinking.

"Yes. Where did you get the stamp in the first place?"

"Oh!" said the young man instantly. "I bought it. A long time ago."

"From whom?"

"Some dealer or other. I've forgotten."

"Liar," said Ellery amiably, and he cupped his hands over a match.

Kirk sank back, scarlet. Big Macgowan was staring from his friend to Ellery, obviously struggling between loyalty and a renascence of suspicion. Miss Temple twisted her handkerchief into a limp ball.

"I don't know," said Kirk with difficulty, "what you mean, Queen."

"Come, come, Kirk," drawled Ellery, blowing smoke, "you're lying. Where did you get that Foochow?"

Miss Temple dropped the ball and said: "Mr. Queen—"

Kirk sprang to his feet. "Jo—don't!"

"It's all right, Donald," she said quietly. "Mr. Queen, Mr. Kirk is being very chivalrous. It's quite like the old times. He's a dear to do it, but it's really unnecessary. No, Donald, I've nothing to conceal. You see, Mr. Queen, Donald got the Foochow from *me*."

"Ah," said Ellery with a smile, "that's better. That's ever so much better. May I point out sententiously that the truth always pays in the long run? I suspected some such situation when I came here. Kirk, you're a gentleman and a scholar. And now, Miss Temple, suppose you enlighten us further."

"You don't really have to, you know, Jo," said Kirk quickly. "There's no compulsion. . . ."

Macgowan touched his friend's arm. "Quiet, Don. It's really better this way. Queen's right."

"Indeed he is," murmured Miss Temple cheerfully. "My father, who as I've said on other occasions was in the American diplomatic service in China, was also—something I neglected to mention to any one but Mr. Kirk, since he seemed the only one interested—a small collector of sorts. Nothing showy, like Donald or Mr. Macgowan. He hadn't enough income to go in for really expensive things, you see."

"Jo, don't you think—"

"No, Donald. It may as well come out now. I can't see that it will help matters to suppress it. And since I'm a babe in the woods, I'm sure justice will—er—triumph." She grinned elfishly, and even Kirk smiled in response. "Father picked up a stamp in Foochow years and years ago from some furtive little Eurasian or other—I never did get straight how the creature had got hold of the stamp. I suppose he was in the local postal service. At any rate, father bought the stamp for a ridiculously small price, and it was in his collection until he died."

"Lord, what luck!" cried Macgowan, his eyes shining.

"And other collectors didn't know he had it?" asked Ellery.

"I'm not sure, but I don't think any one did, Mr. Queen. Father didn't know many collectors, and after a while he lost most of his interest in his own collection. . . . It just mouldered away in our attic. I remember my *amah* used to speak to me reproachfully about it."

"Imagine that," muttered Macgowan. "That's the way the great rarities are lost. Lord, that's—that's almost criminal negligence! I beg your pardon, Miss Temple."

"Oh, it's all right, Mr. Macgowan," said Jo with a sigh. "I suppose it was. When father died I sold most of the collection—it didn't bring much, but I needed money, you see. Somehow, though, I couldn't bring myself to sell the Foochow. It was the only item that father ever talked about with anything like enthusiasm, and I—I suppose I held on to it out of silly sentiment."

"To whom," demanded Ellery, "did you sell the others?"

"Oh, to some dealer in Pekin. I forget his name."

"Tso Lin?" asked Macgowan curiously.

"I believe that was the one. Why, do you know him?"

"I've corresponded with him. Perfectly honest Chinaman, Queen."

"Hmm. You didn't tell him about the Foochow, Miss Temple?"

She frowned prettily. "I don't think so. At any rate, when I began to correspond with Mr. Kirk about my literary plans, somehow it came out that—well, he can tell you about that."

Kirk said eagerly: "It all came about very naturally, Queen. I happened to write once that I collected Chinese stamps, and Miss Temple wrote me about her father's Foochow. I was enormously interested, of course and—" his face darkened—"I was a little better off financially than I am now. While the Foochow, being a local, wasn't in my line, it sounded so extraordinary that I decided I must have it. To make a long story short, I persuaded Miss Temple to part with it."

"It wasn't so hard," said the tiny woman softly. "I realized that I was selfish to hold on to it, since I've not the faintest interest in philately. I suppose I share the usual feminine stupidity about such things. And then, too, I needed money badly. Mr. Kirk offered such an unbelievable sum for it that at first I was suspicious—thought he had sinister designs on the unsophisticated girl from China."

"But then," grinned Ellery, "I suppose his honest letters turned the tide. Well! How much did you pay Miss Temple for it, Kirk?"

"Ten thousand. It's worth it. Isn't it, Glenn?"

Macgowan started slightly out of a reverie. "Oh, unquestion-ably, or I shouldn't have bought it."

"And that's all," sighed Miss Temple. "Now do you see, Mr. Queen? Perfectly innocent story, and I'm sure your suspicions are all banished; aren't they, Mr. Queen?"

"A plethora of Mr. Queens, Miss Temple," said Ellery, rising with a smile, "but it would seem so, wouldn't it? By the way, didn't it occur to you, either, after the crime that there was something backwards about the stamp?"

"I do believe," said Jo ruefully, "that I completely forgot the whole thing. You can't remember everything, you know."

"I suppose not," drawled Ellery. "Especially the important things. Well, good day to you all; I'm afraid I've wasted your time as well as mine. Don't worry, Macgowan; as they say in Silver Gulch, 'It all comes out in the wash.'"

"Ha, ha," said Macgowan.

"Well," grinned Ellery, "at least that was appreciation. Good-bye."

When Hubbell had let him out of the Kirk apartment, Mr. Ellery Queen seemed neither in an unsuspicious temper nor of a disposition to depart. He stood still in the corridor, musing and frowning and chewing a mental cud that apparently offered stub-born resistance.

"Damned funny business, all of it," he muttered to himself. "I'll be switched if I can see light anywhere."

The door across the corridor caught his attention, and he sighed. It did seem like a century ago that he had opened that door and found a room turned topsy-turvy and a dead man in inverted clothing. Struck by a sudden thought, he crossed the hall and tried the door. But it was locked.

He shrugged and was about to turn the corner and proceed

toward the elevators when a movement far down the corridor caused him to jump like a startled kangaroo around the corner and stand still without breathing. He took off his hat and peered cautiously out.

A woman had appeared from the fire-escape stairway beyond and at the other side of the door to Dr. Kirk's study; and she was acting very queerly indeed.

In her arms there was a bulky bundle wrapped in brown paper—a heavy bundle, to judge from the labored progress she made. She was trying to tread softly, and there was no question of the nervousness that animated her, since she kept jerking her head from side to side like a wary animal. It was very odd to see a tall young woman in a modish fur-trimmed suit and a rakish toque and trim gloves staggering under the weight of a badly wrapped bundle of that size. There was something almost humorous about it.

But Ellery did not smile. He watched with a breath-suspended concentration, tingling in every nerve. "Lord," he thought, "what luck!"

The woman turned her head to look his way, and Ellery dodged back out of sight. When he looked again she was fumbling with the knob of Dr. Kirk's door in a sort of desperate haste. Then it swung open and she vanished inside the room.

Ellery sped down the corridor like the wind, topcoat-tails flying. But he made no noise and reached the door without incident. He looked up and down the hall; it was deserted. Dr. Kirk was presumably not in the apartment; he was probably being wheeled about the roof of the Chancellor by Miss Diversey for his morning constitutional, grumbling and cursing in his usual ill-temper. . . . Ellery knelt and peered through the keyhole. He could see the woman moving quickly about the study, but the view was too narrow for panoramic observation.

He scrambled up the corridor to the next door, which he re-

membered led to Dr. Kirk's bedroom. If the irascible old gentleman was out . . . He tried the door; it was unlocked, and he stole
into the room. He flew to the door at his right, which led to another bedroom, and bolted it; and then he hurried to the closed door
leading to the study. It took him many seconds to turn the knob
and open the door to a crack without making any noise.

The woman was almost finished. The brown wrapping-paper
lay on the floor. With feverish haste she was placing the contents
of the bundle—huge heavy books—on the shelf from which Dr.
Kirk's Hebrew books had been stolen.

When she was gone, crushing the brown paper into a ball and
carrying it with her, Ellery stepped calmly into the study.

The books which the woman had just put upon the shelf were,
as he had suspected, all volumes of Hebrew commentaries. Unquestionably they were the books which had been stolen from the
old scholar.

Ellery quietly retraced his steps, unbolted the farther door of
the bedroom, went out by the bedroom door, and slipped down
the corridor just as he heard the foyer door of the Kirk suite slam.

He stood very still in the elevator all the way down to the lobby,
his brow creased in many corrugations of thought.

It was perfectly amazing. Of all developments! Another incomprehensible thread in the fabric of the most puzzling mystery he
had ever faced. . . . And then something sparked in his brain and
he grew very thoughtful indeed. Yes, it was possible. . . . A theory
which covered the facts; at least on the surface. . . . If that was the
case, there was another—

He shook his head impatiently. It would bear thinking about.

For the woman had been Marcella Kirk.

11. UNKNOWN QUANTITIES

PERHAPS THE most precise development in the science of policing is the uncanny ability of the modern detective to trace the movements and establish the identities of so-called unknown persons. Since he is not infallible his score is imperfect; but his percentage of successes is remarkably high, considering the Minotaur's maze of difficulties. The whole complicated mechanism of the police chain hums along on oiled bearings.

And yet, in the case of the mysterious little man who was murdered in the Hotel Chancellor, the police encountered no success whatever. Even in instances of the normal failures something is found—a clue, a trace, a wisp of connection, some last movement which has left its imprint on a casual mind. But here there was nothing but the darkness of space. It was as if the little man had dropped to earth from another planet, accompanied by the chill mysteries of the void.

Inspector Queen, in whose hands—since he was in charge of the murder investigation—the threads of identification refused to assemble, clung to his task with the tenacity of a leech. He refused to concede failure even after the regular channels were drained: the publicized photographs of the dead man, the descriptions and pleas sent to police officials of other cities, the tireless check-up with the records of the Identification Bureau, the unceasing search by plainclothesmen for the last trail of the dead man, the pumping of underworld informers on the theory that the victim might have had criminal affiliations.

The Inspector gritted his teeth and flung more men into the search. The reports of—*Nothing. No Trace. Unknown Here. No Fingerprints*—continued to pour in. All lines of investigation ended in a *cul-de-sac*. The blank wall of mystery leered down, apparently insurmountable.

The Missing Persons Bureau, experts in searches of this kind, formed the inevitable theory. Since all the routine investigations had met with no success, it was not untenable, they said, that the victim was not a New Yorker at all; indeed, perhaps not even an American.

Inspector Queen had shaken his head. "I'm ready to try anything," he said to the weary-eyed official in charge of the Bureau, "but I tell you it's not that. There's something awfully screwy about this business. . . . He may have been a foreigner as you claim, but I doubt it, John. He didn't look foreign. And the people who spoke to him before he died—this woman Mrs. Shane and this man Osborne, and even that nurse on duty at the Kirk place who heard him say a few words—they all insist that he didn't have a foreign accent of any kind, just a funny sort o' soft voice. And that was probably just a speech defect, or a habit." Then he set his little jaw. "However, it won't hurt to try; so go to it, John."

And so the enormous task of notifying the police departments of all the major cities of the world, which had been begun tentatively before, was pushed ahead with thoroughness and dispatch. Full description and fingerprints were forwarded, with due emphasis on the soft-voice characteristic. The dead man's photograph was exhibited to employees of air lines, of Atlantic Ocean liners, of coast steamers, of railroads. And the reports came bouncing back with the hopeless inevitability of a rubber ball: *No Identification. Man Unknown. No Recollection of Appearance on This Line.* Nothing.

It was three days after Miss Temple's confession of ownership of the Foochow stamp that Inspector Queen growled to Ellery: "It may be that we're up against a situation that hits us on the snoot every once in a while. I've found from experience that periodically these transportation people go into a fit of the doldrums if doldrums have fits—and can't remember anything further back than their last yawn. Because we've met with failure along this angle so far doesn't mean that bird—damn his soul!—didn't use a liner, or a train, or a 'plane. Darn it all, he must have got to New York *some* way!"

"If he got to New York at all," said Ellery. "I mean—if he hasn't been in New York all the time."

"There are a lot of 'ifs' in this business, my son. I'm not claiming anything. May've been born and brought up in the city here and never left the Bronx once, for all I know. Or this may have been his first visit to New York. But I'm betting he wasn't a New Yorker."

"Probably not," drawled Ellery. "I just made the point to get it on the record. I think you're right, myself."

"Oh, you do?" snapped the Inspector. "When you use that tone of voice I get suspicious. Come on—what d'ye know?"

"Nothing that you don't know," laughed Ellery. "I've told you every little thing that's happened so far when you weren't around. Can't I agree with you once in a while without being jumped like a horse-thief?"

The Inspector tapped his snuff-box absently, and for some time there was no sound but the shrill whistle of the uniformed officer two floors below who was addicted to *The Sidewalks of New York* out of loyalty to the administration. Ellery stared gloomily through the bars on his father's office-window.

And then something brought his eyes around, and he gaped at his father, who was glaring at him with the mania of discovery. As he watched, the old gentleman leaped out of his swivel-chair and almost fell over trying to press one of his push-buttons.

"Of course!" he cried in a strangled voice. "What a dope, what a dope I am. . . . Billy," he howled at the deskman who ran in, "is Thomas out there?" The desk-man vanished and a moment later Sergeant Velie barged in.

The Inspector inhaled snuff, muttering to himself. "Sure, sure, that's the ticket. . . . 'Lo, Thomas. Why didn't I think of it before? Sit down."

"What is this?" demanded Ellery. "What's the brainstorm?"

The Inspector ignored him elaborately and sat down at his desk, chuckling and rubbing his hands. "How you doin' on the stamp and jewelry lead, Thomas?"

"Not so good," rumbled the Sergeant lugubriously.

"Nothing, hey?"

"Not a smell. They don't know him, any of 'em. I'm sure of that now."

"Curious," murmured Ellery, frowning. "There's something else that baffles me."

"Go baffle a buffalo," said the Inspector jovially. "This is hot. Listen, Thomas. Did you get the last full report on the hotels?"

"Sure. He wasn't registered at any hotel in the city. Dead sure now."

"Hmm. Well, listen here, Thomas, my boy. And you too, son, if you aren't too busy with those grand bafflements of yours. Let's say the little guy wasn't a New Yorker. We're all convinced of that?"

"*I* think he comes from Mars or some place," grumbled Velie.

"I'm not convinced," drawled Ellery, "but it's probably so."

"All right. If he wasn't a New Yorker—and the signs all point to the fact that he didn't come from any of the suburbs, because we've checked all that—then what's the situation?" The Inspector leaned forward. "Then he comes from some outlying spot. American or foreign, but at least outlying. Right so far?"

"Dismally so," said Ellery, nevertheless watching his father intently. "*Alors*?"

"A lor' yourself," retorted the Inspector, in rare good-humor. He tapped his desk with a little click of his finger-nail. "A lor', my son, he was a visitor to New York. A lor', my son, *he must have had baggage!*"

Ellery's eyes widened. The Sergeant's mouth fell open. Then Ellery sprang from the chair. "Dad, that's positively brilliant; that's genius! How on earth could such a simple conclusion have escaped me? Of course! You're perfectly right. Baggage. . . . I bow this proud head in shame. It takes experienced brains, these things. Baggage!"

"Sounds like a good hunch, Inspector," said the Sergeant thoughtfully, stroking his mastodonic jaw.

"You see?" The Inspector spread his hands, grinning. "Nothing to it. Nothing up my sleeve but muscle and hair. I'd bet right now . . ." Then his face fell. "Well, maybe we'd better not count any chickens. The point is he didn't register at a hotel anywhere. And when he walked out of the elevator on the twenty-second floor of the Chancellor he wasn't carrying anything. Yet he must have had baggage. So what?"

"So he must 'a' checked it somewhere," muttered the Sergeant.

"So you're damned right, Thomas. Here's what I want you to do, Carnera, me lad. Put every available man—get the Missing Persons to lend a hand—on a canvass of all the checkrooms in the city, right from the Battery to Vanderveer Park. Everything— hotels, terminals, department stores; the whole shooting-match. Don't forget the airfields, by the way; see that Curtiss Field, Roosevelt, Floyd Bennett—all of 'em are covered. And the Customs House. Get a line on everything that was checked on the afternoon of the murder and that's still uncalled for. And keep in touch with me every hour."

The Sergeant grinned and took himself off.

"Smart," said Ellery, lighting a cigaret. "Intuition tells me that you've finally got your talons into something, Inspector dear."

"Well," sighed the old gentleman, "if that fails I'll be about ready to give up, El. It does beat—"

The deskman came in and flipped an envelope on the Inspector's desk.

"What's that?" demanded Ellery, cigaret suspended in air.

The Inspector seized the envelope. "Ah. Answer from the Yard to my cable!" He read the message quickly and then tossed it to Ellery. "Well," he said in a quieter tone, "seems you were right, El. Seems you were right."

"About what?"

"That woman."

"Indeed!" Ellery reached for the cablegram.

"How'd you guess?"

Ellery grinned, a little woefully. "I never guess; you know that. It was that backwards business, you see."

"Backwards!"

"Of course," sighed Ellery. "It struck me the woman was off-color somewhere; that's why I suggested asking Scotland Yard about a possible *dossier*. But the name—" He shrugged. "When I wrote the name Sewell down on that piece of paper for you, it was because I'd applied the backwards test to the name of Llewes—inevitable, I suppose, my mind being the tortuous organ it is. And then it was too much to ask that Llewes should be Sewell backwards without its also being the woman's alias, you see.

Ellery scanned the cable swiftly. It ran:

IRENE SEWELL BRITISH CONFIDENCE WOMAN WELL KNOWN TO US AND CONTINENTAL POLICE NOT WANTED PRESENT STOP SPECIAL WEAKNESS FOR JEWELS WORKS

ALONE HAS USED NAME LLEWES IN PAST KINDEST PERSON-
AL REGARDS

TRENCH

INSPECTOR SCOTLAND YARD

"Special weakness for jewels," murmured Ellery, putting down the cable. "And there's such an alluring honey-pot in the Kirk direction. . . . Have you been able to find out anything about her, dad?"

"Some. She came from England a couple of months ago and put up at the Chancellor in great style."

"Alone?"

"Except for a maid—Cockney. Looks funny to me. Anyway, Irene struck up an acquaintance with Donald Kirk—don't know just how she managed it, but she did it in short order—and they got pretty chummy. She posed as a sort of globe-trotter who'd had plenty of experiences in queer places—"

"Scarcely a pose, I should judge from Trench's cable."

"I guess not," said the Inspector grimly. "Anyway, the gag seems to have been that she had had a lot of experiences that were just crying to be put into print-travel stuff in faraway places, reminiscences of pretty famous people—she'd spent a lot of time in Geneva, for instance—something like that. So she was thinking of writing a book about it all. Well, you know these young publishers. Kirk's got a sound head on his shoulders and all that, from what I hear, but this dame is beautiful and she has a smooth line, and—well, I guess he fell for it."

"Or her," suggested Ellery.

"It's a toss-up which one. I'd say not, judging from the googoo eyes he's been making at this Temple girl."

"But Jo Temple unfortunately came *after* Miss Llewes," murmured Ellery. "By that time, perhaps, the damage—if there is any—was done. Go on; you excite me strangely."

"Anyway, they began to talk this 'book' over. Kirk began to have 'conferences' with her at odd hours."

"Where?"

"In her suite at the Chancellor."

"Unchaperoned?"

"Pul-ease, *Mr.* Queen!" The Inspector grinned lasciviously. "What d'ye think this is, Old Home Week? Sure! And that maid—she's the one that gave Thomas all the dope—is ready to testify to goings-on."

Ellery raised his eyebrows. "Goings-on? Kirk and the Llewes wench?"

"Put your own construction to it," snickered the Inspector. "*I'm* a pure-minded old cuss who always believes the best of everybody. But at night with a raving beauty in the kind of clothes she wears, or rather doesn't wear . . ." He shook his head. "And, after all, this Kirk lad is young and he looks normally lusty to me. He began to take her around to parties and he introduced her to all his friends and to his family—regular tea-party, it was. Then came the dawn."

"Meaning?"

"The dawn," repeated the Inspector dreamily. "He woke up, I guess. Got tired of playing tiddledywinks, or whatever the hell it was he *was* playing. Anyway, he started to try to avoid her. Well, fawncy that. What d'ye think happened? The usual thing. She hung on with that damn' smile of hers. I'll bet she hangs pretty!"

"It's not difficult to see what must have happened," said Ellery thoughtfully, "and I suppose you yourself could see it if you'd stop playing the vicarious satyr—which is sheerest pose, my dear pater, as only I can know—and get back to normal. When Jo Temple appeared on the scene young Donald must have suffered a complete change of heart. From the tender and slightly unorthodox love-scene I inadvertently blundered into with Macgowan three days ago he fell in love with her on the spot. Naturally, exit Miss Llewes as far as young Lothario is concerned. And Miss Llewes—who's playing a deep and dirty game—pleasantly refuses to exit. Result— Mr. Kirk has headaches and goes about with a Help!-the-tigress-is-after-me sort of look on his honest young pan."

"This Sewell woman has a hold on him, I'm positive," said the Inspector. "A hold he can't wriggle out of. He's in a tough spot. And then if she's trying to bleed him . . . Say, he *is* in a tough spot! Or do you think he's strapped financially because he's been paying her heavy sugar for blackmail?"

"It's possible that that may have contributed, dad, although I feel sure his financial troubles antedated the advent of Miss Llewes. I know one thing, however, which was dark mystery before."

"Well?"

"The secret of that scribbled message Glenn Macgowan left for Kirk the evening of the murder. Remember what it said? 'I know now. You're dealing with a dangerous character. Go easy until I can talk to you aside. Don, watch your step.'"

"Maybe," grumbled the Inspector. "I was half-hoping Macgowan was referring to our fat little corp-us."

"No, no, I'm sure that's not the case. Macgowan obviously was suspicious of the Llewes woman from the beginning—he's a shrewd chap, Macgowan, and with his strong streak of moral rectitude would probably have been suspicious of such a dazzling worldly creature under any circumstances. . . ."

"Macgowan?" said the Inspector dubiously. "Never struck me that way. I thought he's sort of a regular guy."

"Oh, he's regular enough; but there are some things one can't live down, and one of them is a moral streak. His family burned witches in Salem Town. I don't mean that Macgowan's above affairs

of the flesh, to put it politely; but he is above—or below—the notoriety and scandal that sometimes result from them. It's a pragmatic
morality."

"All right, all right; I give up. So what?"

"He must have looked the Llewes wench up quietly and dis-
covered something about her the very afternoon of the murder.
I suspect his source of information may have been identical with
Velie's—the woman's maid. At any rate, he felt that he had to warn
Kirk against her at the earliest opportunity—*ergo*, the note. Yes,
yes, I'm sure that's it."

"Sounds plausible," admitted the Inspector grudgingly.

"Shows you that it never pays to use strong-arm methods, father dear. You've been reading too much Hammett. I've always said
that if there's one class who should be excluded from the reading of
contemporary blood-and-thunder of the so-called realistic school
of fiction it's our worthy police force. Breeds shocking illusions of
grandeur. . . . Where was I? Yes; here we've solved a mystery without so much as a suspicion in the minds of the principals that we
know where the body is—er—buried."

"Don't you think Donald Kirk has discovered his note from
Macgowan is missing?" grinned the Inspector.

Ellery murmured: "I doubt it. He was in a terrific stew that
night. And even if he has discovered it's missing, he must think he
lost it somewhere. Certainly he doesn't suspect *me* of burglarious
methods. That's one advantage of looking scholarly."

"He hasn't acted funny towards you?"

"That's precisely why I made that really scintillant assertion."

"Hmm." The Inspector watched Ellery struggle into his coat. "I
have the funny notion something's due to break on this case."

"Baggage?"

"You wait," said the Inspector slyly, "and see."

Ellery had not long to wait. He was lounging comfortably before his fire that evening reading aloud to Djuna—who looked fiercely bored—the Mock Turtle's oration when the Inspector burst into their apartment.

"El! What d'ye think?" The old gentleman flung his hat down and thrust his jaw at Ellery.

Ellery put the book down and Djuna, with a huge sigh of relief, slipped away. "It's broken?"

"It's broken. Busted wide open, my son. Wide open!" The Inspector strutted up and down in his coat like some latter-day Napoleon. "We searched the Sewell woman's rooms at the Chancellor this afternoon."

"Do tell!"

"I'm giving it to you. She was out somewhere and we worked fast. What d'ye think we found?"

"I haven't the remotest idea."

"Jewelry!"

"Ah."

The Inspector sneezed cheerfully over his snuff. "Well, it was a plain figure. Trench cables that the woman's got a yen for jewels; and here we find a slew of the stuff hidden in her apartment. Damned good stuff, too; no junk. So we assumed it wasn't hers and I sent the boys hot on the trail to try and trace the ice. Know what we found?"

Ellery sighed. "I suppose this is vengeance. Am I as exasperating to you at times as you are to me now? No! What?"

"We hit the regular jewelry trade and found that the ice is unique. Old pieces in rare settings with histories attached to 'em. Collectors' items."

"Good lord!" exclaimed Ellery. "Don't tell me the fool stole them!"

"As to that," murmured the Inspector, "I wouldn't know, y'see.

But one thing I do know." He yanked at Ellery's lapel. "Get out of that chair; we're going places. One thing I do know. . . . The trade to a man told us who's supposed to own that stuff. Matter of common knowledge, they said."

"Not—" Ellery began slowly.

"Sure. To a piece, they all come from the jewelry-collection of Donald Kirk!"

12. A GIFT OF GEMS

SERGEANT VELIE, who had been hurriedly superseded in his direction of the search for the dead man's baggage in order that he might be at hand for the raid on Irene Llewes's apartment, reported to the Inspector in the lobby of the Chancellor.

"Clear coast, Chief. I had a man—Johnson—in the dame's apartment after the raid dressed up as a hotel porter fixin' the plumbing. The maid's okay, too. She didn't come in from her afternoon off till just before six."

"She doesn't know what happened?" asked the Inspector sharply.

"Not her."

"How about Irene?"

"She trots in, Johnson says, around half-past six and dressed in doodads, like she's goin' on a party. She never even looked for the ice in the wall-safe. Her own stuff—in her jewel-box in the vanity—she did look at, though. Wore some of it."

"Did she put her wrap on when she left her rooms?" demanded Ellery.

The Sergeant grinned. "But she *didn't* leave 'em, Mr. Queen."

"Is she alone?"

"Not so you could notice it. She's throwin' a party for the Kirk crowd—cocktail party, Johnson reports he heard her say. They're all up there now."

"Hmm," said the Inspector. "Well, one place is as good as another. Before we tackle her, though, I want to go up to the twenty-second."

"Now why on earth," said Ellery, "do you want to do that?"

"Just a notion."

The elevator was jammed and they were crushed against the rear bronze wall. The Inspector whispered: "If this Marcella girl's at the shindig, I'll kill two birds with one stone and pump her about those books of her old man's. I don't know why you told me to lay off the other day."

"Because I hadn't quite figured it out," snapped Ellery.

"Oh, then you know now why she did it?"

"On examination it's simplicity itself. I was stupid not to have thought of it instantly."

"Well, why?"

But they had reached the twenty-second floor, and Ellery preceded his father and the Sergeant from the elevator without replying.

Mrs. Shane gulped a frightened, bosom-raising greeting from her desk. But the Inspector ignored her and strode straight to the door of Donald Kirk's office and opened it without knocking. Sergeant Velie grunted: "Hey, wake up, flattie," to a uniformed officer who had been drowsing on a chair near the door to the death-room.

Osborne rose from his desk and dropped his stamp-tongs. "Inspector—Mr. Queen! Is anything wrong again?" He was a little pale.

"Yet," growled the Inspector. "Listen, Osborne. Is there a piece of jewelry in Kirk's collection known as the Grand Duchess's Tiara?"

Osborne looked puzzled. "Why, certainly."

"And one called the Red Brooch?"

"Yes. Why—"

"A beaten-silver *lavallière* with an emerald pendant?"

"Yes. But what's happened, Inspector Queen?"

"Don't *you* know?"

Osborne looked from the old man's grim face to Ellery's, and slowly sank back into his chair. "N-no, sir. I don't have much to do with Mr. Kirk's collection of antique jewelry, as he can tell you. He keeps them in a vault at the bank, and only he has access to them."

"Well," barked the Inspector, "they're gone."

"Gone?" gasped Osborne. He was utterly and sincerely flabbergasted. "The entire collection?"

"Just some choice pieces."

"Does—does Mr. Kirk know?"

"That," said the Inspector with a sour smile, "is what I'm going to find out." He jerked his head at his two companions. "Come on. I just wanted Osborne's corroboration. Just in case." He chuckled and started for the door.

"Inspector!" Osborne clutched the sides of his desk. "You're—you're not going to question Mr. Kirk now, are you?"

The Inspector stopped short, whirled around, and cocked his head at Osborne with an expression of complete unfriendliness. "And suppose I am, Mister Osborne? What's it to you?"

"But they're all—I mean," said Osborne, licking his pale lips, "Mr. Kirk's having a little celebration, Inspector. It wouldn't be nice—"

"Celebration?" The Queens regarded each other. "In the Kirk rooms?"

"No, sir," said Osborne eagerly. "In Miss Llewes's suite on the floor below. You see, she invited them all to a cocktail party when she heard that Mr. Kirk had become engaged. So that's why I—"

"Engaged!" murmured Ellery. "Will wonders never cease, O

Power of Darkness? I take it, Ozzie, that this is a Sino-American alliance?"

"Eh? Oh, yes, sir. Miss Temple. Under the circumstances you couldn't very well go—"

"The Temple girl, huh?" muttered the Inspector.

"While we're here," drawled Ellery. "Ozzie, did you ever hear of a postage stamp—" his eyes swept lazily over the stamp-littered desk—"of Foochow, $1 denomination, ochre and black, with the black erroneously printed on the gum-side of the stamp?"

Osborne sat very still. His weary eyes shifted, and his knuckles became a dirty white. "Why—I can't—remember any such error," he muttered.

"Liar," said Ellery cheerfully. "We know all about it, Ozzie. If I may call you Ozzie. . . ."

"You—know?" said Osborne with difficulty, raising his eyes.

"Oh, certainly. Don Kirk himself told us."

Osborne took out his handkerchief and wiped his forehead. "I'm sorry, Mr. Queen. I thought—"

"Come on," snapped the Inspector impatiently. "You, there!" he bellowed at the policeman, who started and went pale. "You see that this man Osborne here doesn't touch that house 'phone for five minutes. Be good, Osborne. . . . Well, come on, boys. If there's any fun we might's well be in on it, too!"

The three rooms of the Llewes suite were directly below the Kirk apartment. The door was opened in response to the Inspector's ring by an angular maid with cubistic cheeks and an unlovely pointed nose. She began to protest in a weak whining Cockney voice, but then she saw the Sergeant and fell back gaping. The Inspector pushed past her without ceremony and strode through a small reception-foyer into a sitting-room, which was noisy with laughter and conversation. Both ceased magically.

They were all there—Dr. Kirk, Marcella, Macgowan, Berne, Jo Temple, Donald, Irene Llewes; and there were two women and a man whom the Queens had never seen before. One of the strangers was a tall flashing woman of foreign appearance who clung to Felix Berne's arm with a queer possessiveness. All were in evening attire.

Miss Llewes came swiftly forward, smiling. "Yes?" she said. "Yes? You see, I have guests, Inspector Queen. Perhaps another time . . ."

Macgowan and Donald Kirk were staring at the silent trio very intently. Dr. Kirk, his old nose purple, wheeled himself furiously forward. "What's the meaning of this latest intrusion, gentlemen? Can't decent people ever have protection from meddling busybodies in this confounded madhouse?"

"Take it easy, Dr. Kirk," said the Inspector mildly. "Sorry, folks, to butt in this way, but business is business. We won't be but a minute. Uh—Mr. Kirk, I want to see you about something. Miss Llewes, have you another room we can use for a couple of minutes?"

"Is anything wrong, Inspector?" asked Glenn Macgowan quietly.

"No, no; nothing serious. Just go on with your party. . . . Ah, that's fine, Miss Llewes."

The woman had led them to a door which opened into a living-room. Donald Kirk, silent and pale, walked in like a prisoner approaching the execution chamber. And tiny Jo Temple followed him with head held high and a firm step. The Inspector frowned and was about to say something when Ellery touched his arm. So the Inspector held his tongue.

Donald did not see Jo until the door of the living-room was shut and Sergeant Velie's expansive back was set against it.

"Jo," he said harshly. "You don't want to be mixed up in this—in anything. Please, dear. Go out and wait with the others."

"I'll stay," she said; and she smiled and squeezed his hand. "After all, what good is a wife—or a near-wife—if she doesn't share a little of her husband's responsibilities?"

"Oh," said Ellery. "Things happen so suddenly these days. May I offer my very sincere congratulations?"

"Thank you," they both murmured submissively; and both lowered their eyes. Strange lovers! thought Ellery.

"Well, now, look here," began the Inspector. "I don't have to tell you, Kirk, that you haven't been strictly on the level with us. You've held back certain information and you've acted very funny throughout. I'm going to give you a chance to clear yourself."

Kirk said very slowly: "I don't know what you mean, Inspector." And Jo flung him a sidewise glance that was as puzzled as it was swift.

"Kirk, did you have a robbery recently?" snapped the old gentleman.

"Robbery?" He seemed completely taken by surprise. "Of course not. . . . Oh, I suppose you mean about father's books. Well, you know they've been returned rather mysteriously—"

"I don't mean about father's books, Kirk."

"A robbery?" frowned Kirk. "I can't—No."

"You're sure? Think hard, young man."

Donald jammed his hands nervously in the pockets of his tuxedo. "But I assure you—"

"Do you own certain pieces of antique jewelry—collectors' items—known as the Red Brooch, the Grand Duchess's Tiara, an emerald-pendant *lavallière*, a Sixteenth Century Chinese jade ring?"

Quick as a flash Kirk said: "No, I've sold them."

The Inspector regarded him calmly for a moment, and then went to the door. Sergeant Velie stepped aside and the old man opened the door and called out: "Miss Llewes. One moment, please." Then the tall woman was in the room, smiling a little uncertainly, her slender brows inquiring. She was dressed in something long and curved and intimate and clinging, cut so low that the cleft between her breasts narrowed and widened with the slow surge of her breath, perfectly visible, like a crevasse on a tumbled shore uncovered periodically by the action of the surf.

The Inspector said gently: "Don't you think you'd better step out for a few minutes, Miss Temple?"

Her tiny nose twitched a little, almost humorously. But she said nothing, nor did she release her grip on young Kirk's hand.

"All right," sighed the Inspector. He turned on the tall woman and smiled. "We may as well know each other by our right names, my dear. Now why didn't you tell us that you're really Irene Sewell?"

Kirk blinked uncomprehendingly; and the tall woman drew herself up and blinked, too, like a green-eyed cat faintly startled. Then she smiled in response, and Ellery thought that it was the fourth-dimensional smile of the Cheshire Cat, remote and disembodied. "I beg your pardon?"

"Hmm," said the Inspector with a grin of admiration. "Good nerves, Irene. But it won't do you any good to keep acting. Y'see, we know all about you. My friend Inspector Trench of Scotland Yard informed me only this evening by cable that you and he are old, old buddies. Notorious British confidence-woman, I think he said. But that's Trench for you; no politeness at all. Did you know that, Kirk?"

Donald licked his lips, regarding the woman apparently through a sick haze. "Confidence-woman?" he faltered. But there was something unconvincing in his hesitation; and Ellery sighed and turned away a little, blushing for the good sense of mankind. The only genuine character in the drama, he reflected, was little Miss Temple; she was being herself, not acting a part. And she was studying the tall woman with a sort of distant horror.

The tall woman said nothing. And while there was something

wary in the depths of her green eyes, there was something elusive and mocking in them, too, as if she were indeed the Cheshire Cat having her enigmatic little jest with a faintly bewildered Alice.

"Might's well come clean, Irene," murmured the Inspector. "We know you down to the ground. We know, for instance, that you had in your possession a number of valuable pieces of jewelry which came from the collection of Mr. Kirk. Eh, Irene?"

For an instant her guard came down and she flashed a look in the direction of a door at the farther side of the room. Then she bit her lip and smiled again, and this time it was not the smile of the Cheshire Cat at all but the smile of a dying hope.

"Oh, it won't do you any good to look for 'em in your bedroom wall-safe," chuckled the Inspector, "because they aren't there any more. We routed 'em out this afternoon while you were away. Well, Irene, are you going to tell all about it or do I have to put the nippers on you?"

"Nippers?" she murmured, frowning.

"Now, now, Irene. That's what they call 'em in your country, and I don't doubt but that you've had 'em on your pretty wrists more than once in the past." He lost patience with her suddenly. "You stole those gems!"

"Ah," she said; and this time she was smiling broadly, the hope miraculously revived. "Really, Inspector, you speak such an incomprehensible jargon! You're quite sure they belong to Mr. Kirk?"

"Sure?" The Inspector stared. "What's your game now?"

"If they do, why do you insist there's a crime involved, Inspector? Is it a crime for a gentleman to present a lady with gifts of jewelry? For a moment I thought you meant that Mr. Kirk had stolen them. Heavens!"

There was a moment of thick silence. Then Ellery said swiftly: "Well, Kirk?"

Jo Temple was wrinkling her tiny nose in the most complete

puzzlement. She tightened her grip on Donald's arm. "Donald. Did you give her—those things?"

Kirk stood still, and yet Ellery got the impression that inside he was a caldron of seething little feelings twining about and grappling with one another like a miniature snake enveloping the miniature sons of Laocoön. There was no color whatever in his normally tanned face; it looked washed out, gray.

Almost absently he lifted Jo's hand from his arm and said. "Yes." He had not once looked directly at Irene Llewes.

"There!" cried Miss Llewes gaily. "You see? Much ado about nothing. I trust you, Inspector, to return my jewels at once. I've heard the most shocking stories about the dishonesty of the American police that—"

"Stop it," said the Inspector curtly. "Kirk, what is this? You mean to say that you actually made a gift of those expensive pieces to this woman?"

His control collapsed like a stuck balloon. Under the steady eyes of Jo he sank into the nearest chair and buried his face in his hands. His voice came muffled, miserable. "Yes. No. . . . I don't know what I did."

"No?" said Irene Llewes swiftly. "Ah, Donald. You've such a poor memory," and without a further word she hurried into her bedroom. The Sergeant, scowling, relaxed at the Inspector's headshake. In a moment she was back, bearing a sheet of notepaper. "I'm sure Donald didn't realize what he was saying, Inspector Queen. I don't care, as a rule, to display these intimate—things, but then I've no choice, have I, Inspector? Donald, shame on you!"

The Inspector stared at her, hard; and then took the note from her fingers and read it aloud:

Dear Irene:
I love you. I feel that I can never do enough to con-

vince you of that. My gems are among my most precious possessions. Isn't it a proof of my feeling that I have given you the Tiara, which adorned the head of a Grand Duchess of Russia; the Red Brooch, which belonged to Christina's mother; the jade, which graced the finger of a daughter of a Chinese emperor—all those other pieces which I have had for years? But I give them willingly to the most glamorous woman in the world. Tell me you'll marry me!

DONALD.

Miss Temple quivered perceptibly. "What," she asked in a cold voice, "is the date on that—that piece of erotica, Inspector Queen?"

"You poor dear," murmured Miss Llewes. "I know exactly how you feel, darling. But you can see for yourself that Donald wrote me that before you came to the city, before he knew you. When he met you . . ." She shrugged her magnificent bare shoulders. "*C'est la guerre, et j'y tomba victime.* I harbor no ill feeling, I assure you. Certainly my invitation to you and Donald tonight is proof of that?"

"Clumsy," sneered the Inspector. "If that's the passionate letter of a lover asking his Juliet to get hitched, I'm a monkey's uncle. More like a historical essay. It's a frame, and I'll have the truth if I have to sweat it out of you—both of you! Kirk, what the devil hold has this woman over you that would make you write a note like this at her dictation?"

"Dictation?" Miss Llewes frowned. "Donald. This is becoming quite stupid. Please tell them. Talk, Donald." She stamped her foot. "Talk, I say!"

The young man rose and faced the woman squarely for the first time. There was a veil over his eyes. And although he faced her he addressed the Inspector. "I see no point in continuing this farce," he said in a voice that rasped from his throat. "I'm in for it and

I might as well take my medicine. I lied." Ellery saw a vast relief flood into the tall woman's eyes, to be shut out instantly by her lids. "I wrote the note and I gave Miss Llewes—or Miss Sewell, if that's her real name—the jewels. I didn't know anything about her past. What's more, I don't care. This is a private matter and I see no reason why it should be dragged up now in this—this murder investigation, which hasn't the least connection with my personal affairs."

"Donald," choked Jo, "you—you asked her to marry you?"

Miss Llewes was smiling her faintly triumphant smile. "Don't be silly, now, my dear. What if he did? I'm not exactly the most hideous object in the world? Put it down to an infatuation. I'm sure that's all it was; wasn't it, Donald? At any rate, it's all over now, and you have him. You're not going to be provincial about this, are you?"

"Such heroism," murmured, Ellery.

"Donald! You—you admit it?"

"Yes," he said in the same harsh tone. "I admit it. For God's sake, how long do I have to submit to this torture?" He did not look at the tiny woman from China. "I'm willing to call it all quits if there's no publicity of any kind. It's over now—finished, done. Why don't you let me alone?"

"I see," said the Inspector frigidly. "And the jewels, Kirk?"

"I gave them to her."

Jo stepped quietly in front of the tall woman and said: "Of course you're just the vilest creature. N-not even Donald could really have been taken in . . ." She whirled on the frozen young man. "Don, you *know* I don't believe all this—all this mumbo-jumbo! You—I know you so well, darling. You couldn't have done anything really wrong. Oh, I don't care about a—a petty affair with a cheap adventuress; it hurts me, I suppose, but . . . What is it, Don? What has she done to you, darling? Can't you tell me?"

He said in a queer soft voice: "You'll have to take me as I am, Jo."

The tall woman kept smiling. But there was something strong and sure and arrogant in her voice. "I think I've been *most* patient. Another woman would have made a scene. As for you, Jo Temple, I'll overlook that nasty epithet and give you some advice based on very wide experience: Don't be a silly fool. You have him, and he's a very nice young man." Jo ignored her; she still stared at the averted face of the young man. "And now, Inspector, I must insist that you call your dogs off. I won't have this perpetual persecution. If you persist, I shall leave at once."

"That's what *you* think," said the Inspector sourly. "But you're not leaving until I give you permission to. If you make the slightest move to get out of the country, I'll arrest you on suspicion. It's a swell word, and it's very elastic. Matter of fact, I could slam you behind bars this minute for being an undesirable character. So you stay put in this apartment of yours, Sewell, and be a nice girl. Don't try any tricks on *me*." He squinted at the silent pair before him. "As for you, Kirk, some day you're going to be mighty sorry you didn't make a clean breast of the whole miserable mess you're in. I don't know what devilment this woman is up to, but she seems to have hooked you good and proper. Bad business, young man. . . . Come on, boys."

Ellery sighed, stirring. "But aren't you going to question Marcella Kirk on that little matter of philology?" he murmured.

He was frankly astounded to see wildest alarm leap into Donald Kirk's haggard eyes. "You let Marcella alone, do you hear?" the young man shouted, livid. "Don't drag her into this! Let her alone, I tell you!"

Inspector Queen studied him with a coolly sudden renascence of interest. Then he said gently: "So. I was going to say I'd got a bellyful of the lot of you. But on reconsideration I can stand a little more. Thomas, get Miss Marcella Kirk and her father in here!"

Donald sprang like a released missile toward the door as Velie turned to open it, catching the Sergeant wholly by surprise and shoving him roughly aside. He stood trembling but determined before the door. "No, I tell you. Queen, for God's sake. Don't let him do it!"

"Why, you cocky little weasel—" the Sergeant began to growl, lunging forward.

"Whoa, Velie," said Ellery in a drawl. "Why the dramatics, Kirk, old fellow? No one means to hurt your sister. It's a little misunderstanding that must be cleared up. That's really all." He stepped forward and put his arm in friendly fashion about Kirk's rigid shoulders. "Let Miss Temple take you upstairs, Kirk. You're sadly in need of a drink and some rest for those jumpy nerves of yours."

"Queen, you won't—" There was something pathetic in his voice.

"Of course not," said Ellery soothingly. He glanced at the tiny woman, and she sighed and went to the young man and took, his hand and said something to him in a soft murmur. Ellery felt Kirk's muscles go limp. The Sergeant, scowling, opened the door and permitted the pair to leave. Staring eyes met them from the other room.

"You too, Irene," said the Inspector with curt emphasis. She shrugged and sauntered after Kirk and Jo. But there was something wary about the set of her handsome shoulder-blades, quite as if she were steeling herself against a blow from behind. Sergeant Velie followed her.

"What the devil's eating the youngster?" muttered the Inspector, staring after them.

Ellery started. "Eh? Oh—Kirk." He produced a cigaret and slowly struck a match. "Very interesting. I just caught a glimmer. The barest glimmer . . . Here they are."

It was not two who came in, but three. Sergeant Velie glowered fiercely.

"This Macgowan guy wouldn't stay put," he rasped. "Shall I kick him in the pants, Inspector?"

"I shouldn't advise the attempt, Sergeant," said Ellery with an amused smile, glancing at Macgowan's formidable bulk.

"Well, if he wants to get the works," growled the Inspector, "that's his funeral. Listen, sister—"

Marcella Kirk stood slim and breathlessly quiet between her *fiancé* and her father, who leaned heavily on her arm. The old man was shrunken within the dry bones of his gaunt frame, strangely quiescent and unlike his usual belligerent self. There was a furtive gleam in his old eyes.

Macgowan said softly: "Take it easy, Inspector. My *fiancée* happens to be a sensitive young lady. And I'm not sure I'd be able to stand your strong-arm stuff myself. What's on your mind besides breaking up a perfectly respectable cocktail party?"

"That'll be enough out of you, Mr. Macgowan—"

Dr. Kirk quavered: "What have you done to Donald, damn you?"

"He looked—" whispered Marcella.

"I'll do the asking," said Inspector Queen grimly. "Dr. Kirk, the other day you reported the return of your stolen Hebrew books. Is that correct?"

"Well?" The old scholar's voice was cracked.

"They were *all* returned?"

"Certainly. I told you I wanted no fuss made. I have my books back, which is the only consideration." He stroked his daughter's bare arm with his bony fingers, absently. "Why, have you discovered who—took them?"

"You bet your sweet life."

Marcella Kirk sighed. Her lips were very red against her skin.

Macgowan opened his mouth to speak, changed his mind, and glanced from the face of the girl to the face of his future father-in-law. And he, too, went pale under his tan; and he bit his lip and tightened his grip on Marcella's hand.

"If I may," murmured Ellery. They stared at him, three pairs of fearful eyes. "I think we're all reasonably adult people. Miss Kirk, may I say first of all that I have nothing but admiration for you?"

She swayed suddenly, closing her eyes.

"What do you mean?" said Macgowan hoarsely.

"Your *fiancée*, Macgowan, is a brave, loyal girl. I know precisely what her mental processes were. . . . I had been harping on the strange backwards nature of the crime. There leaped into her mind an instant panoramic picture—her father . . . you, Doctor . . . poring over—" Ellery paused—"Hebrew books. A language whose prime characteristic, she knew, is its literal backwardness. And so—"

"I stole them," she said with a strangled sob. "Oh, I was afraid—"

Dr. Kirk's face altered strangely. "Marcella, my dear," he said in a soft voice. And he pressed her arm and drew himself a little straighter.

"And you forgot, Miss Kirk," Ellery went on, "that Chinese, which is represented in your father's library by many manuscripts, is also a backwards language, so to speak. Isn't that so?"

"Chinese?" she gasped, her eyes widening.

"I thought so. Dad, there's no need to go into this thing any more fully. It's basically my fault. Perfectly understandable, Miss Kirk's reaction to my oral cogitations about the backwardness of the crime. Now that it's cleared up I think it's best we all forget it."

"But Hebrew *is* backwards—"

"Alas," sighed Ellery. "And a great lack. *I* don't know what any of it means. And am I my brother's keeper?" He grinned at Marcella and Macgowan. "Go, and sin no more."

"Oh, all right," growled the Inspector. "Let 'em out, Thomas."

The Sergeant stood aside as the three passed by—all very quiet, and Macgowan hiding something behind his eyelids.

"While we're here," muttered the Inspector, "I might as well clean up one more thing."

"What now?" murmured Ellery.

"This bird Felix Berne. Thomas—"

"Berne?" Ellery's eyes narrowed. "What about Berne?"

"We finally got a check-up on his movements the day of the murder. There's one element . . . Thomas, get Mr. Berne in here, and also that foreign-looking dame who was hanging on his arm when we came in. If my hunch is correct, she's got something to do with this."

"With what?" asked Ellery swiftly as the Sergeant tramped out.

The Inspector shrugged. "That's what I don't know."

Berne was very drunk. He lurched in, his bitter eyes inflamed and a sneer on his sharp keen features. The woman with him looked frightened. She was a tall supple brunette with a body that leaped with life. She pressed her full breasts against Berne's black-sleeved arm as if she were afraid to release it.

"Well?" drawled Berne, his thin lips writhing humorously. "What is it tonight—the *sjambok*, the *bastinado*, or the bed of Procrustes?"

"Good evening, Berne," murmured Ellery. "I will say that detective work is broadening. Pleasure to meet such cultured people. *Sjambok*, did you say? Sounds faintly African-Dutch. What is it?"

"It's a whip made out of rhinoceros hide," said Berne with the same fixed drunken smile, "and if I had you on the South African *veldt*, my dear Queen, I'd like nothing better than to give you a taste of it. I dislike you intensely. I don't know when I've disliked a

fellow-creature more. Go to hell. . . . Well, you vest-pocket Lucifer,"
he snapped suddenly at Inspector Queen, "what's on your mind?
Speak up, man! I haven't all night to waste answering idiotic questions."

"Idiotic questions, hey?" growled the Inspector. "One more
crack like that out of you, wise guy, and I'll sick the Sergeant here
on you, and what he'll do to that pan of yours I'll leave to your
own imagination." He whirled on the woman. "You. What's your
name?"

She pressed closer to the publisher and looked up at him with
a childlike faith.

Berne drawled: "Tell him, *cara mia*. He looks bad, but he's
harmless."

"I—am," said the woman with difficulty, "Lucrezia Rizzo." She
spoke with a strong Italian accent.

"Where d'ye come from?"

"*Italia*. My home—it is—in Firenze."

"Florence, eh?" murmured Ellery. "For the first time I grasp the
essential inspiration behind the vigor of Botticelli's women. You
are very lovely, and you come from a lovely city, *ma donna*."

She flashed him a long low look that had nothing in common
with the fear that had filled her eyes a moment before. But she said
nothing, and continued to cling to Berne's arm.

"Listen, I'm in a hurry," barked Inspector Queen. "How long
you been in New York, *Signora*?"

Again she glanced at Berne, and he nodded. "It is—a week or
so, I think," she said, her sibilants soft and warm.

"Why do you ask?" drawled Berne. "Thinking of pulling *Si-
gnorina Rizzo* into the well-known can on a charge of murder,
Inspector? And I might also point out that you either leap to
conclusions or else possess a shocking ignorance of the simplest
Italian. My friend Lucrezia is unmarried."

"Married or not," snarled the Inspector, "I want to know what she was doing in that bachelor apartment of yours on East Sixty-fourth Street the day of the murder!"

Ellery started slightly, but Berne did not. The publisher showed his teeth in the same fixed drunken smile. "Ah, our metropolitan police now flourish the banner of moral purity! What d'ye think she was doing? You must have a good notion or you wouldn't be asking. . . . Always incomprehensible to me, this stupid habit of asking questions you know the answers to. You didn't think I'd deny it, did you?"

The Inspector's bird-like face was growing redder with every passing instant. He glared at Berne and said: "I'm mighty interested in your movements that day, Berne, and don't think you'll pull the wool over my eyes with that gab of yours. I know that this woman came over on the *Mauretania* with you, and that you cabbed straight from the boat to your apartment with her. That was before noon that day. How'd you spend the rest of the day before you turned up at the Kirk layout upstairs?"

Berne continued to smile. There was a glassy calm in his inflamed eyes that fascinated Ellery. "Oh, you don't know, do you, Inspector?"

"Why, you—"

"Because obviously, if you did know," murmured Berne, "you wouldn't have put the question that way. Amusing, very amusing. Eh, *cara*? The naughty policeman who protects our wives and homes and civic honor doesn't know, and, simple soul that he is, apparently doesn't even suspect. Oh, perhaps I'm being faintly astigmatic; he *does* suspect, let us say, but he hasn't been able to find out definitely." The woman was staring up at him with bewildered, adoring eyes. It was evident that the rapid interchange of English had taxed her simple knowledge of the language. "And, putting his faith in the comfortable labyrinth of our Anglo-Saxon laws, he realizes that without evidence he is like a child without its mother, or," Berne drawled, "a lovely piece of feminine Italian flesh without a chaperon. Eh, Inspector?"

A deadly quiet settled over the room with the extinction of Berne's last word. Ellery, glancing at his father, felt uncomfortably aware of the possibilities. The old gentleman's face had turned to marble, and there was a pinched look about his little nostrils that made his face seem even smaller and harder than it was. There was danger, too, from the direction of Sergeant Velie; his huge shoulders were hunched pugilistically and he was glaring at the publisher with a candid menace that startled Ellery.

Then the moment passed, and the Inspector said in almost a matter-of-fact voice: "Then your story is that you spent the whole day in your apartment with this woman?"

Berne, coolly indifferent to the threatening atmosphere, shrugged. "Where did you think a man would spend the day with this enchanting morsel to keep him company?"

"I'm asking you," said the Inspector quietly.

"Well, then the answer is sweetly in the affirmative." Berne smiled the old ghastly smile and said: "The inquisition is over, Inspector? I may go with lovely Lucrezia to bear me company? *La politesse* calls. Mustn't keep our hostess waiting, you know."

"Go on," said the Inspector. "Beat it. Beat it before I choke the ugly smile off your face with my own hands."

"*Bravo*" drawled Berne. "Come, my dear; it seems that we're no longer wanted." And he drew the bewildered woman closer to him and swung her gently about and steered her toward the door.

"But, Felicio," she murmured, "what—is—"

"Don't Italianate me, my dear," said Berne. "Felix to you." And then they were gone.

None of the three men said anything for some time. The Inspector remained where he was, staring expressionlessly at the door. Sergeant Velie was drawing deep breaths, as if he had been laboring under tremendous strain.

Then Ellery said gently: "Oh, come, dad. Don't let that drunken boor get the best of you. He *does* raise the hackles, I confess. I've felt, myself, a prickling at the nape of my neck that's as old as man's enemies . . . Get that look off your face, dad, please."

"He's the first man," said the Inspector deliberately, "in twenty years who has made me feel like committing murder. The other one was the bird who raped his own daughter; and at least *he* was crazy."

Sergeant Velie said something venomous to himself in a soft mutter.

Ellery shook his father's arm. "Now, now! I want you to do something for me, dad."

Inspector Queen turned to him with a sigh. "Well, what is it now?"

"Can you hale that Sewell woman downtown late tonight on some pretext or other? And get her maid out of the way?"

"Hmm, What for?" said the Inspector with a sudden interest.

"I have," murmured Ellery, sucking thoughtfully on a cigaret, "an idea based on that phantom glimmer I mentioned a few moments ago."

13. BOUDOIR SCENE

Mr. Ellery Queen, not having been reared in that dark quarter of the cosmopolis which breeds those whimsical Raffles who steal in and out of people's homes and manage still to preserve a certain *savoir-faire*, peered nervously up and down the corridor of the Chancellor's twenty-first floor. The coast being clear, his shoulders quivered once or twice beneath his bundling topcoat and he slipped a skeleton key into the keyhole of the Llewes front door. The bolt turned over with a sharp squeak and he pushed the door open.

The reception-foyer was inky black. He stood very still and listened with an intentness that made his ears ache. But the suite was quite silent.

He cursed himself for a cowardly fool and advanced boldly into the darkness toward the spot on the wall where memory told him the electric switch lay. Fumbling, he found it and pressed. The foyer sprang into being. A quick glance through the sitting-room to the door of the living-room for orientation, and he switched off the light and made for the far door. He tripped over a hassock and swore again as he flailed wildly to keep his balance. But at last he reached his goal and opened the door and stole into the living-room.

By the vague flickering light of a hotel electric sign across the canyon of the street he made out the door to the bedroom and went toward it.

The door stood ajar. He poked his head through, held his breath, heard nothing, and slipped into the room shutting the door behind him.

"Not so bad after all," he said to himself, grinning in the darkness. "Maybe I've neglected a natural talent for house-breaking. Now where the deuce is that switch?"

He groped around in the jumpy quarter-light, straining his eyes. "Ah, there you are," he grunted aloud, and extended his hand to the wall.

And his hand froze in midair. An instantaneous prickle climbed up his spine. A hundred thoughts raced through his head all at once. But he did not move, did not breathe.

Some one had opened the front door. There could be no mistake. He had heard the telltale squeak of the unoiled bolt.

Then movement surged back in a wave, and his arm dropped, and he whirled on the balls of his feet and sped toward a Japanese-silk screen which he had dimly perceived a moment before during his hunt for the switch. He reached its shelter and crouched low behind it, holding his breath.

It seemed an eternity before he heard the cautious metallic rasp of the bedroom knob being turned. He heard a scraping, too, as of a shoe over the sill of the door. And then the unmistakable panting intake of a human breath. The metallic sound occurred again; the prowler had closed the door behind him.

Ellery strained his eyes through a crack between two of the leaves of the Japanese screen. Oddly, his nose became sensible of a faraway odor which made him think of the perfumed flesh of a woman. But then he realized that the odor had been there before the prowler, before himself; it was the odor of Irene Sewell. . . . His pupils, enlarged by immersion in the darkness, began to make out a human form. It was the figure of a man, so muffled that not even the skin of his face glimmered in the pulsating dusk of the room. The man was moving about swiftly and yet nervously, jerking his head from side to side, breathing in hoarse gulps, almost sobbing.

And then he pounced upon a low vanity built along modern lines and began pulling drawers open with wild swoops of his arms, apparently careless of the clatter he was making.

Ellery tiptoed from behind the screen and made his way noiselessly across the thick Chinese rug to the wall near the door.

With his arm raised he said in a pleasant unhurried voice: "Hello there," and in the same instant pressed the switch.

The prowler whirled about like a tiger, blinking and silent. In the brilliant light Ellery made out his features clearly as the upturned lapels of the man's coat dropped stiffly back.

It was Donald Kirk.

They measured each other for an eon, as if they could not tear their eyes away, as if they could not believe what their eyes saw. They were both shocked into silence by surprise.

"Well, well," said Ellery at last, drawing a grateful breath and advancing toward the tall motionless young man. "You *do* get about, don't you, Kirk? And what's the meaning of this horribly trite nocturnal visit?"

Donald relaxed completely all of a sudden, as if he could not bear the tension an instant longer. He sank into a nearby white plush chair and with trembling fingers pulled out a cigaret-case and lit a cigaret.

"Well," he said with a short despairing laugh, "here I am. Caught red-handed, Queen—and by you, of all people."

"Fate," murmured Ellery. "And a kind fate for you, my careening young bucko. A more vigorous operative might have—what's the phrase? ah, yes—plugged you first and asked questions afterward. Fortunately, having a sensitive stomach, I don't carry firearms. . . . Fearfully bad habit, Kirk, prowling about ladies' bedrooms at this time of night. Get you into trouble."

And Ellery seated himself comfortably on a zibeline *chaise-longue* opposite the plush chair and produced his own cigaret-case and selected a cigaret with dreamy abstraction and lit it.

They smoked thoughtfully and in silence for some time, regarding each other without once lowering their eyes.

Then Ellery swallowed a mouthful of smoke and said: "I suffer a bit from insomnia, too. What do you do for it, old boy?"

Kirk sighed. "Go on. Say it."

Ellery drawled: "Care to talk?"

The young man forced a grin. "Curiously enough, I'm not in a conversational mood at the moment."

"Curiously enough, I am. Peaceful atmosphere, two intelligent young men alone, smoking—perfect background for small talk, Kirk. I've always said—a most original observation, of course—that what America needs is not so much a good five-cent cigar as the civilizing influence of inconsequential conversation. Don't you want to be civilized, you heathen?"

The publisher let smoke dribble out of his nostrils. Then he leaned forward suddenly, elbows on his knees. "You're playing with me, Queen. What d'ye want?"

"I might ask you," said Ellery dryly, "substantially the same question."

"Don't get you."

"Well, since I must be specific: What were you looking for so strenuously in Miss Irene Sewell's vanity a few moments ago?"

"I won't tell you, and that's final," snapped Kirk with a defiant flare of his pinched nostrils.

"Pity," murmured Ellery. "I seem to have lost all power of persuasion." And there was a long and pregnant silence.

"I suppose," muttered Donald at last, studying the rug, "you'll turn me in."

"I?" said Ellery with elaborate astonishment. "My dear Kirk, you grieve me. I'm not—er—official, you see. Who am I to go about making people unhappy?"

The cigaret burned down to Kirk's fingertips and he crushed the fire out between his fingers unconsciously. "You mean," he said slowly, "you'll pass it up? Won't tell any one about it, Queen?"

"I had some such thought," drawled Ellery.

"By George, that's white of you!" Kirk sprang to his feet, a revitalized man. "Damned decent, Queen. I—I don't know quite how to thank you."

"I do."

"Oh," said the young man in a different voice, and he sat down again.

"Look here, you dithering fool," said Ellery cheerfully, flipping his cigaret-butt out one of the open windows. "Don't you think you've tortured yourself with that secret of yours just about to a sufficiency? You're essentially honest, Kirk; haven't either the flair or the technique for intrigue. Why can't you get it through that stubborn young skull of yours that the biggest mistake you've made in this miserable business was in not confiding in me?"

"I know it," muttered Donald.

"Then you've come to your senses at last? You'll tell me?"

Kirk raised haggard eyes. "No."

"But why not, man, for God's sake?"

The young man rose and began to pace the rug with hungry strides. "Because I can't. Because—" the words came reluctantly—"because it's not my secret, Queen."

"Oh, that," said Ellery quietly. "That's scarcely news to me, old chap."

Kirk stopped short. "Just what . . . You know?" There was a deep sounding of pain and tragic despair in his voice.

Ellery shrugged. "If it had been your secret you would have come out with it long ago. Kirk, my lad, no man would stand by and permit the woman he loves to get a horribly distorted impression about him without taking the obvious defensive measures—unless his tongue was paralyzed by the necessity of protecting some one else."

"Then you don't know," murmured Kirk.

"Protecting some one else." Ellery looked sympathetic. "I'd scarcely be worth my salt as an observer of human beings if I couldn't perceive that the one you're protecting is—your sister Marcella."

"Good God, Queen—"

"I was right, then. Marcella, eh? . . . Does she know what threatens her, Kirk?"

"No!"

"I thought not. And you're saving her from it. Perhaps from herself. Stout fellow, Kirk. Knight-in-shining-armor business. I'd no idea lads like you still paced the earth. I suppose Kingsley was right when he said that the age of chivalry is never past so long as there's a wrong left 'unredressed.' And that, of course, is what attracts the female of the species. Your tiny Jo is apparently no exception. . . . No, no, Kirk, don't clench your fists; I'm not poking fun at you. I mean it. You're adamant in your refusal, I suppose?"

The veins at Donald's temple were angry knots. Perspiration materialized on his forehead. But he choked: "No," and said at once: "I mean—yes!" and tossed his head about like a restless horse, chafing at the rein of circumstances.

"And still I'm morally certain you were going to tell Papa Queen all about it on the night of the murder. Then we found the body and you pulled in your horns. You were going to ask my advice, weren't you, Kirk?"

"Yes, but not about—this. About this Llewes—Sewell—woman . . ."

"Ah, then the secret that concerns your sister has nothing to do with your charming Irene?" asked Ellery quickly.

"No, no, I didn't say that. Oh, good God, Queen, don't make it so hard for me. I just can't say any more."

Ellery rose and went to the open window to stare out inscrutably over the flickering dark canyon below. Then he turned and said lightly: "Since we've reached the climax of our little bout of dialectic, I suggest we get out of here before the mistress of this boudoir returns with excursions and alarums. Ready, Kirk?"

"I'm ready," said Kirk in a muffled voice.

Ellery held the door open for him and then switched off the light. In the darkness they went through the apartment to the front door and passed out into the corridor. There was no one about. They stood still for a moment.

Then Donald Kirk said: "Well, good night," in the dreariest of tones and trudged off down the corridor toward the stairs without once looking back.

Ellery watched his drooping shoulders until they vanished.

He turned in a seemingly aimless motion and peered sharply out of the corner of his eyes at the turn of the corridor behind him. There had been . . . But there was nothing to be seen.

For five long minutes Ellery waited without stirring from the spot. No one turned up, no one even looked his way from the far length of the corridor. He strained his ears and kept his eyes open. . . . But the corridor was as still as a cathedral.

And so, this time without hesitation, he inserted his skeleton key in the lock of the door and swiftly reentered the Llewes suite.

But even in the isolation of the darkness there he was troubled. He *had* seen some one, he felt sure. And, from the tininess of the ankles, that some one who had watched them emerge from the apartment had been Jo Temple.

14. THE MAN FROM PARIS

MISS IRENE Sewell, alias Llewes, came swiftly into her apartment at two o'clock in the morning, humming a waltz. She did not look like a woman who had spent several hours under the searching scrutiny of the police.

Under her arm she carried a small package done up in brown paper.

"Lucy!" she called gaily. "Lucy!" Her voice echoed through the sitting-room. But there was no answer, and with a shrug she let her mink coat slip to the floor and glided into the living-room. She turned on the light, still humming, and looked about with a slow sweep of her remarkable brown eyes. The hum ceased abruptly. An expression of suspicion disturbed her large beautiful features. A sixth sense told her subtly that something was wrong. What it was she could not conceive, and yet... Her eyes blazed, and she strode forward and yanked open the bedroom-door and snapped on the light.

Mr. Ellery Queen sat smiling in the plush chair facing the door, his legs comfortably crossed. At his elbow lay an ashtray overflowing with butts.

"Mr. Queen! What's the meaning of this?" she demanded in her throaty voice.

"Good entrance, Miss Llewes," said Ellery cheerfully, getting to his feet. "I mean the business. The speech wasn't so good. Hackneyed, don't you think?"

"I asked you," she said sharply, "what you're doing in my bedroom at this hour of the morning!"

"Implying, I trust, that at an earlier hour you would have no objection whatever? Thank you. . . ." He stretched his lean arms and yawned politely. "That was a long wait, Miss Llewes. I was beginning to believe that you'd found my father a positively enchanting host."

She clutched the back of the nearest chair, her mask stripped off. The bundle was still under her arm. "Then it was a trick," she said slowly. "He returned Kirk's jewels to me and kept asking me questions. . . ." Her eyes travelled over the furniture, probing for signs of disturbance. They widened a little when she saw that the lowest drawer of the vanity was open. "Then you've found it," she said with bitterness.

Ellery raised his shoulders. "Very clumsy, my dear. I should think that a woman of your experience would have chosen a more subtle hiding-place. Yes, I've found it; and that's why I've waited in this damnably sleepy chair."

She advanced toward him with oddly uncertain steps, as if she did not quite know what to do or say. "Well?" she murmured at last. Her peculiar progress was taking her in a sidling way to the vanity.

"The .22 isn't there any more," said Ellery, "so you may as well sit down, Miss Llewes."

She went a little paler, but she said nothing and obediently turned and went to the *chaise-longue*, upon which she sank in a tired way.

Ellery began to pace the rug thoughtfully. "The time has come—to paraphrase the immortal Walrus—to discuss fundamentals. You've been playing a dangerous game, my dear. Now you've got to pay the price."

"What do you want of me?" she asked huskily; there was no defiance in her voice.

Ellery cocked a shrewd eye at her. "Information. Explanation. . . . I must say I'm inexpressibly astonished, even a little disappointed in you, Irene. No resistance beyond that instinctive groping toward the little .22? *Tch, tch.* I suppose you've decided that submission is the better part of conflict."

"What can I say?" She leaned back, and the folds of her evening gown draped her in long clean curves. "You've won. I've been stupid. *Voila!*"

"Much as it goes against the gentleman in me," murmured Ellery, "I must agree with you. You've not only been stupid, Irene, but criminally stupid. To keep those letters so carelessly in your bedroom! Why didn't you put them in the wall-safe?"

"Because the wall-safe or any safe is the first place people examine," she replied with an unnatural smile.

"The Dupin principle, eh?" Ellery shrugged. "And then, too, people like you place too great reliance upon firearms. I suppose you thought the .22 was protection enough."

"I usually," she murmured, "carry it in my bag."

"But tonight, of course, you left off the lethal jewelry for purposes of your visit to Headquarters. Quite so. Perhaps I've been hasty in my judgment, Irene. . . . Well, my dear, it's late; and much as I enjoy the intimate nature of this *tête-à-tête*, I should relish sleep more. Why," he snapped suddenly, "did you change your name to Llewes from Sewell?"

"It seemed an interesting surname," she said brightly.

"I suppose you realize that Llewes is Sewell spelled backwards?"

"Oh, that. Of course. That was how . . ." She sat up in alarm. "You don't mean—you don't think—"

"What *I* mean or think, dear lady, is inconsequential. I'm just a cog in the machine."

"But it happened so long ago—years ago," she faltered. "I assure you there wasn't—there couldn't be the slightest connection between the name and the—"

"That remains to be seen. Now, Miss Llewes, to get down to business. I've found those letters and the copy of the certificate. It's unnecessary for me to point out that your little game has been played, and that you've lost."

"Possession of those—isn't documents the technical word, Mr. Queen?" she murmured with a sudden sparkle in her eyes—"merely establishes the proofs, you know. But you can't eradicate from my brain the knowledge of what happened, you see. And it's quite evident that Mr. Donald Kirk is anxious that I keep quiet. What do you say to that?"

"Awakening resistance," chuckled Ellery. "Wrong again, my dear. Your word—the word of a woman with a long criminal record—wouldn't stand for an instant against mine if I should testify that I found these papers in your possession. And Kirk, knowing you no longer possess them, will be willing to testify in his turn that you blackmailed him. So—"

"Oh," smiled the woman, rising and stretching her long white arms, "but he won't, d'ye see, Mr. Queen."

"Resistance stretches. I apologize for the accusation of stupidity. You mean, I presume, that with or without the papers in your possession, Kirk's only concern is to keep you silent, and that if it came to a matter of arrest and trial he couldn't prevent your telling the story in open court?"

"How clever you are, Mr. Queen."

"Now, now, no flattery. But let me point out in rebuttal," said Ellery dryly, "that if it does come to a showdown in court, the story must come out anyway. And since it must come out and Kirk will be powerless to prevent its coming out, he'll testify against you with a grim and enthusiastic vengeance, my dear, that will put that fetching body of yours behind bars—ugly American bars—for years and years and years. And what do you say to that, Irene?"

"Am I to understand," she murmured, coming closer to him, "that you're proposing an *entente*, a conspiracy of silence, Mr. Queen? That you won't prosecute in return for my silence?"

Ellery bowed. "I beg forgiveness again; I underestimated the acuteness of your perceptions. Precisely what I'm proposing. . . . And please don't come any nearer, my dear, because while I can exercise stern self-control on occasion, this is not one of the occasions. I'm still human. At two o'clock in the morning my moral resistance is at its lowest ebb."

"I could like you—very much, Mr. Queen."

Ellery sighed and hastily retreated a step. "Ah, the Mae West influence. Dear, dear! And I've always said that the Hammetts and the Whitfields are wrong in their demonstrated belief that a detective has countless opportunities for indulging his sex appeal. Another credo blasted. . . . Then it's agreed, Miss Llewes?"

She regarded him coolly. "Agreed. And I have been a fool."

"A fascinating fool, at any rate. Poor Kirk! He must have had the very devil of a time with you. By the way," murmured Ellery, and his eyes belied the smile on his lips, "how well did you know that man?"

"What man?"

"The Parisian."

"Oh!" Her mask slipped on. "Not very well."

"Did you ever meet him?"

"Once. But he was unshaven—wore a beard, in fact. And he was foully drunk when he sold me the letters. I met him only when the letters and money changed hands. For an instant. All previous negotiations had been conducted by letter."

"Hmm. You saw the face of the corpse, Miss Llewes, upstairs the other day." Ellery paused. Then he continued slowly: "*Could the man from Paris have been the man murdered upstairs?*"

She stepped back, dazed. "You mean—that little . . . Good heavens!"

"Well?"

"I don't know," she said hurriedly, biting her lips. "I don't know. It's so hard to say. Without the beard . . . It was a bushy beard that concealed most of his features. And he was horribly seedy and dirty, a wreck. But it's possible. . . ."

"Ah," frowned Ellery. "I'd hoped for a surer identification. You can't be certain?"

"No," she murmured in a thoughtful tone, "I can't be certain, Mr. Queen."

"Then I'll bid you good night and pleasant dreams." Ellery snatched up his coat and wriggled into it. The woman was still thoughtful, standing in the middle of the room like a draped tree. "Oh, yes! I knew I'd forgotten something."

"Forgotten something?"

Ellery walked over to the *chaise-longue* and picked up the brown-paper package. "Donald Kirk's precious antiques. Dear, dear! It would have been a beastly oversight to leave without them."

The color ebbed out of her face. "Do you mean to say," she demanded in a furious voice, "that you're taking those, too? You—you brigand!"

"Lovely, my dear. Anger becomes you. But surely you didn't think I'd leave them in your care?"

"But then I have nothing left—nothing!" She was almost sobbing in her rage. "All these weeks, months. The expense . . . I'll tell the whole story! I'll call in the press! I'll splatter that story all over the world!"

"And spend the best part of the remainder of your life behind cold gray walls, in a narrow cell, and with coarse—I assure you it's unreasonably coarse—cotton underwear next to your skin?"

Ellery shook his head sadly. "I think not. You're about thirty-five now, I should say—"

"Thirty-one, you beast!"

"I beg your pardon. Thirty-one. When you're out you'll be— let's see—Well, in your case, considering the plenitude of your *dossier*, you should get—"

She flung herself on the *chaise-longue*, panting. "Oh, get out of here!" she screamed. "Get out! Or I'll tear your eyes out!"

"Heavens, you'll wake the neighbors," said Ellery with horror; and then he smiled and Bowed and went away with the package under his arm.

He startled the night-clerk at the desk in the lobby of the Chancellor by reaching for one of the house-telephones.

"Here, man!" cried the night-clerk. "What do you think you're doing? Don't you know it's almost half-past two?"

"Police," said Ellery portentously, and the man fell back, gaping. Ellery murmured to the hotel operator: "Ring Mr. Donald Kirk on the twenty-second, please. Yes, important." He waited, whistling a merry tune. "Who's this? Oh, Hubbell. This is Ellery Queen. . . . Yes, yes, man; Queen! Is Donald Kirk in? . . . Well, get him out of bed, then! . . . Ah, Kirk. . . . No, no, nothing's the matter. Actually, I've rousing good news for you. You'll be glad I woke you up at this obscene hour. I've something for you—call it a little engagement gift. . . . No, no. I'll leave it for you at the desk. And let me tell you, Kirk, that your troubles are over. About M., I mean. . . . Yes! Well, don't shout my ears off, old chap. And, as far as I. L. is concerned, her claws are permanently trimmed. She won't bother you again. Stay away from her like a good little boy and devote yourself—you lucky devil!—to the lady known as Jo. Night!"

And, chuckling, Ellery deposited the package with the clerk and marched out of the Chancellor, reeling a little from sheer fatigue but glowing with the consciousness of a good deed exceedingly well done.

Ellery astounded his father and Djuna by appearing at the Inspector's breakfast table at the Inspector's usual breakfast hour, which was an early hour indeed.

"Well, look who's here," said the old gentleman a little brokenly, because his mouth was full of eggy toast. "Sick, El? Must be something wrong to get you up this early."

"Something right," yawned Ellery, rubbing red-rimmed eyes. He sank into a chair with a groan.

"What time did you get in?"

"About three. . . . Djuna, the royal oofs, if you please."

"Oofs?" said Djuna suspiciously. "What's them?"

"What are those, my lad; this association with the youth of 87th Street is contaminating you. Oofs, Djuna, is a sort of bastardized French for eggs. I could stomach a right good egg at the moment. Turn 'em over and slap 'em in the behind; you know—the usual style."

Djuna grinned and vanished into the kitchen. The Inspector grunted: "Well?"

"You may well say well," murmured Ellery, reaching for the cigarets. "I am happy to report unmitigated success."

"Hmm. If you'll tell me what you're talking about, maybe I'll understand you."

"The situation is briefly this," said Ellery, leaning back and blowing smoke. "I asked you to get the Llewes woman—fascinating wench!—out of the way so that I could pursue a little hunch of mine. It was obvious that she had a hold on Kirk—something she was waving over his head which was keeping that harassed young idiot quiet and which he would have given the remnants of his fortune to get back. Well, what was she waving over his head? Obviously, again, something of a tangible nature. Such being the case,

I said to myself in the typical rococo style of a vanished literary era, it was in her possession and very close to her charming person. Where? Her apartment, of course. She's too foxy and experienced a creature to get mixed up with safety-deposit vaults and the consequent records. So—you obliged me and engaged her in Centre Street chit-chat while I burgled her rooms."

"And without a warrant, too!" gasped the Inspector. "That's the second time, you fool. Some day you're going to step into a nasty mess of trouble. Suppose it hadn't been there? By the way, did you find it?"

"Certainly I found it. A Queen, as the saying goes in Centre Street, never fails."

"Never mind how the saying goes in Centre Street," growled the old gentleman. "You ought to hear how the saying goes in City Hall. Well, give!"

"Of course, I neglected to mention that I bumped into young Kirk on my prowl. It seems we both had something of the same brilliant idea—"

"What!"

"Don't look so startled; it's unbecoming. The poor boy's desperate, or at least he was until about two-thirty this morning. I packed him off to bed and returned to Miss Llewes's American lair and found the—ah—papuhs; and I waited for the admirable lady to return to said lair from her visit to Headquarters, where I fancy you were entertaining her with tiffin. I blush to confess that I made her see the light. Would you believe it? She even returned the loot she got from Kirk!"

"Surprising you were smart enough to think of that," snapped the Inspector. "It broke my heart to have had to hand it over to her. Come on, come on; let's see those—well, whatever they are."

"That's the funniest thing," drawled Ellery. "I can't for the life of me remember where I put them. I was so damned sleepy last night—"

The old gentleman glared. "What—Say, look here, El, stop making a fool out of yourself. Let's see those papers!"

"Perhaps," said. Ellery quietly, "it's better that you don't. I can tell you what's in them and still retain the evidence."

"But why don't you want me to have them, for cripe's sake?" snarled the Inspector.

"Because you've such a confounded loyalty to duty. They remain in my possession. So you won't be placed in the position of succumbing to the temptation of dragging a very sad and pitiful story out into the light of day."

The Inspector sputtered incoherently for a moment. "Why, you presumptuous young dope! I thought you were going to be a help. . . . Well, tell me, then."

"I must exact a promise first."

"Exact your Aunt Tillie!"

"It's between us exclusively? You won't spill it to any one—the press, the Commissioner, the Chief Deputy Inspector?"

"Boy, it sure must be a honey," said the Inspector sarcastically. "All right, I promise. Now what's it all about?"

Ellery puffed reflectively on his cigaret. "It concerns Marcella Kirk. It's a howling little tragedy, and it's the sort of thing a vulture like this Llewes woman would snap up in her filthy beak.

"Marcella's not quite as adolescent as she looks. Several years ago—in her pre-deb days—she met a man. He seems to be—or to have been—an American expatriate who'd spent most of his recent time in Paris among the wolves. But Marcella met him in New York and fell in love with him. He was apparently old enough to be her father, but she was extremely impressionable and he swept her off her feet. Anyway, with an eye on the Kirk money, I suppose, he carried her off and married her secretly in Greenwich."

"So what?" growled the Inspector.

"It wasn't until it was all over that Donald Kirk learned of even the existence of this man, let alone what followed. The man went by the name of Cullinan, Howard Cullinan. Kirk instituted a feverish but quiet inquiry and discovered that Cullinan was already married; had a wife in Paris."

"Good Lord," said the Inspector.

Ellery sighed. "Nasty mess, as nasty as they come. Nobody else apparently knew. Not even old Dr. Kirk. Donald found Marcella alone in Greenwich—the man was out somewhere—disclosed to her what he knew, and took the poor girl away, more dead than alive. Cullinan seems to have possessed a certain amount of bravado; he shrewdly guessed that Kirk would rather hush the affair than prosecute him for bigamy. And the upshot of the sordid business was that Kirk paid him a sizeable sum to keep his mouth shut and clear out."

"Well, even so—" muttered the Inspector, knitting his bushy brows.

"Tut, tut. The worst is yet to come; this is a story for the ages. That would have been bad enough, you understand. But Marcella kept writing Cullman letters on the sly, as she had written him before they eloped. The girl was desperate, unbalanced, on the verge of suicide. She was afraid to tell even her brother what actually had happened."

"Oh," said the Inspector in a low tone. "She was pregnant?"

"Exactly. Which made it an altogether different story. Cullinan naturally washed his hands of her. Marcella's being pregnant only complicated matters for him; he'd got his cut and that's all he was interested in. So Marcella, in a pitiable state, went to Donald with the news. You can imagine poor Kirk's feelings."

"I wouldn't blame him if he'd cut that skunk's throat," growled the Inspector.

"Odd, isn't it?" murmured Ellery with a queer smile. "I had the same thought. . . . Anyway, he trumped up some story of a breakdown for the benefit of his family and friends, let this Dr. Angini in on it—he's a very old and trusted friend—and the doctor and Kirk took Marcella away to Europe. She had her baby there, the wheels of progress being oiled by the worthy physician. Unfortunately the child was born quite healthy, and it's still in Europe in the care of a trusted nurse."

"So that was the hold Sewell had on Kirk," muttered the Inspector.

"Quite a hold, eh? One the Strangler would be proud of. . . . I don't know precisely how she first got wind of it, but somehow she found out—probably through the intercession of some underworld intermediary—and negotiated with Cullinan, who had drifted back to Paris and was of course on his uppers, for the sale of the letters and the marriage certificate. The letters incidentally tell enough of the story to permit a complete reconstruction of what happened. . . . Then Miss Irene Llewes came to the Hotel Chancellor, making the crossing from France for the sole purpose of squeezing Donald Kirk to within an inch of his last dollar. What happened then is history. Poor Kirk was caught properly—"

"Macgowan, of course," said the old gentleman gloomily.

"Precisely. In the meantime Marcella, with the resilience of youth, had rehabilitated herself. No one suspected. She'd almost forgotten the whole dreary horrible business. And then Macgowan, Kirk's best friend, suddenly realized that Donald had a beautiful grown-up sister. It developed into a romance; they were engaged. Next scene: the Llewes creature turns up and Kirk was in for it with a vengeance."

"Doesn't Marcella Kirk know what's been going on?"

"Not the faintest vestige of the breath of a minute suspicion, as far as I can make out. From the internal evidence of the letters she seems to have gone half-potty from the pressure of conscience and shame—I mean during the time she was pregnant. I suppose Kirk has felt that a reopening of the mess would put the finishing touch on her. And then Macgowan, for all his worldliness, is a puritanical soul, and he comes from one of those blue-plush-and-carryall families who would insist on his breaking off the engagement at the first breath of scandal. Poor Kirk has had his hands full."

"And the ice he gave Sewell?"

"Blackmail. It wasn't what she had expected, but she made the best of it. Wasn't so bad, since she's specialized in gem swindles and probably has connections with 'fences' in Amsterdam. . . . He had to give her parts of his collection, you see, because unfortunately he was in straitened circumstances when she popped onto the scene. He gave her what cash he could scrape together and then when the cash gave out—he even borrowed from Macgowan in his desperation—he gave the woman jewels from his collection. What she got makes a sizeable sack, I'll tell you that. But then you saw it yourself."

"And she forced him to write that note to cover her up in case something went wrong," mused the Inspector. "Smart. I s'pose the touch about asking her to marry him in the note was another little nest-egg for the future—if he ever recovered financially she'd sue him for breach of promise. But when the murder occurred and the police started nosing around, she got a little scared and generously handed Kirk over to his new lady-love. Well, well! So now where are we?"

"As regards the murder?" murmured Ellery.

"Sure."

Ellery rose and went to the window. "I don't know," he said in a puzzled way. "I really don't. And yet I have a fugitive idea—"

"Sa-a-ay!" The Inspector bounced from his chair, wildly excited. "Oh, what fools we are! Listen to this, El; just listen to this." He began to trot about the room, hands gripped behind his back, head low. "Just struck me. It all ties in. Swell! Listen. *The bird who was bumped off at the Chancellor was Marcella Kirk's boyfriend!*"

Ellery said slowly: "You've caught the fugitive. You think so?"

"Well, isn't it a perfect set-up?" The Inspector waved his spindly arms about. "Here's a man on his uppers; we can't trace him here; Marcella's man hung out in Paris; it's possible. . . . He came over here to put the screws on Kirk himself, see? Soon as he got off the boat; there was a boat from France that day. . . . He's desperate, see; he was afraid before, with the girl having a kid, and all that; but he needs money bad, and he's decided to go back for more. He beats it to the Chancellor to see Kirk. . . . Great!" Then his face fell. "But Kirk should have recognized him, if he's the one. Maybe—"

"Curiously enough," muttered Ellery, "Kirk never met Cullinan. He paid the man off by mail."

"But then there's Marcella. . . . She fainted, didn't you say, when she first got a look at the dead man?"

"Yes, but that may have been merely shock."

"At the same time, if it *was* the Parisian guy," mused the Inspector in a fierce undertone, "she naturally would shut up; naturally wouldn't admit she knew him. Didn't the Sewell woman know Cullinan by sight, either?"

"She says she saw him only once, and then under unfavorable circumstances. She can't be sure of anything, she maintains. Yes, yes, it's a possibility; no doubt about it."

"I like it," said the Inspector with a ferocious grin. "I like it, El. It ties in. First time in this blasted case I've got the feeling of co—co—what d'ye call it?"

"Cohesion?"

"That's it. It's tightened up, the whole thing. Because now we can establish a strong connection—"

"In theory," said Ellery dryly.

"Sure. Between this dead palooka and the people, most of 'em, involved in this thing. Motive's clear as crystal against almost any of 'em."

"As?"

"Well, now take Donald Kirk, poor young squirt. He's in the hotel that afternoon—I don't doubt seeing the Sewell animal on her demand for a powwow. He knows in some way that—we'll call him by the Paris feller's name—that Cullinan is upstairs waiting, or is coming to see him. He dodges up the stairway from the twenty-first floor, waits for a clear field, sneaks into the anteroom, bumps off Cullinan, goes back. . . . Then there's Marcella. Ditto for her. And for the old walrus, Dr. Kirk. All had the same reason—to shut Cullinan's mouth. Of course none of 'em except Donald and Marcella knew that there were two people floating around with knowledge of the affair."

"And Macgowan?" murmured Ellery, squinting at his smoke.

"Even he's a possibility," said the Inspector argumentatively. "Suppose in some way he'd found out Marcella's story but hadn't let on? I'll make it better! Suppose he'd found out through Cullinan *himself* who, let's say, read in the papers about Macgowan's engagement to Marcella and promptly wrote asking blackmail?"

"Superb," said Ellery.

"So Macgowan brings this bird over from the other side and kills him in—in—"

"In his best friend's office?" Ellery shook his head. "Doesn't wash, dad. That's the last place he would have selected for the job."

"Well, all right," grumbled the Inspector, "Macgowan's out. But Llewes, or Sewell, or whatever the hell her name is, had a motive, too. She showed up in the office after the murder, didn't she? Well, suppose she did that just as a sort of cover-up? She was certainly on the twenty-second floor that afternoon. Suppose she'd seen Cullinan in the anteroom—suppose she's lying about not being able to remember what he looked like—suppose she found out from him his plan to blackmail Kirk, or Macgowan, or somebody. So what? So she kills him to cut him out of the gravy, or keep him from spoiling her game. How's that?"

"Masterly," murmured Ellery, "as are your speculations about the others. In classic terminology you've put your finger on probably an epic motive. But there's just one little element which puts the damper on the boodle of 'em, especially if the motive is what you claim it to be."

"What?"

"The fact that the murderer turned everything backwards. I might add," continued Ellery reflectively, "another. The fact, too, that the murderer thrust those *Impi* spears up the dead man's clothes."

"Well, even so," said the Inspector irritably, "I don't see that because we don't know why the killer did those fool things it cuts out my theory. Might still fit."

"Conceivable."

"But you don't think so?"

Ellery stared out at the sky over 87th Street. "Sometimes I get a furtive glimpse of what might be the last outpost of the truth. It's the damnedest thing. Keeps eluding me, like a piece of wet soap in the dark. Or like a dream you've forgotten but are conscious of. That's all I can say."

They were silent for a long time. Djuna made a cheerful clatter at the kitchen-stove. "Oofs!" he cried.

The Inspector said stubbornly: "I can't trust your glimpses, or whatever y'call 'em. I've got to be sure. El, I tell you this is the first really hot lead we've had in this case." He went to the telephone and dialed Police Headquarters. "Hello. This is Inspector Queen. Get me my deskman. . . . 'Lo! Billy? Listen, I want you to get a cable off to the Prefect of Police in Paris right away. Take it down. Message:

'Send me full information Howard Cullinan, American believed in Paris. Telephoto on way for verification.' Sign my name and rush it. . . . What's that?"

The Inspector bent over the instrument with a sudden jerk, a startled look springing into his small hard eyes.

Ellery, at the window, turned about with a frown.

The old man listened for what seemed ages. Then he rapped: "Swell. Cut off. I've got to work fast." He broke the connection and feverishly dialed Operator.

"What's up?" demanded Ellery curiously.

"Hello! Get me the Hotel Chancellor desk. . . . Can't stop, El. Something big's broken at last. Better throw your things on. Quick. Into your pants." Ellery stared, and then without a word ran into the bedroom, throwing off his dressing-gown as he ran. "Hello! Desk-clerk, Chancellor? This is Inspector Richard Queen, Police Headquarters. . . . Sergeant Velie of the Homicide Squad is there, isn't he? . . . Fine, let me talk to him. . . . Hello! Thomas? Queen. Listen. I just got the flash from h.q. Don't hold the boy. . . . *No, don't*, you big lummox! Let him finish that little job of his. . . . Don't ask questions, idiot! Did you check with the local telegraph office to make sure he isn't a ringer of some kind? . . . Good. Now get this. Give the boy the bag, as if it's on the level, see? Then let him follow his instructions and take it down to Grand Central, where he's supposed to meet this party. Follow the boy and nab the one who picks the bag up from the boy. Go easy, Thomas; this may be the wind-up. . . . No, no! Don't stop to examine the bag. It'll be safe enough. If you hold the kid up too long this bird'll get suspicious. . . . Right. Scoot! I'll be down at Grand Central in less than fifteen minutes."

The Inspector slammed the receiver and yelled: "Ready?"

"For the love of Peter," panted Ellery from the bedroom, "what d'ye think I am—a fireman? What is this, anyway?" He appeared in the living-room doorway in unlaced shoes, trousers with hanging suspenders, unbuttoned shirt, necktie in hand. Djuna gaped from the kitchen.

"Grab your hat and coat and finish dressing in the cab!" shouted the Inspector, yanking Ellery toward the foyer. "Come on!" And he dived through the door.

Ellery made a strangled sound and scrambled after, the tongues of his oxfords flapping dismally.

"But the oofs?" moaned Djuna.

There was no answer except the thunder of feet running down the stairs.

15. THE TRAP

A POLICE CAR was chugging at the curb. One of the officers was on the sidewalk holding the door open.

"Jump in, Inspector," he said quickly, saluting. "We just got the flash on the short-wave to call for you."

"Glad somebody had a brainstorm. Good work, Schmidt," said the Inspector. "'Lo, Raftery. Here, pile in, El. . . . Grand Central, Raf. Keep that siren of yours howling."

They shot away from the curb leaving Officer Schmidt behind, skidded round the corner on two wheels, and headed south, the siren screaming its head off.

"Now," panted Ellery, cramped between his father and the door as he struggled to tie his shoelaces, "suppose you tell me what prompts this aborted Ride of the Valkyries."

The old man faced grimly ahead, watching the traffic rush by. It was as if all other cars in the world stood still. Officer Raftery drove with a magnificent nonchalance while the radio droned in his car. Ellery groaned and stooped lower; they had missed a pedestrian by the proverbial cat's whisker.

"Here's the pay-off. A few minutes ago a Postal Telegraph messenger presented a baggage-check at the checkroom of the Hotel Chancellor. One of the regular brass checks they issue there. The clerk hauled out the bag called for by the check. As he was slippin' the tag off, he suddenly remembered something. Like a shot, he said. Seems this is a funny sort of bag—big canvas valise, like those carpet-bags the farmers used to carry—and a clerk messing around with modern luggage would remember a thing like that."

"Don't tell me—" grunted Ellery, fumbling with his necktie.

"I am telling you," growled the Inspector. "This clerk saw from the stamped date on the tag that the valise had been in the check-room for a long time—much longer than usual, because most of their checking is transient-overnight, more'n likely. But the date on this bag was the day of the murder."

"So your hunch was correct," said Ellery, going into a violent contortion to slip his suspenders over his shoulders. "What—"

"Keep quiet, will you? You want the story, don't you?" The Inspector winced suddenly as the radio-car twisted like a bolt of lightning around a startled Cadillac. "Anyway, this clerk remembered in a flash who had left the bag with him—the man whose face, he said, the detective had shown him in a photo only yesterday. That was when Thomas's boys got around to the Chancellor in that city-wide canvass of all the checkrooms I'd ordered."

"Then it's definitely the murdered chap's bag?" murmured Ellery.

"Seems to be."

"But why on earth didn't he identify the victim from the photograph? If he remembered today—"

"Well, his story is that the face on the picture didn't mean a thing to him. He'd completely forgotten all about the little fat guy. But it was hauling out the bag that brought it all back to him—"

"Not implausible, at that," muttered Ellery. "There! I'm all in one piece at last. Raftery, you fiend, for God's sake be *careful*. . . . The point is that it took the bag to bridge the gap of association—a bridging not effected by sight of the man's photograph. Hmm. Well, go on."

"So," grunted the Inspector, "bein' a smart lad, he held the boy there and called Nye, that sweet-smelling house manager. He didn't want to take any of the responsibility himself, I suppose. Nye and Brummer, their dick, heard the clerk's story and Brummer called the police. The boys were working in midtown and the call was relayed to Thomas, who hotfooted it to the Chancellor. The messenger boy stuck to his story and Thomas checked it by 'phone with the Postal Telegraph branch where the kid works."

They swung into 59th Street, the siren clearing the way like a machine-gun.

"Well, well?" said Ellery impatiently. "And what did the Postal people say?"

"The branch-manager said that earlier today a package had come into the telegraph office containing the Chancellor baggage-check and a typed note. In the envelope with the note was a five-dollar bill; and the note instructed the Postal people to send a messenger with the check to the Chancellor, pick up the bag, and deliver it to the signer near the information desk at the Upper Level in Grand Central. That's their personal service, or something."

"Good Lord," groaned Ellery. "What an opportunity! I suppose the signature doesn't mean anything?"

"Not a thing. It was signed 'Henry Bassett,' or some such phony. Wasn't even written for that matter. The name was just typed out. Oh, this bird isn't taking any chances. It's just that he fell into something he couldn't have foreseen." They jerked around the Plaza and roared down Fifth Avenue, traffic opening magically before them. "It was his tough luck that the clerk has a good memory. Otherwise he'd have got away with it."

Ellery lighted a cigaret and squirmed about, seeking a comfortable position for his shoulders. "Velie didn't open the bag?"

"No time. I told him to let the kid take the bag and beat it down to Grand Central, as per instructions." The Inspector smiled grimly. "We didn't lose much time. There's only plainclothesmen on the job, and with the crowds in the terminal it ought to be a pipe. Thomas didn't let anything stand in his way; he sent one of the boys off to the Postal Telegraph office to pick up the note—that's evidence, or I'll eat my hat. Didn't lose more'n a half-hour all told. It ought to work."

They switched east on Forty-fourth Street, making for the taxi-cab entrance to Grand Central Terminal. Cross-traffic on Madison parted for them as if they were a comb running through a tangled *coiffure*. Another moment, and they were streaking across Vanderbilt into the vehicle-entrance. The siren had stopped at the Inspector's command at Fifth and Forty-fourth. There were a few careless stares from taxicab drivers as the Queens jumped out of the police-car, but that was all. Officer Raftery touched his visor, grinned angelically, and swung the car away. The Queens walked briskly into the Terminal.

It was still early, and most of the traffic in Grand Central was incoming. The huge chamber was murmurous with the usual sounds; occasionally a hollow shout echoed; there were few people at the ticket windows; porters scuttled about; a little crowd of people waited before one of the remoter track-entrances; from two others streams of commuters flowed.

The Queens descended the marble staircase from the Vander-bilt Avenue side with unhurried steps, their eyes focusing instantly on the round marble booth in the center of the Terminal—Information. Without difficulty they made out the slender figure of the Postal Telegraph boy in the characteristic blue uniform waiting on the north side of the booth, a large, roughly triangular valise of stained canvas at his feet. Even from their distant position they could discern signs of nervousness in the lad. He kept jerking his head from side to side spasmodically, and his face under the blue cap seemed peaked and pale.

"Damn that kid," muttered the Inspector as they reached the floor of the station. "He'll spoil everything. Nervous as a cat." They strolled toward the south wall, where the ticket offices were. "We'd better make ourselves scarce, El. Better not take a chance on being spotted by this bird. He's bound to be careful, and it's a sure bet he's somebody that knows us. One peep at us and he'll run like hell."

They sauntered to the central exit giving upon Forty-second Street and took up their stand quietly to one side, out of sight of people coming and going through the exit but with a perfect command both of the exit and the boy beyond the information desk.

"Where's Velie?" murmured Ellery, smoking. He was very nervous himself and unusually pale.

"Don't worry; he's around," said the Inspector without taking his eyes off the telegraph messenger. "And so are the others. There's Hagstrom now. With that old suitcase. Standing near the booth talking to one of the Information men. Good boy!"

"What time—"

"The boy was a little early. Ought to come off any minute now."

They waited for what seemed to Ellery, at least, an eternity.

He kept shifting his attention from the fidgety boy in blue to one of the four huge gilded docks above the information booth. The minutes sucked by lazily. He had never realized before how long a minute could be; how long and empty and nerve-racking.

The Inspector watched without change of expression. He was accustomed to these interludes and from years of experience had developed a patience with anticipated events which was, to Ellery, little short of marvelous.

Once they caught sight of Sergeant Velie. The giant was on the balcony on the east wall of the Upper Level, his hard eyes fixed on the scene below. He was either sitting or crouching, for from the floor where they stood he did not seem a big man.

The minutes slogged past. Hundreds of people came and went. Hagstrom had vanished from the information booth; apparently he felt that it was unwise to linger too long. But his place was instantly taken by Detective Piggott, also a veteran member of the Inspector's personal squad.

The boy waited.

Porters scurried by. There was an amusing interlude: a woman carrying a fat sleepy dog became involved in an altercation with a porter. Once a celebrity arrived: a diminutive woman decked in fresh orchids and surrounded by clamoring reporters and cameramen. She posed at the gate to Track 24. She smiled. There were blue streaks from flashlights. She disappeared; the crowd disappeared.

Still the boy waited.

By this time Detective Piggott was gone from the round booth, and Detective Ritter—burly and positive, smoking a cigar—was demanding information in a loud voice from one of the gray-haired attendants.

Quiet Detective Johnson sauntered over and consulted a time-table.

And still the boy waited. Ellery, gnawing his fingernails, consulted the clock for the hundredth time.

When two and a half hours had elapsed with no result the Inspector crooked his finger at Sergeant Velie on the balcony, shrugged philosophically, and without a word stalked across the marble floor to the information desk. The boy was sitting on the valise now in an attitude of hopeless resignation; the canvas was crushed beneath his slight weight. He looked up eagerly at the approach of Sergeant Velie.

"Get off that," rumbled the Sergeant, and he shoved the boy

gently aside and lifted the bag and joined the Inspector and the group of men who had miraculously materialized from all parts of the terminal.

"Well, Thomas," said the Inspector with a wry grin, "it's no dice, I guess. Scared our man off." He eyed the bag with interest.

"Guess so," said the Sergeant gloomily. "But how the hell he got wise *I* don't know. We didn't slip anywhere, did we?"

"Well, you handled it, Thomas," murmured the old man. "However, there's no sense in crying over spilt milk."

"It's probably infantile enough," said Ellery, frowning. "He suspected a trap at once. At the source."

"How could he, Mr. Queen?" protested Velie.

"It's easy to be clever after the event. It occurred to me two hours ago that the person who sent the five-dollar bill and the note with instructions was taking excellent care indeed to keep himself invisibly in the background."

"So?" said the Inspector.

"So," drawled Ellery, "what do you think he'd do? Leave matters to chance?"

"Don't get you."

"Well, good heavens, dad," said Ellery impatiently, "you're obviously not dealing with an imbecile! Wouldn't it have been extraordinarily simple for him to have been lounging about the lobby of the Chancellor keeping an eye on the checkroom *while the messenger was presenting the baggage-check*?"

Sergeant Velie went crimson. "By crap," he said hoarsely, "I never thought of that."

The Inspector stared at Ellery with a solemn conviction mounting in his marbly little eyes. "That sure sounds kosher to me," he said in a rueful voice.

"Disgusting," said Ellery bitterly. "I didn't think of it, either, until it was too late. Golden opportunity. And yet I don't see how else. . . . Of course he'd be on the alert. Just to make sure nothing went wrong. He was safe there—"

"Especially," muttered Velie, "if he lived there."

"Or normally had business there. But that's beside the point. His plan patently was to watch the boy pick up the bag in the Chancellor and then follow him to Grand Central. In that way he'd be absolutely sure everything was all right."

"So he saw the clerk call Nye and Brummer, saw Thomas, saw the boys. . . ." The Inspector shrugged. "Well, that's that. At least we've got the valise. We'll go back to Headquarters and give it the once-over. Wasn't a total loss, anyway."

It was on the journey downtown that Ellery suddenly exclaimed: "I'm witless! I'm the world's biggest idiot! I should have my head examined!"

"Granting," said the Inspector dryly, "the truth of all that, what's eating you now? You hop around inside that head of yours like a flea."

"The bag, dad. It's just struck me. My mental processes seem to have slowed down with the years. Hardening of the cerebrum. I remember the time when a thought like that would have been instantaneous with the event. . . . It was perfectly logical of you to conjure up a possible bag from the fact that the victim doesn't seem to have been a native of New York. And so to institute a search for it. But," frowned Ellery, "why does the murderer want it?"

"You *are* running down," snorted the Inspector. "Why d'ye suppose? I'll admit I hadn't foreseen that eventuality myself, but still it's easy enough to explain when you think of it. This killer took every precaution against our finding out the identity of the dead man, didn't he? So if the dead man's valise is floating around and liable to be picked up by the police, do you think the killer's going to sit back and let it be picked up? Not if he can help it! He's afraid, or else he positively knows, that there's something in that bag that will establish the dead man's identity!"

"Oh, that," said Ellery, eying the bag at their feet with suspicion.

"So what are you yelping about? I'm surprised at you, asking a question like that!"

"Rhetorical question purely," murmured Ellery, his eyes still on the bag. "The mere existence of the brass check is enough to point to the answer. He found the Chancellor check on the victim's body after the murder when he was cleaning out the little fellow's pockets. The check tells its own story. The murderer took it away with him. But why hasn't he picked up the bag before this? Why has he waited so long; eh?"

"Afraid," said the Inspector contemptuously. "No guts. Scared to take the chance. Especially since the bag was checked at the Chancellor. It's that fact itself that convinces me our man has some connection with the hotel, El. I mean he's known there. He knew damn' well that we have the Chancellor under observation. If he were an outsider altogether he wouldn't have had any hesitation in making a play for the valise. But if we knew him he'd be scared."

"I suppose so." Ellery sighed. "I'm itching to get my claws inside that thing. Lord knows what we'll find."

"Well, it won't be long now," said the Inspector placidly. "I've got the funniest feeling that even if we did miss out in, our chance to collar the killer, this bag is going to tell a sweet story."

"I sincerely," muttered Ellery, "hope so."

There was a solemn moment in Inspector Queen's office before the valise, so shabbily innocent-appearing from the outside, was opened. The door was shut, their coats and hats were flung helter-skelter in a corner, and the Inspector, Ellery, and Sergeant Velie stared at the bag on the Inspector's desk with varying expressions of emotion.

"Well," said the Inspector in a rather hushed voice, at last, "here goes."

He picked up the valise and examined its worn, grimy canvas exterior carefully. It bore no labels of any kind. Its metal hasps were rather rusty. The canvas was eaten away in the creases. There were no initials or insignia.

Sergeant Velie growled: "Sure has seen service."

"Sure has," murmured the Inspector. "Thomas, hand me those keys."

The Sergeant silently offered his superior a ringed bunch of skeleton keys. The Inspector tried a half-dozen before he found one that fitted the rusty lock of the valise. The tiny bolt turned over inside with a grating little noise; the Inspector pulled up the clamps on each side, pressed the central section of metal, and yanked the two halves of the bag apart.

Ellery and Velie leaned over the desk.

Inspector Queen began to pull things out of the bag, like a prestidigitator over a silk hat. The first object he brought out was a black alpaca coat, creased and worn-looking, but clean.

Ellery's eyes narrowed.

The old gentleman fished the things out swiftly, ranging them in piles on his desk. When the bag was empty he scrutinized its interior closely, holding it up to the light, grunted, tossed the bag aside, and turned back to the desk.

"If we have to we can try to trace that thing," he said in a slightly disappointed voice. "Well, let's see what it comes to. Isn't much, is it?"

The coat was part of a two-piece suit, the other being a pair of trousers of faintly foreign cut. The Inspector held it up against himself; it was just right for his own short legs. "That looks like it might have been his," he muttered. "Nothing in the pockets, darn the luck."

"Or in the coat, either," reported the Sergeant.

"No vest," said the Inspector thoughtfully. "Well, there wouldn't be with this summer suit. Don't see many of 'em in these parts."

The next series of exhibits consisted of shirts—linen and cotton, all with collarless neckbands and all, from their crisp appearance, fairly new.

The next pile was of hard collars, narrow and shiny and old-fashioned.

Beside it lay handkerchiefs.

A little heap of clean, light tropical underwear.

A half-dozen pairs of black cotton socks.

A pair of worn black shoes, knobby and old.

"That's Doc Prouty's corn-and-bunion diagnosis," murmured Ellery.

All the garments from the bag were cheap. And all, with the exception of the suit and shoes, were new and bore the label of a Shanghai haberdasher.

"Shanghai," said the Inspector thoughtfully. "That's China, El," in a wondering tone. "China!"

"So I see. What's remarkable about that? Bears out the Missing Persons Bureau's guess that the man didn't hail from the United States."

"I still think—" Then the Inspector stopped with a curious light in his eyes. "Say, this couldn't be a plant!"

"Is that a question or an assertion?"

"I mean, is it possible it is?"

Ellery raised his eyebrows. "I don't see how, if that clerk in the Chancellor checkroom maintains that it was really the victim who checked the bag."

"I guess you're right. S'pose I'm just naturally suspicious." The Inspector sighed and looked over the assortment of clothing on his desk. "Well, it gives us something to work on, anyway. Sa-a-ay!" He eyed Ellery shrewdly. "What's coming off here? I thought it was you who were always so soft on that China tie-up in this case. Now you say it's not remarkable, or something. How come?"

Ellery shrugged. "Don't interpret everything I say literally. Let's see that Bible."

He delved among the miscellaneous objects from the bag and fished out a torn, worn, coverless book. It looked as if it had been used as ammunition in a major conflict.

"Not a Bible. Ordinary cheap little breviary," he muttered. "Hmm. And those pamphlets—ah, religious tracts! We seem to have struck a very godly old gentleman, dad."

"Godly old gentlemen rarely get themselves bumped off," said the Inspector dryly.

"And this." Ellery put down the book and picked up another. "An ancient edition—London—of Hall Caine's *The Christian*. And here's Pearl Buck's *The Good Earth* in the original American edition that looks as if it had been kicked from here to Peiping. Who says that never the twain shall meet? . . . Queer."

"What's queer about it? He'd probably read that Buck book if he came from China."

Ellery started from a reverie. "Oh, certainly! I'm just communing with myself. I didn't mean the books." He fell silent, sucking his thumb and staring at the littered desk.

"Might 'a' known," grumbled Sergeant Velie, looking disgusted, "that this would be a dud. Not even a clue to his monicker."

"Oh, I wouldn't say that," said the Inspector with a faraway expression. "It's not so bad, Thomas. We'll know soon enough who he is." He sat down at his desk and pressed a button. "I'll cable the American consul in Shanghai right off, and I'll bet you it won't be long before we've got the whole story of this bird's life. After that it ought to be a cinch."

"How d'ye figure that?"

"The killer took the devil of a lot of pains to keep the dead man's identity a secret. So when we find it out I figure we'll strike something real hot. Oh, come in, come in. Take a cable to the American consul in Shanghai, China—"

While the Inspector was dictating his cable Sergeant Velie drifted out of the office. Ellery folded his lean length in the Inspector's best chair and pulled out a cigaret and lit it and smoked away with a deep frown. There was the most extraordinary expression on his face. Once he opened his eyes and re-examined what lay on the desk. Then he closed them again. He snuggled back in the chair until he rested on the nape of his neck—a favorite position with him, which he assumed chiefly during his more passionately concentrative moments—and he remained that way without stirring until his father's deskman went out and the old gentleman turned back with a chuckle, rubbing his hands briskly together.

"Well, well, it won't be long now," said the Inspector genially. "Just a question of time. I'm sure we've got it now, El. Everything clears itself up, when you think it out. For instance, that business of our check-up with all the shipping people. We concentrated on the Atlantic. That was a mistake. He probably came by the Pacific route and then took a train across the continent from San Francisco."

"Then why," murmured Ellery, "didn't some genius like your Chancellor clerk remember him? I thought you'd rather thoroughly canvassed the railroad people."

"I told you once that that's a tough job. Nothing wrong there. He was an ordinary-looking little coot, and I s'pose nobody noticed him, that's all. These people see thousands of faces every day. In a story I guess he'd have been spotted. But things don't always work out that way in real life." He leaned back, gazing dreamily at the ceiling. "Shanghai, eh? China. Guess you were right."

"About what?"

"Oh, nothing, nothing. I was just thinking. . . . I s'pose we were wrong, at that, about this guy Cullinan. Can't sort of connect Paris and Shanghai. We'll be hearing from Chiappe soon, and then we'll know definitely." He chattered on.

He was brought to an abrupt realization of his surroundings by a sudden crash. He jerked upright, startled, to find Ellery on his feet.

"What's the matter, for God's sake?"

"Nothing's the matter," said Ellery. There was a rapt expression on his face. "Nothing at all. God's in His heaven, the morning's dew-pearled, all's right with the world. Good old world. Best little world. . . . I've got it."

The Inspector gripped the edge of his desk. "Got what?"

"The answer. The ruddy, bloody answer!"

The Inspector sat still. Ellery stood rooted to the spot, his eyes clear and excited. Then he nodded to himself several times, vigorously. He smiled and went to the window and looked out.

"And just what," said the Inspector in a dry voice, "is the answer?"

"Most remarkable thing," drawled Ellery without turning round. "Perfectly amazing how things come to you. All you have to do is think about them long enough and, pop! something bursts and there it is. It's been there, staring us in the face from the very beginning. All the time! Why, it's so simple it's childish. The whole thing. I can scarcely believe it yet, myself."

There was a long silence. Then Inspector Queen sighed. "I suppose that long string of chatter means you don't want to tell me."

"I haven't begun to glimpse all the possibilities as yet. It's just that I've discovered the key to the whole business. It explains—"

The Inspector's deskman came in with an envelope. Ellery sat down again.

"Well, the dead man isn't Cullinan," growled the old gentleman. "Here's a wire from the Prefect of Police in Paris. Chiappe says Cullinan's in Paris. On his uppers, but alive right enough. So that's that. What were you saying?"

"I was saying," murmured Ellery, "that the key explains virtually every important mystery."

The Inspector looked skeptical. "All that turning-around business—the clothes, the furniture in the room, all that?"

"All that."

"Just one little key, hey?"

"Just one little key."

Ellery rose and reached for his hat and coat. "But there's still something eluding me. And until I figure it out I can't do anything drastic, you see. So I'm going home, *mon père*, and I shall get into my slippers and root myself before the fire and dig in until I catch that slippery fugitive. I've got only part of the answer now."

There was another silence, this time distinctly awkward. It had always been a bone of contention between them that Ellery was stubbornly uncommunicative until the very *dénouement* of a case. Neither pleas nor wild horses could drag a single explanatory word out of him until he was mentally satisfied that he had built up a flawless and impenetrable argument. So there was really no point in asking questions.

And yet the Inspector felt chagrined. There all the time! "What gave you the tip-off, then?" he demanded with irritation. "I'm not the world's biggest dope, and yet I'll be switched if I can see—"

"The bag."

"The bag!" The Inspector looked at the top of his desk in bewilderment. "But I thought you said the answer was there all the time. And we only found the bag a couple of hours ago."

"True," said Ellery, "but the bag served the double purpose of setting off the spark of association and confirming what went before when the result of the conflagration was assimilated." He went to the door thoughtfully.

"Talk English, will you? Just how much *do* you know? Who is the dead man?"

Ellery laughed. "Don't let me dazzle you with my display of mental pyrotechnics. I'm not a crystal-gazer. His. name is the least important part of the solution. On the other hand, his title—"

"His title!"

"Precisely. I think I know why he was murdered, too, although I haven't given that phase of it sufficient thought. The big thing bothering me at the moment is *how*, not who or why."

The Inspector gasped. "Do you realize what you're—. What d'ye mean, El, for jiminy's sake? Have you gone batty?"

"Not at all. There's a vital problem tied up there somehow; I don't know exactly how at the moment. That's going to be my job until I get the answer."

"But you *do* know how he was murdered!"

"Strangely enough, I don't."

The Inspector bit his fingernails in a fever of baffled uncertainty. "You'll be the death of me yet with your damn' puzzles. Why, you act as if you didn't even care what the American consul is going to cable me!"

"I don't."

"Cripe! You mean to say it doesn't make any difference to you what he finds out about the dead man?"

"Not," said Ellery with a smile, "a particle." He opened the door. "I could tell you right now, as a matter of fact, what his reply in substance will be."

"Either I'm crazy or you are."

"Isn't lunacy a question of point of view? Now, now, dad, you know how I am. I'm not entirely sure of my ground yet."

"Well, I guess I'll have to burn up waiting. You're sure, now, you *do* know who pulled the murder? You haven't gone off half-cocked on some wild notion?"

Ellery tugged at the brim of his hat. "Know who did it? What put that idea in your head? Of course I don't know who did it."

The Inspector sank back, utterly overwhelmed. "All right, I give up. When you start lying to me—"

"But I'm not lying," said Ellery in a hurt voice. "I really don't know. Oh, I might hazard a guess, but. . . . That doesn't say, however," he went on, his lips compressing, "that I *won't* know. I've a remarkable start; simply unbelievable. I must find the answer now. It would be unthinkable that after this—"

"According to what you say," said the Inspector bitterly, "you don't know any of the really important things. I thought you had something."

"But I have," said Ellery in a patient tone.

"Well, what the devil did those two African spears sticking up the dead man's backside mean, then?" The Inspector half-rose from his chair, shocked by the look on Ellery's face. "For the love of Mike! What's the matter now?"

"The spears," muttered Ellery, staring blindly at his father. "The spears."

"But—"

"Now I do know how. . . ."

"I know, but—"

Ellery's face came alive. His cheeks screwed up, and his eyes blazed, and his lips trembled. Then he howled like a maniac: "Eureka! That's the answer! Those blessed spears!"

And with a whoop he dashed out of the office, leaving a dazed and collapsed Inspector behind.

CHALLENGE
TO THE READER

Somewhere along the trail, during the creation of my past novels, I lost a good idea. Those kindly persons who—it seems ages ago—discovered that there was a gentleman named Queen writing detective stories and who continued to read that worthy's works will recall that in the early books I made a point of injecting at a strategic place in each hook a challenge to the reader.

Well, something happened. I don't know precisely what. But I remember that after one novel was completed and set up and the galleys corrected some one at the publisher's—a discerning soul indeed—called my attention to the fact that the usual CHAL-LENGE was missing. It seems that I had forgotten to write one. I supplied the deficiency hastily, rather abashed, and it was stuck into the offending volume at the last moment. Then conscience pricked me and I engaged in a little research. I found that I had forgotten the CHALLENGE in the book BEFORE that, too. LONGA DIES NON SEDAVIT VULNERA MENTIS, either, believe me.

Now my publisher is very firm about the integrity of the Queen books, and so I give you . . . the CHALLENGE. It's really a simple matter. I maintain that at this point in your reading of *The Chinese Orange Mystery* you have all the facts in your possession essential to a clear solution of the mystery. You should be able, here, now, henceforward, to solve the puzzle of the murder of the nameless little man in Donald Kirk's anteroom. Everything is there; no essential clue or fact is missing. Can you put them all together and—not make them spell "mother," to be sure—by a process of logical reasoning arrive at the one and only possible solution?

—ELLERY QUEEN

16. THE EXPERIMENT

THE HUMAN brain is a curious instrument. It is remarkably like the sea, possessing deeps and shallows—cold dark profundities and sunny crests. It has its breakers dashing in to shore, and its sullen backwashes. Swift currents race beneath a surface ruffled by minor winds. And there is a constant pulsing rhythm in it very like the tides. For it possesses periods of ebb, when all inspiration recedes into the blind spumy distance; and periods of flow, when strong thoughts come hurtling in, resistless and supreme.

In another metaphor Daniel Webster once said that mind is the great lever of all things; that human thought is the process by which human ends are alternately answered. But a lever suggests action, which inevitably suggests reaction; and Webster points out by indirection that the entire process is one of alternation, of fluctuation between a period of inertia and a period of activity.

Now Mr. Ellery Queen, who labored habitually within the confines of his skull, had long since found in his researches that this was a universal law, and that to achieve intellectual light it was mandatory that he struggle through a phase of intellectual darkness. The problem of the queer little dead man was a singular example in his experience. For days on end his brain wrestled through a slippery fog, groping for signposts; willing, even eager, but impotent. And suddenly there was the light staring coldly into his puckered eyes.

He wasted no time or breath on gratitude to the Wielder of the Cosmic Balance. The reaction had come. The light was there. But the light was still obscured by the whipping tails of the fog. The fog must be dissipated, and it could be dissipated by only one process—concentration.

And so, being a logical man, he concentrated.

Ellery spent the rest of that momentous day draped in his favorite dressing-gown, a fetid garment redolent of old nicotine and haphazardly studded with tiny brown-edged holes, the visible signs of thousands of long-perished cigaret sparks. He lounged on the nape of his neck before a fire in the living-room, his toes toasting cosily, eying the ceiling with bright distant eyes and automatically flinging cigaret-butts into the flames as they burned down to his fingertips. There was no pose in this; for one thing, there was no one to pose for, since the Inspector was sulkily occupied with another case at Headquarters and Djuna was seated somewhere in the musty darkness of a motion picture theatre following the hectic fortunes of one of his innumerable bowlegged heroes. For another, Ellery was not thinking of himself.

It was curious, for instance, that occasionally he screwed his eyes downward a little to study the long crossed swords hanging above the fireplace. They were aged relics of his father's past—a gift to the Inspector from a German friend harking back to student days in Heidelberg. Certainly they could have no connection with the case in hand. And yet he studied them long and earnestly; although it is to be confessed that to his transfiguring eyes they assumed the menacing shape of *Impi* spears, broad-bladed and wicked.

Then the period of inspection passed, and he snuggled deeper into the chair and gave himself up wholly to disembodied thought.

At four in the afternoon he sighed, roused himself, creaked out of the chair, flung another cigaret into the fire, and went to the telephone.

"Dad?" he croaked when Inspector Queen answered. "Ellery. I want you to do something for me."

"Where are you?" snapped the Inspector.

"Home. I—"

"What the devil are you doing?"

"Thinking. Look here—"

"About what? I thought you'd settled the whole business in your mind." The Inspector sounded faintly bitter.

"Now, now," said Ellery in a weary voice, "don't be that way. I didn't mean to offend you, you sensitive old coot. I really have been working. Anything new, by the way?"

"Not a blessed thing. Well, what is it? I'm busy. Some tramp was shot up on Forty-fifth Street and I've got my hands full."

Ellery gazed dreamily at the wall above the fireplace. "Have you any connections with some reliable theatrical costumer who can be trusted to do a confidential job and keep his mouth shut?"

"Costum—! What's up now, for cripe's sake?"

"An experiment in the interests of justice. Well, have you?"

"I suppose I can rustle one," grumbled the Inspector. "You and your experiments! Johnny Rosenzweig over on Forty-ninth once did a job for me. I guess you can rely on him. What's the dope?"

"I want a dummy."

"A what?"

"A dummy. Not the human kind," chuckled Ellery. "A stuffed shirt, inarticulate, will do. Here, I'm confusing you. Get this Rosenzweig friend of yours to make up a dummy of the same general size and height as the murdered man."

"Now I know you've gone nuts," complained the Inspector. "You sure this is for the case? Or are you workin' on some far-fetched, crazy detective-story idea for a book? If it's that, El, I can't take time off to bother—"

"No, no, I assure you this will prove a stepping-stone toward the high place in which New York justice sits enthroned. Can you get him to work fast?"

"I s'pose so. Just a dummy the size and height of the dead man, hey?" The old gentleman sounded sarcastic. "Anything else? How about a little bridgework? Or some artistic modelling on the nose?"

"No, seriously. There *is* something else. You've got the weight of the dead man, haven't you?"

"Sure. It's in Doc Prouty's report."

"Very good. I want the all-over weight to be identical with the victim's. He'll have to do a clever job. See if he can't approximate the same weight of limbs, torso, and head. Especially the head. That's most important. Think he can do it?"

"Might. He'll probably have to get Prouty's help in the weights."

"Be sure to tell him to keep the dummy flexible—"

"What d'ye mean?"

"I mean I don't want it in one stiff straight piece. Whatever he uses for the weighting—iron, lead—should not run in a single piece from head to foot. Let him use separate weights for the feet, the legs, the torso, the arms, and the head. In that way we'll have a dummy which in virtually every particular will be a facsimile of the dead man's body. That's vital, dad."

"I guess he can string 'em together with wire or something," muttered the Inspector, "which'll bend. Anything else?"

Ellery chewed his lower lip. "Yes. Have the dummy dressed in the dead man's clothes. That's the theatre in me coming out."

"Put on backwards?"

"Good heavens, yes! The dummy should look precisely like our little corpse."

"Say," snapped the Inspector, "don't tell me you're going to pull one of those old psychological gags of confronting the suspects with what seems to be the corpse risen from the dead! By thunder, El, that's—"

"Now that," said Ellery sadly, "is the most unkindest cut of all. Have you really such a low estimate of my mentality? Of course I haven't any such notion. This is an experiment in the name of science, dear father. No hocus-pocus about it. The theatre I referred to was an afterthought. Understood?"

"I don't know what you're talking about, but I guess so. Where d'ye want the thing?"

"Have it sent up here, to the apartment. I have work for it."

The Inspector sighed. "All right. *All* right. But sometimes I think that all that thinking you say you do has gone to your head. Ha, ha!" And with a sad chuckle he hung up.

Ellery smiled, stretched, yawned, wandered into the bedroom, flung himself on his bed, and fell asleep within sixty seconds.

The dummy was delivered by Sergeant Velie at 9:30 that night.

"Ah!" cried Ellery, seizing the end of the long heavy crate. "Lord, that's heavy! What's in this, a gravestone?"

"Well, the Inspector said it was supposed to weigh as much as the stiff, Mr. Queen," said the Sergeant. "All right, bud," and he nodded to the man who had helped him carry the crate upstairs. The man touched his cap and went away. "Here. Let's dig him out of that."

They set to work and under Djuna's awestruck eyes removed something that might have been a man. It was swathed in brown paper like an Egyptian mummy. Ellery stripped the wrappings away and gasped in astonishment. The dummy slipped out of his arms and promptly proceeded to crumple section by section in a heap on the living-room rug, quite like a dead man.

"Lord, it's—it's *he!*"

For there, smiling up at them, was the unctuous face of the stout little man.

"Papeer mashay," exclaimed the Sergeant, gazing proudly at the dummy. "This guy Rosenzweig knows his onions. Reconstructed that there face from the photos and did one swell job with his paints and brushes. Look at that hair!"

"I'm looking," murmured Ellery, fascinated. It was, as the Sergeant had said, a most artistic job. The pink smooth skull with its fringe of gray hair was quite life-like. Even the crushed blackish area where the brass poker had struck was there, and the jelly-like radiations of dried blood.

"Look," whispered Djuna, stretching his thin neck. "He's got his pants on backwards. An' his coat 'n' everything!"

"Quite in order. Well!" Ellery breathed deeply. "Rosenzweig, my friend, I salute you. I'm certainly in the debt of that genius, whoever he is. Couldn't have conceived a more perfect dummy for my purposes. Here. Let's get him—"

"Gonna throw a scare into them?" growled Velie, stooping and tugging at the dummy's shoulders.

"No, no, Velie; nothing so crude as that. Let's sit him in that chair near the bedroom door. There. That's the idea. . . . Now, Sergeant." He straightened, flushed a little, and stared into the giant's hard eyes. The Sergeant scratched his chin and looked suspicious.

"You want me to do somethin'," he said accusingly, "somethin' you don't want no one to know about."

"Exactly. Now—"

"Not even the Inspector, I bet."

"Oh," said Ellery airily, "why not surprise him? He doesn't get much fun out of life, Velie." He took the giant's arm and steered him into the foyer. Djuna, a little hurt, stalked back to his kitchen. He kept his sharp ears cocked, however, and he could hear Ellery murmur earnest words and at least once an explosive exclamation from the mountainous Sergeant. The Sergeant, it appeared, was stupefied. Then there was the slam of the front door and Ellery was back, smiling and rubbing his hands.

"Djuna!"

Before the name was out of his mouth Djuna was at his side, panting and eager as a charger.

"You gonna do somepin'?"

"And, my chief of the Baker Street Division," said Ellery, eying the smiling face of the dummy thoughtfully, "how. You're hereby appointed First Special Laboratory Assistant, young man. We're alone, there are no prying eyes and ears—" He fixed a stern eye on Djuna. "You take your oath as a Romany gentleman that what passes between us this night is henceforth and forever a secret, writ in words of blood? Cross your heart and hope to die?"

Djuna crossed his heart hastily and hoped to die.

"Settled! Now, first." Ellery sucked his thumb. "Ah, yes! That small mat from the storage-closet, Djuna."

"Mat?" Djuna's eyes opened wide. "Yes, *sir.*" And he sped away, to return a moment later with the commandeered mat.

"Next," said Ellery, crossing the room and gazing up at the wall above the fireplace, "the step-ladder."

Djuna brought the step-ladder. Ellery mounted it and with the solemnity and dignity of a high priest performing a sacred rite unhooked the somewhat dusty long swords from their brackets on the wall and brought them down. These he placed beside the rolled mat and smote his palms together, chuckling.

"We progress, Djuna. Finally, a commission."

"Com—"

"An errand. Don your legate's robes, O Assistant."

Djuna frowned a moment, and then grinned and vanished and reappeared in hat and coat. "Where to?"

"The hardware store on St. Nicholas Avenue. That monstrous emporium."

"Yes, sir."

Ellery handed him a bill. "Procure, O Assistant, a small roll of every kind of cord and twine in the establishment."

"Yep."

"And," added Ellery, frowning, "also thin pliable wire—a few lengths. We must overlook no possibility in our quest for the Holy Grail in which truth lies enshrined. *Comprends*?"

Djuna ran.

"A moment, young limb. Perhaps you'd better buy us a new broom, too."

"Why?"

"I might say platitudinously because it sweeps clean, but that would be aborting the facts. Rest content, my friend, with the bare wording of the commission."

Djuna shook his head stubbornly. "But we got a new broom."

"We must have another. Nothing's happened to our saw, Djuna, I trust?"

"It's in the tool-chest in the storage-closet."

"Superb. The brooms may serve if the swords fail us. *Alors*, avaunt, then, my fine churl; science waits upon the vigor of your muscles!"

Djuna set his small mouth in desperate lines, stuck out his thin chest, and scudded out of the apartment. Ellery sat down and stretched his legs.

Then Djuna popped his head back. "You won't do nothin' till I get back, will you, Mr. El?" he asked anxiously.

"My dear Djuna," said Ellery in a reproachful voice. And then Djuna was gone again, and Ellery leaned back and closed his eyes and laughed aloud.

At 11:15, when Inspector Queen tramped wearily into the apartment, he found Djuna and Ellery in excited discussion before the fire—a discussion which ended abruptly with his entrance. The dummy was packed in his coffin and laid out in the center of the room. The mat, the assorted rolls of twine, and the brooms were not in evidence. Even the long swords had found their way back to their accustomed places above the fireplace.

"Well, what's the whispering about?" grunted the old man, flinging his hat and coat down and coming to the fire to chafe his hands.

"We found a—" Djuna began hotly, when Ellery clapped his hands over the boy's mouth.

"Is that the way, O Assistant," he said severely, "you keep to your sacred oath? Dad, I beg to report—*we* beg to report—success. Complete, utter, final success."

"'Zat so?" said the Inspector dryly.

"You don't seem immoderately elated."

"I'm worn out."

"I'm sorry." There was a little silence. Djuna, sensing intrafamiliar trouble, slipped off to his bedroom. "I mean it, though."

"Glad to hear it." The Inspector sat down, groaning. He cast a long sidewise glance at the coffin-like crate in the middle of the room. "I see you got the dummy all right."

"Oh, yes. Thanks loads." There was another silence. Ellery's spirits seemed dampened; he rose and went to the mantelpiece and rather nervously fingered one of the iron candlesticks on it. "How did your Forty-fifth Street tramp come out?"

"With a slug in her belly," sniffed the Inspector. "It's all right, though. We got the guy who plugged her. Dippy MacGuire, the coke. That ends *one* spectacular career."

And again a silence. "Aren't you going to ask me," said Ellery at last in a plaintive tone, "what success means in terms of Queenian syllables?"

"I kind of figured," drawled the Inspector, dipping into his snuff-box, "that if you were over your fit of hush-mouth, you'd tell without my asking."

"It's solved, you know," said Ellery bashfully.

"Congrats."

"I know the whole story now, you see. All the essential things. Except the little chap's name, and that's *not* important. But who murdered him, why, and how it was done—especially how it was done—they're quite settled in my mind."

The Inspector said nothing; he placed his small hands behind his head and gazed gloomily into the fire.

Ellery grinned suddenly and seized a chair and dragged it over to the fire and sat down. He leaned over and smacked his father's knee resoundingly. "Come on, old growler," he chuckled. "Come out of it. You know you're putting on an act. I do want to tell you, now that I'm convinced. . . . Or perhaps you'd rather not—?"

"It's up to you," said the Inspector stiffly.

So Ellery put his hands between his knees and squatted and talked.

He talked for an hour. All the while Inspector Queen remained motionless, gazing steadily into the flames, his bird-like little face screwed up and his brows flanking a frown.

And then, all at once, he grinned all over his face and cried: "Well, I'll be double-damned!"

17. LOOKING BACKWARD

Mr. Ellery Queen had never set a stage more carefully in the whole of his variegated experience than he did the morning after the great experiment in his living-room. And, for once, he had Inspector Queen with him.

Why they deemed it necessary to be so thoroughly cautious and painstaking about their preparations neither took the trouble to explain to any one. And the only other person who might have been able to account for it was missing. Sergeant Velie, normally the soul of punctuality, had vanished. And again, for once, Inspector Queen accepted his vanishment with equanimity.

When it began it proceeded very smoothly indeed. Early in the morning a grim-faced detective from Headquarters called on each of the persons associated with the case and constituted himself a gratuitous bodyguard thenceforward. There were no explanations or excuses. Beyond a curt: "Orders of Inspector Queen," each detective remained silent.

Consequently, when 10:00 o'clock rolled round, the anteroom to Donald Kirk's office—the scene of the crime—began to fill with curious, rather shaken, people. Dr. Hugh Kirk, faintly blustering, was wheeled into the anteroom by a subdued Miss Diversey under the watchful eye of Detective Hagstrom. Donald Kirk and his sister Marcella were marched in by Detective Ritter. Miss Temple, distinctly mauve-complectioned, entered with Detective Hesse.

Glenn Macgowan stamped in, furious but unprotesting, under the wing of Detective Johnson. Felix Berne was a reluctantly early comer, prodded along by Detective Piggott, who seemed to have developed an abrasive dislike for his charge. Inspector Queen attended to Irene Sewell himself. Osborne found himself hustled into the anteroom by a brawny policeman. Even Nye, the Chancellor's manager, and Brummer, the black-browed house-detective, were there in firm if polite custody; as were Mrs. Shane, the floor-clerk, and Hubbell, Kirk's valet-butler.

When they were all assembled Mr. Ellery Queen briskly shut the door, smiled at the silent seated company, cast a professional eye over the detectives ranged against the wall, nodded to Inspector Queen, who had taken up a silent station before the corridor door, and strode to the center of the room.

Through the windows streamed a pale morning light, sluggishly emanating from an overcast, depressing sky. The coffin-like crate lay before them, its lid loosely on; the contents of this remote sarcophagus had not been revealed to them, and more than one puzzled disturbed glance was directed at it.

"Ladies and gentlemen," began Mr. Ellery Queen, resting one neat shoe on the crate, "I suppose all of you are wondering at the peculiar character of this morning's little convention. I shan't keep you in doubt. We've gathered this morning to unmask the murderer of the man who met his death in this room not so long ago."

They were sitting rigidly, staring at him with a sort of fascinated horror. Then Miss Diversey whispered: "Then you know—" and bit her lip and blushed in confusion.

"Shut up," snarled Dr. Kirk. "Are we to understand, Queen, that this is to be one of those fantastic exhibitions of crime-nosing you're reputed to be so addicted to? I must say that—"

"One at a time, please," smiled Ellery. "Yes, Dr. Kirk, that's precisely what this is intended to be. Let's say: a practical demonstration of the invincibility of logic. Mind over matter. The self-taught brain victorious. And as for your question, Miss Diversey: we shall argue certain points of interest and see where they lead us." He raised his hand. "No, no, no questions, please. . . . Oh, before I begin. I suppose it's futile to request the murderer of our little corpse to step forward and save us both time and cerebral wear-and-tear?"

He looked at them gravely. But no one replied; every one kept his eyes fixed guiltily before him.

"Very well," he said in crisp tones. "To work. . . ." He lighted a cigaret and half-closed his eyes. "The crux of this case was the astounding fact that everything on the scene of the crime, including the very clothes of the victim, had been inverted, turned backwards. I say 'astounding.' Even in my mind, trained in the observation and diagnosis of just such phenomena, there was a distinct reaction of amazement. I daresay not even the murderer, conceiving the backwards business and carrying it into effect, realized just how amazing it was going to appear.

"After the shock had passed I proceeded to analyze the facts, or rather the fact. Experience has taught me that rarely does a criminal do something positive—as opposed to an unconscious act—without purpose. This was a positive, a conscious act. It required hard work and the expenditure of precious time in the accomplishment. I was justified in saying at once, therefore, that there was *reason* behind it; that while its manifestations seemed insane its purpose, at the least, must have been rational."

They were listening with painful attention.

"I will confess," continued Ellery, "that until yesterday that purpose eluded me. I pursued it mentally with the tenacity of desperation, but for the life of me I couldn't see why everything had been turned backwards. I assumed, of course, that the backwardness of the crime pointed to something backwards about somebody in the case. It seemed the only possible tack. And yet it enmeshed me in strands of philology, philately, and nomenclature so confused that more than once I was tempted to throw the whole puzzle up. There were all sorts of bewildering questions to be answered. If everything was turned backwards to point to a backwards significance about somebody, then that somebody must have been criminally involved. What was the real backwards significance, then? Whom was it intended to involve criminally? And, more important, who had turned everything backwards in the first place? Who was pointing to whom?"

He chuckled. "I see confusion here, and I can't say I blame you. I found plenty of leads. They performed the function of leading, to be sure, but unfortunately in the direction of obfuscation, not toward a lucid solution of the problem. As for who had done the job, was it the criminal? Was it some one who had inadvertently witnessed the killing? But if it was the criminal pointing to some one else, then that some one was being framed. And yet it was the sorriest frame-up conceivable, since it was so inconclusive, so vague, so really, incomprehensible. If everything was turned backwards by some one who had witnessed the crime, why didn't that witness come forward with his knowledge instead of taking that hideously tangled, complex method of leaving a clue to the murderer's identity? You see what I was up against. Wherever I turned I met darkness.

"And then," murmured Ellery, "I saw how simple it was, how easily I had led myself astray. I had made a mistake. I had misread the facts. My logic had been imperfect. I hadn't taken into consideration the startling fact that there were two general explanations for the backwardnesses, not one!"

"I can't say I understand this Ciceronian oration," said Felix Berne suddenly. "Is this something characteristically esoteric, or do you know what you're talking about?"

"The gentleman from The Mandarin," said Ellery, "will please to observe the amenities and preserve the peace. You'll find out soon enough, Mr. Berne. . . . For you see, I found on reconsideration that there were two possible answers to the riddle. The first I've already related: that everything had been turned backwards *to point to* something backwards about somebody in the case. Its alternative, which had escaped me," continued Ellery, leaning forward, "was that everything was turned backwards *to conceal* something backwards about somebody in the case!"

He paused to light a fresh cigaret. Cupping his hands about a match, he scrutinized their faces. But he saw only bewilderment.

"I see expansion is required," he drawled, puffing away. "The first possibility led *away* from the crime; the second led *to* the crime. The first possibility involved *re*vealment; the second *con*cealment. Perhaps I can make it clearer by asking you: By everything about the body and the crime-scene being turned backwards, *against whom* could concealment have conceivably been directed? What about whom in the case could have been meant to be hidden, camouflaged, disguised?"

"Well, if everything was turned backwards on the body," ventured Miss Temple in a low voice, "then it must have been the victim about whom something was being concealed, I should think."

"*Brava*, Miss Temple. You've put your finger on the precise point. There was only one person in the case against whom concealment could have been effected by turning everything backwards. And that was the victim himself. In other words, instead of seeking a backwards significance involving the murderer, or a possible accomplice, or a possible witness to the crime, it was necessary to look for a backwards significance *involving the victim.*"

"That sounds pat when you say it fast, and all that," said Berne, "but I fail to see—"

"As Homer said," murmured Ellery: "'Give me to see, and Ajax asks no more.' Classics to the classical, Mr. Berne. . . . The obvious question was: What could this backwards significance be which centers about the victim? Was it something backwards *about him* literally? Yes, from our theorem something backwards about the victim which the murderer wanted to conceal, to disguise, to cover up. That is to say, if the victim had something, some one thing, backwards about him, then the murderer by turning *everything else about him* backwards would conceal the backwardness of that one thing!—would make it very difficult indeed to discern what that backwards element about the victim had been to begin with."

A startled expression sprang into the publisher's eye, and he sank back with compressed lips. Thereafter he studied Ellery in a new and faintly puzzled way.

"Once I had reached that stage of my cogitations," continued Ellery with a quizzical look, "I knew I was on solid ground at last. I had something to work on—the most tangible thing in the world: a positive clue. It at once confirmed everything that had gone before and dissipated the fog like magic. For I had merely to ask myself if there was any indication on the victim's body that pointed to the possible nature of the *original* backwards phenomenon, the one that was meant to be concealed by the murderer's turning everything else backwards. No sooner asked than answered. There was."

"Clue?" muttered Macgowan.

"I saw the body myself," began Donald Kirk in a wondering voice.

"Please, gentlemen. The hour ageth. What was this indication, this clue? *The fact that there was no necktie on the man's body or on the scene of the crime!*"

If Ellery had uttered in a loud voice the word: "Abracadabra!" he could not have evoked a more general expression of dazed inquiry than flickered from the faces of his audience.

"No necktie?" gasped Donald. "But what—"

"Our instinctive presumption," said Ellery patiently, "was that the victim *had* worn a necktie, but that the murderer had taken it away because somehow it permitted identification of the victim or traceability. But it was evident to me now *that there never was a necktie;* that the victim had not worn a tie at all! Remember, when he spoke to Mrs. Shane, and to Mr. Osborne in the presence of Miss Diversey, he wore a scarf bundled closely about his neck. In other words, there was no tie for the murderer to take away!"

"But at best," protested Dr. Kirk, fascinated despite himself, "that was a pragmatic conclusion, Queen. It was a theory, but not necessarily the truth."

"A theory, my dear Doctor, resulting inevitably from the argument that the backwards process had been employed to conceal something. But I agree that, as it stood, it was unsatisfactory. Fortunately, a fact existed which offered positive corroboration." Ellery related briefly the incident of the canvas valise, and listed its contents. "For there were the necessary garments of the victim—everything from a suit to shoes—and yet the only familiar article of apparel missing from the bag was—*a necktie*. I felt certain then that the reason it was missing was that the owner of the bag habitually *did not wear* neckties. You see?"

"Hmm," muttered Dr. Kirk. "Corroboration indeed. A man who didn't wear neckties . . ."

"The thing was child's play after that," Ellery shrugged, waving his cigaret about. "I asked myself: What type of man never wears a necktie with ordinary street-clothes?"

"A priest!" burst out Marcella. She sank back, blushing.

"Precisely, Miss Kirk. A Catholic priest—or, to be accurate, either a Catholic priest or an Episcopalian clergyman. And then I remembered something else. All three of the witnesses who had seen and spoken with the victim remarked about the peculiar quality of his voice. It had a soft queer timbre, almost unctuous in its sugary tones. And while this was by no means conclusive, or for that matter even a good clue, it did fit with the character of a priest after I'd deduced one. And then there was the very worn breviary in the bag, and the religious tracts . . . I couldn't doubt it any longer.

"So here I had the kernel of the entire process of inversion. For to what backwards phenomenon—meant to be obscured, buried among the irrelevant backwardnesses—did the neck-tie-clue point? And then it struck me like a physical blow that a Catholic or Episcopalian man-of-God wears his collar turned around. *Backwards!*"

There was a stifling silence. Inspector Queen, at the corridor door, did not stir. He had his eyes fixed oddly upon the door oppo-site him, the door to the office which stood shut.

"So I had finally smelled out the backwards significance of the crime," sighed Ellery. "Everything had been turned backwards by the murderer to conceal the fact that his victim was a priest, to conceal the fact that his victim wore no necktie and wore a turned-around collar."

They erupted all at once, springing into life as if some one had given a signal. But it was Miss Temple's soft voice which somehow caught on. "There must be something wrong, Mr. Queen. It was an ordinary collar, wasn't it? Couldn't the murderer have merely turned the collar around on the dead man's neck into the usual lay position?"

"Excellent objection," smiled Ellery. "Naturally that occurred to me, as it certainly occurred to the murderer. I should point out, incidentally, that the cravatless victim must have been a great shock to the murderer. For it is true that no one in this case, including the murderer himself, had ever actually seen that stout little man before he emerged quietly from the elevator on this floor. Muffled up to the chin in the scarf, he was killed before the murderer realized that he was a priest. . . . But to reply to your question. If the murderer had turned the collar around—that is, turned it into the lay position—it would have stood out like a sore thumb. And the missing tie would have only called further attention to the one thing about the victim the murderer wanted to conceal."

"But why the devil," objected Macgowan, "didn't this murderer solve the whole problem by getting a tie somewhere and putting it on the dead man's neck?"

"Why indeed?" said Ellery, his eyes gleaming. "And that question, too, occurred to me. In fact, it was one of the most important indications in the whole logical structure! I shan't answer it fully now, but you'll see later why the murderer *couldn't* get a necktie. Of course he couldn't use his own—" Ellery smiled maliciously, "if he were a man, since he had to meet other people; and if he, so to speak, were a woman he naturally, also so to speak, couldn't provide one from his own person. But most important, he couldn't get out of the anteroom, as I'll show you later. At any rate, take my word for it at this point that his best course was to leave the collar as it was—turned around—and then as a blind to turn everything else on the body and in the room around, thereby concealing the significance of the inverted collar and the lack of a necktie and thereby leading the police astray." Ellery paused, and continued thoughtfully. "As a matter of fact, at this point in my deductions it was evident that we were dealing with a person of great imagination, even brilliance, and also with a large cranial capacity and a strictly methodical temperament. It took genius of a sort to conceive the idea of inverting all the clothes; and it took brain-power and logic to foresee that to turn *only* the clothes about was not sufficient, since the very strangeness of the appearance of the clothes would call dangerous attention to them. So he turned the furniture and everything else movable around as well, diverting attention from the clothes and therefore from the collar—the whole thing a perfectly inspired logical chain of reasoning. And it very nearly worked."

"But even so, even if you knew the victim was a priest—" began Donald.

"Where did it get me?" Ellery grimaced. "It's true that merely knowing the victim was a priest, while it narrowed the field of search, was hardly vital. But then there was the business of the valise."

"Valise?"

"Yes. I didn't visualize baggage myself; Inspector Queen did, to his eternal credit. But the murderer knew all along what he was up against. When he emptied the priest's pockets he found the baggage-check, bearing the inscription of the Hotel Chancellor itself. Since his main objective was to prevent identification of the victim, it was apparent that he had to get hold of the luggage held by the Chancellor checkroom to prevent its falling into the hands of the police. Yet he was afraid. The Chancellor was under close surveillance. He dillydallied, apprehensive, timid, worried, until it was too late. Then he conceived the scheme of gaining possession of the valise by way of the falsely signed note, the five-dollar bill, and the instructions to the Postal Telegraph office. As it happened, we caught the trail instantly; he was watching and saw the game was spoiled, made no effort to claim the bag in Grand Central, and the bag fell into our hands.

"Now observe what that fatal procrastination of the murderer led to. When the bag was opened we found the dead man's clothing with Shanghai labels in them. Since the clothes were all fairly new those garments must have been purchased recently in China. I put this together with the fact that despite the most thorough search no trace of the man had been found in this country. Had the priest lived in the United States but was merely returning from a visit to China, I reasoned that some one in this country would have come forward to identify him—a friend, a relative. But no one did. So it was not at all improbable that he had been a permanent resident in the East. But if he was a Catholic priest *from* China, what did we have? There is only one great class of Christian men-of-God in the land of Buddhism and Taoism."

"A missionary," said Miss Temple slowly.

Ellery smiled. "Right again, Miss Temple. I felt convinced that our benevolent-appearing, soft-speaking little corpse with the breviary and religious tracts in his bag had been a Catholic missionary from China!"

Some one rapped thunderously on the door against which Inspector Queen's slender shoulderblades were resting, and the old man turned quickly and opened the door. The visitor was Sergeant Velie, hard-bitten and grim as usual.

Ellery murmured: "I beg your pardon," and hurried to the door. They watched the three men conferring with open expressions of anxiety and apprehension. The Sergeant was rumbling something ominous-sounding, the Inspector was looking triumphant, and Ellery was nodding vigorously at every murmur. Then something passed from Velie's beefy hand to Ellery's, and Ellery turned his back and examined it, and turned and smiled and put what he was holding into his pocket. The Sergeant leaned back against the door, towering beside Inspector Queen.

"I'm sorry about the interruption," said Ellery placidly, "but Sergeant Velie has made an epochal discovery. Where was I? Oh, yes. I knew then roughly who Donald Kirk's visitor was. A little thought then convinced me that I had found the key to—as it were the *casus belli*—to the direct motive which inspired the murderer. It was quite obvious that the priest himself, as a flesh-and-blood personality, was unknown to any one in this room. Yet he had come to visit Donald Kirk, asking for him by name. Only three classes of persons frequent Mr. Kirk's office here; stamp people, gem people, and people on publishing business, chiefly authors. Yet the priest had refused to tell Mr. Osborne, Kirk's confidential assistant, anything about his business; not even his name. This did not sound like a publishing contact, and it struck me that it was most probable the point of contact between Kirk and the priest was one of Kirk's two hobbies: stamps or gems.

"Now I reasoned that, if this was true, the missionary had come either to sell stamps or jewels, or to buy them—the two all-inclusive classifications. The cheapness of the man's attire, his vocation, the long journey he had made, convinced me that he was not a buyer. Then he was a seller. This fitted well, too, with his general air of secrecy. He had something in a stamp or jewel to sell Donald Kirk, something valuable, to judge from his reticent attitude. It was therefore evident that he must have been murdered for possession of the stamp or jewel he had come all the way from China to sell. It was even possible to infer that, since Kirk is a specialist on stamps of China, the missionary was probably the owner of a Chinese stamp rather than a jewel. This wasn't certain, but it seemed the better possibility. Ergo, having solved the case in my own way, I instructed Sergeant Velie to ransack the premises of the murderer with an eye to finding this Chinese stamp; although I did tell him to look out for a jewel." Ellery paused to light another cigaret. "I was right, and the Sergeant reports success. He has found the stamp."

Some one gasped. But when Ellery searched their faces he met only stubbornly furtive stares.

He smiled and took from his pocket a long manila envelope. From this envelope he took another, smaller envelope of queer foreign appearance, with an address (presumably) in Chinese and a cancelled stamp in one corner. "Messrs. Kirk and Macgowan." The two men rose uncertainly. "We may as well call upon our two philatelists. What do you make of this?"

They came forward, reluctant but curious. Kirk took the envelope slowly, Macgowan peering over his shoulder. And then, simultaneously, they cried out and began to talk to each other excitedly in undertones.

"Well, gentlemen?" murmured Ellery. "We're panting for enlightenment. What is it?"

The stamp on the envelope was a small rectangle of thin tough paper printed in a single color, bright orange. Within its rectangular border there was a conventionalized coiled dragon. Its denomination was five *candarins*. The printing of the stamp was crude, and the envelope itself was ragged and yellow with age. A message in Chinese—the letter—had been written on the inside of the envelope, which was of the old-fashioned type still used in Europe and elsewhere for both address and message, folding up neatly for postage.

"This," muttered Donald, "is the most remarkable thing I've ever seen. To a China specialist it's a find of monumental proportions. It's the earliest official postage stamp of China, antedating by many years the accepted first-issue design which is in the standard catalogue. It was an experimental issue of extremely small quantity and was used postally only for a few days. No copy on cover, as we call it, which is to say on the envelope—or off, for that matter—has ever been found. God, what a beauty!"

"It's not even listed in specialized Chinese catalogues," said Macgowan hoarsely, eying the envelope with rapacity. "It's barely mentioned in one old stamp treatise, rather affectionately referred to by color, just as philatelists refer to the first national authorized issue of Great Britain as the One-Penny Black. Lord, it's beautiful."

"Would you say," drawled Ellery, "that this is a valuable piece of property?"

"Valuable!" cried Donald. "Why, man, this should be even more valuable philatelically than the British Guiana! That is, if it's authentic. It would have to be expertized."

"It looks genuine," frowned Macgowan. "The fact that it's on cover, and the cancellation is clear, and the message is written inside . . ."

"How valuable would you say?"

"Oh, anything. Anything at all. These things are worth what a collector will pay at top. The Guiana's listed at fifty thousand." Donald's face darkened. "If I were stable financially, I'd probably pay as much as that for it myself. It would make top price for any stamp; but, Lord, there's nothing like this in the world!"

"Ah. Thank you, gentlemen." Ellery returned the envelope to its manila container and tucked it into his pocket. Kirk and Macgowan slowly went back to their seats. No one said anything for a long time. "This Chinese stamp, then," resumed Ellery at last, "may be characterized as *deus ex machina*. It brought our friend the missionary all the way from China; I daresay he had made the find in some obscure place, visualized suddenly a wealth which would keep him in luxurious comfort for the rest of his days, lost his grip on the spiritual consolations of his profession, and resigned from the mission. Inquiry in Shanghai would have informed him of the great collectors of Chinese stamps who might be in the market for such a rarity; I suppose it was there, or perhaps in Peiping—more probably Shanghai—that he learned of Mr. Donald Kirk. . . . And it killed the priest, too, for the murder was committed in its name."

Ellery stopped to look thoughtfully down at the coffin-like crate at his feet. "Having identified the victim, then—except for name, which was unimportant—and come to a satisfactory conclusion about the motive (although this was also unimportant from the logical standpoint), I proceeded to consideration—the supreme consideration—of the murderer's identity.

"For some time, comparatively speaking, this most essential point escaped me. I knew the answer was there, if only I could spot it. Then I remembered one or two apparently inexplicable phenomena of the crime which no one, including myself, had been able to interpret. An impetus was provided by a chance question of the Inspector's. And an experiment revealed the whole thing."

Without warning he stooped and removed the lid of the crate. Sergeant Velie silently stepped forward; and between them they raised the dummy to a sitting position in the crate.

Marcella Kirk uttered a faint shriek and shrank against Macgowan beside her. Miss Diversey gulped noisily. Miss Temple lowered her eyes. Mrs. Shane breathed a prayer and Miss Llewes looked sickish. Even the men had turned pale.

"Don't be alarmed," murmured Ellery, rising. "Just a pleasant fancy of mine, and a rather interesting sample of the dummy-maker's art. Please pay the very closest attention."

He went to the door leading to the adjoining office, opened it, vanished, and an instant later reappeared with the paper-thin Indian mat which had lain in front of the door on the office side. This he deposited carefully over the threshold, one-third in the anteroom and the other two-thirds in the office. Then he got to his feet, took from his right pocket a coil of thin tough-looking cord, and held it up for their inspection. He nodded, smiled at them, and proceeded to measure off one-third the length of the cord. He then wound the cord at that point about the protruding metal knob of the bolt on the anteroom side of the door. The cord now dangled from the knob—a short length and a long length, held to the metal protrusion by the single winding. There was no knot of any kind, as he demonstrated in pantomime. Ellery took up the short end and passed it through the crack under the door, over the mat into the office beyond. He closed the door without touching the knob. It was shut but unbolted.

They were watching him like children at a puppet-show, wide-eyed, eager, puzzled. No one spoke, and all that could be heard were the soft sounds of Ellery's movements and the heavy uneven breathing.

Ellery continued his demonstration in the same pregnant silence. He stepped back and surveyed the two sections of bookcase which flanked the doorway. He studied them for a moment, and then sprang forward and began to tug at the case to his right as he faced the door. He pulled the case back along the right-hand wall about four feet. He returned and began to move the bookcase on the left of the doorway, as they saw it. He tugged and shoved until he had it jutting out into the room—pulled toward the door until its left side at the rear touched the hinges of the door, its right side swung outward into the room a short way, the whole bookcase forming an acute angle with the door. Then he stepped back with a nod of satisfaction.

"You will observe," he said briskly in the silence, "that both bookcases are now exactly as we found them when the body was discovered."

As if this were a signal, Sergeant Velie stooped and lifted the dummy out of the crate. Despite its weight he carried it as he might have borne a child. They saw now that the dummy was dressed in the dead man's garments, and that they were on backwards. Ellery said something to the Sergeant in a low voice and Velie set the body upright on its feet. He balanced it erect, grotesquely, with one huge splayed finger.

"Let go, Sergeant," drawled Ellery.

They stared. Velie withdrew his finger and the body collapsed, sinking vertically until it lay in a heap on the floor where an instant before it had been standing.

"The muscleless inertia of the very dead," said Ellery cheerfully. "Good work, Sergeant. We assume that *rigor mortis* has not yet set in. Our demonstration has proved it. Now for the second stage."

Velie lifted the dummy and Ellery went to the crate and came up with the two *Impi* spears which had been found on the body. These he thrust up the dummy's trouser-legs and under the coat until they emerged from behind the head, their wicked blades far above the *papier-mâché* skull. Then the Sergeant carried the dummy over and propped it up in the angle made by the door and the left-hand bookcase, facing toward the right. It stood erect very stiffly, the two spearheads jutting like horns from the coat. The feet barely rested on the edge of the Indian mat.

Sergeant Velie stepped back with a hard grin on his lips.

Then Ellery proceeded about a curious business. He took the dangling end of the cord—the long end—and began carefully to wind it about the haft of the spear nearer the door, just below the blade. He wound it about the spear twice. They saw then that there was a slight slack in the length leading from the spear to the bolt of the door—a graceful dip in the suspended cord.

"Observe, please, that there is no knot or noose in the cord about the spear," said Ellery. Then he stooped and pushed the remaining end now dangling from the spear—pushed it, as he had pushed the short end some time before—through the crack between the mat on the threshold and the bottom of the door until its end vanished into the office.

"Don't move, any one," snapped Ellery, rising. "Just keep your eyes on that dummy and the door."

He reached over, grasped the knob, and gently pulled the door to him. As he pulled, the slack in the cord grew looser. When the door was sufficiently ajar, Ellery very cautiously stooped, wriggled under the cord, and squeezed through the narrow opening, disappearing from view. Then the door softly clicked back—shut but unbolted.

They watched.

For thirty seconds nothing happened.

And then the mat under the door moved. It was being jerked out of the anteroom into the office beyond the door.

It caught them completely off guard. Their mouths opened and remained open. They strained to see what was apparently a miracle. It happened so quickly that it was over almost before they could realize the significance of the process.

For with the jerk of the mat several things occurred simultaneously. The dummy trembled, began to topple, and its stiffly speared body began to slide along the top edge of the jutting bookcase in the direction of and a little outward from the door. But a split-second later something happened to correct the sideward slip. The slack in the cord from the spear to the bolt tightened and pulled the dummy back, halting it. For a moment it swayed, then started to fall rigidly forward on its face parallel with the door. The slack in the cord from the spear to the bolt diminished until the head was about a foot from the floor. At this point the cord became taut and the miracle occurred. With the tightening, the pull of the dummy's weight exerted as the dummy fell forward *caused the bolt to slide in the same direction, from left to right as they viewed it, into the catch on the jamb!*

The door was securely bolted.

And while they gaped, incredulous, they saw something else that was in itself almost as profound a miracle. They saw the short end of the cord begin to move, as if it were being pulled from the other side of the door. There was a moment of resistance at the coil about the bolt-knob, and then the cord broke at the point of resistance. Since there was no knot there, the broken piece—still attached to the spear—fell dangling to the floor between the dummy and the door. The remaining piece, whose end had been jerked, vanished under the door as it was pulled from the other side.

And then they saw the other length—the two-thirds length wound about the spear—tighten about the haft of the spear for a moment and then very smoothly begin to slide around, the dangling end which had just broken off from the knob of the bolt growing shorter and shorter as the same invisible hand pulled the two-thirds length into the office from the other side of the door. And finally the dangling end reached the haft, and glided around, and fell free, and in its turn vanished through the crack under the door. A moment later the mat which had caused the body to fall in the first place also vanished.

And the dummy lay just as the body had lain, and the door was bolted, and nothing remained but the bookcases and the spears and the position of the body to show how it was possible for a door to have been bolted from its other side.

Ellery came running back and dashed into the anteroom from the corridor. They were still glaring at the dummy and the door.

The detectives stood against the wall. The Inspector had his hand near his hip-pocket.

Some one had risen, pale as the sullen morning sky through the window, and was whispering in a cracked voice: "But I—don't see—how you—could have known."

"The spears told me," said Ellery in the stupefied silence. "The spears and the position of the two bookcases flanking the doorway to the office. When I assembled the facts I saw the truth. The missionary was murdered not where we found him but in another part of the room; that was established very early by the traces of blood on the floor. So the question arose: Why had the murderer moved the body to the door? Obviously because he had a use for the body at that point. The next question was: Why had the murderer shoved the right-hand bookcase along the right-hand wall farther away from the door? The answer to that could only be: to make room in front of the right-hand wall near the door. The third question was: Why had the murderer moved the left-hand bookcase up to the hinge-side of the door and pulled the right side out into the room, making an acute angle with the door? And the answer to that puzzled me until I remembered the spears. . . .

"The spears were stuck through the victim's clothes from shoes to head. They are solid wood; they made the body almost like an animal's corpse strung on stout poles. *They stiffened the body*; they produced, in a way, artificial *rigor mortis*. A dead man falling from an upright position would crumple in sections to land in a shapeless heap. This dead man, with the spears to stiffen his limp corpse into one piece, would fall in one piece, rigidly. But the right-hand bookcase had been moved back to leave space on the right of the door. Then the dead man was intended to fall before the door, at least part of him coming to rest in that cleared space. And he was intended to fall *parallel* with the door, otherwise there would have been no necessity for clearing a space to the side of the door. What was the left-hand bookcase moved for? Why that angle, patently deliberately made? I saw then that if the dead man had been set on his feet in that angle he would, if something occurred to move his body, have had to fall roughly toward that cleared space on the other side of the doorway!

"But why should the murderer want him to fall *precisely that way*, let alone fall at all?" Ellery drew a long breath. "And, impossible as it seemed, the only logical answer I could give to that question was: The murderer, who had removed the body from another part of the room *to* the door, wanted the dead man to do something *to* that door *in falling*. . . . The rest was a matter of concentration and experiment. The only thing that can be done to a door which might conceivably be of importance to a criminal would be to lock it; in this case, to bolt it. But why, for heaven's sake, make a dead man bolt the door when the murderer himself could have bolted it from this room and made his escape by the other door, that one leading to the corridor from this room?"

The cracked voice said: "I—never—thought—"

Ellery said deliberately: "The only possible answer was that the murderer couldn't or wouldn't leave this room by that corridor door. The murderer wanted to leave this room by way of *the door to the office*. And he wanted every one to believe that he had left by the corridor door, that the office door had been bolted all the time, that *whoever was in the office and had not appeared in the corridor outside the office therefore could not apparently have been the criminal!*"

James Osborne covered his face with his hands and said: "Yes, I did it. I murdered him."

"You see," said Ellery a moment later, regarding the cowering man with pitying eyes as the others, transfixed by horror, stared at Osborne, "the problem resolved itself simply into a logical analysis. The use of the spears and the shifting of the bookcases and the moved body of the dead missionary proved that the murderer must have left the anteroom after the crime by the office door. The murderer, therefore, was in the office directly after the murder. But, by his own admission, Osborne was the only constant tenant of that office during the murder-period! The visitors—Macgowan, Miss Sewell, Miss Temple, Miss Diversey—were eliminated because had one of them been the murderer he or she could have left the scene of the crime by the corridor door from this room and therefore could have bolted the office door

from the inside of this room without having to resort to the mechanical method Osborne used. Or, to put it another way, since
any one who could have left this room by the corridor door could
have bolted the office door without resorting to the mechanical
method, then any one who could have used the corridor door, instead of being suspect for the crime, as we had assumed all along,
became actually innocent.

"The only one who could not use the corridor door of the anteroom without being seen by Mrs. Shane as he returned to the
office was Osborne. You, Osborne, were therefore the only possible
suspect, the only one for whom the door trick and the spears were
necessary, and the only one who benefited from the creation of the
illusion that the criminal had to leave the murder-room via the
corridor door. Why didn't you leave well enough alone—leave that
office door unbolted?"

"Because," choked Osborne, "then I knew I would be the first
one suspected. But if it was bolted from the other side, they'd—
you'd never suspect me. Even now I can't see how—"

"I thought so," murmured Ellery. "The complex mind, Osborne. As to how, it was a matter of trial and error until I hit the
winning combination; I simply put myself in your place and figured out what you would have to do. . . . Now you see, ladies and
gentlemen, why it was impossible for Osborne to do the simple
thing and get a necktie somewhere to put on the tieless dead man.
He couldn't use his own, of course, and he had no place to get
another, because he couldn't afford to be seen leaving that office
of his in sight of Mrs. Shane, even casually. He might have slipped
out by the anteroom-corridor door, but then he couldn't risk all
the time required and the almost certain eventuality that he would
be seen—if, say, he went downstairs to buy a tie. He couldn't go to
Kirk's apartment, either, for the same reason. And he didn't live at
the Chancellor—Kirk once told him in my presence to 'go home'—

so he couldn't secure one of his own ties. . . . I suppose, Osborne, you took the dead man's vest and secreted it in the office there somewhere until you could safely burn it with all the other things you took from his clothes?"

"Yes," sighed Osborne in the queerest, mildest way. And Ellery noted, with a faint perplexity, that Miss Diversey looked like death and seemed about to faint.

"You see," he murmured, "if the man was a priest and wore the clerically inverted collar and no necktie, he must also have been wearing the special clerical vest which comes up to the neck. I knew then that the murderer had to take it away with him, since a clerical vest would have given the whole thing away; but I knew it much too late to prove anything by it. The opportunity to search every one had long since gone. . . . Osborne, why did you kill an inoffensive little man—you, who aren't the killer type at all? You did it for a poor return, Osborne; you would have had to sell the stamp undercover. But even if you *could* have got fifty thousand—"

"Ozzie—Osborne, for God's sake," whispered Donald Kirk, "I didn't dream—"

"It was for her," said Osborne in the same queer mild way. "I was a failure. She was the first woman who ever paid any attention to me. And I'm a poor man. She even said that she wouldn't think of marrying a man who couldn't provide the—the comforts. . . . When the opportunity came—" He licked his lips. "It was a temptation. He—he wrote a letter months ago addressed to Mr. Kirk from China. I opened the letter, as I open all—all Mr. Kirk's mail. He wrote all about the stamp, about resigning from his mission, about coming to New York—he was an American originally—to sell the stamp and retire. I—I saw the opportunity. I knew that the stamp, if what he said was true, would . . ." Osborne shuddered. No one said anything. "I planned it then, from the beginning. I corresponded with him, using Mr. Kirk's name. I never told Mr. Kirk a word about him. I didn't tell her. . . . We conducted a long correspondence. So I learned that he didn't have any relatives or friends in this country who could inquire about him if he disappeared. I learned when he was coming, told him when to come, gave him—sort of—advice. I never knew till he actually showed up—till I had killed him, when his scarf fell off—that he was a priest, with no tie, with a turned-around collar. I'd thought he was just a missionary—an ordinary missionary. A Methodist, maybe, or Baptist."

"Yes?" prompted Ellery gently, as the man fell silent.

"When I let him into this room I went back after a while, told him I hadn't realized it before, but he must be the man from China, and that I knew all about the stamp, that Mr. Kirk had told me, and all that. Then he got friendly and unbent and said that his brother-missionaries at the Chinese mission knew all about the stamp and that he had gone to America to sell it to Mr. Kirk. So when I killed him I had to make sure nobody could find out who he was."

"Why?" asked Ellery.

"Because if the police could trace him to that Chinese mission—it was very likely they could if they knew he was a priest and just arrived—they'd learn from the other priests about the stamp and why he had come—and they'd investigate Mr. Kirk and me, and Mr. Kirk really wouldn't know about the stamp and I'd be accused. . . . Maybe they'd find some of my letters, and trace the handwriting of the signatures back to me. . . . I—I couldn't face all that. I'm not an actor. I knew I'd give way. . . . So I thought of all that backwards business in a flash. But about the door and the cord and the body and things I—I'd figured out long before and had everything ready. When it was all over and I had him—him dead standing there, I tried to get it to work, but it wouldn't at first—the cord wasn't just right—and I tried and tried until finally it worked. I couldn't get a tie. . . ." His voice was growing fainter and fainter until it died away entirely. There was a dazed expression on his face; he seemed unable to grasp the horror of his position.

Ellery turned aside, sick at heart. "The woman was Miss Diversey?" he murmured. "If you didn't tell her, then she couldn't have had anything to do with this, of course."

"Oh," said Miss Diversey, and she fell back in a faint.

It happened before any of them realized his intention. He had been so mild, so dazed, so humble. It was only later that they knew it had been a last desperate, clever pose. . . . Ellery's back was turned. The Inspector was standing at the door with Sergeant Velie. The detectives . . .

Osborne lunged forward like a deer and scrambled past Ellery before he could turn. Inspector Queen and the Sergeant cried out and sprang simultaneously, both missing the man by inches. And Osborne vaulted the sill of the open window and screamed once and vanished.

"Before I go," drawled Mr. Ellery Queen a half-hour later in the almost deserted anteroom, "I should like to speak to you, Kirk, alone."

Donald Kirk was still motionless in his chair, hands dangling hopelessly between his knees, staring at the empty open window. Little Miss Temple sat quietly by his side, waiting. The others had gone.

"Yes?" Donald raised heavy eyes. "Queen, I can't believe it. Old Ozzie . . . He was always the most loyal, the most honest chap. And he finally came a cropper over a woman." He shivered.

"Don't blame Miss Diversey, Kirk. She's more to be pitied than blamed. Osborne was a victim of circumstances. He was repressed, at the dangerous age. His laboring imagination became

excited . . . and the woman possesses a certain virile attractive-
ness. Some strain of weakness in his character came to the surface. . . . Miss Temple, I wonder if you'd understand—Will you
leave me alone with your *fiancé* a moment?"

She rose without a word.

But Donald grasped her wrist and pulled her down to him and
said: "No, no, Queen. I've made up my mind. This is one woman
who can't bring a man anything but luck. I shan't keep anything
from Jo. I think I know—"

"Sensible resolution." Ellery went to his coat, which was flung
over a chair, and dug into one of the pockets. Then he returned
with a small packet.

"I gave you," he smiled, "an engagement gift not so long ago.
Now permit me to give you a wedding gift."

Kirk licked his lips once. "The letters?" Then he swallowed hard,
glanced at Miss Temple, set his chin, and said: "Marcella's letters?"

"Yes."

"Queen . . ." He took them and held them tightly. "I never
thought I'd get them back. Queen, I'm in your debt so much—"

"Tut, tut. Obviously, a little arson ceremony is called for,"
chuckled Ellery. "I suppose it's *au fait* to confide in your future
wife, but I should consign them to the flames and confide in no
one else." He sighed a little. "Well," he said, reaching for his coat,
"that's over. There's always a silver lining, *et cetera*. I trust you'll
both be very happy, but I doubt it."

"Doubt it, Mr. Queen?" murmured Miss Temple.

"Oh," said Ellery hastily, "don't take that personally. I was making the usual misogynist's observation about marriage."

"You're a darling, Mr. Queen." Miss Temple eyed him suddenly.
"You've been rather regal about all this ghastly business and I fancy
I shouldn't ask too many questions—should be thankful for how
everything's turned out. But I'm curious—"

"With your intellect, my dear, that's easily understood. Haven't I made everything clear?"

"Not quite." She linked her arm in Donald's and pressed it to her. "You made an unconscionable fuss about that tangerine, Mr. Queen. And here you've neglected to mention it at all!"

A shade passed over Ellery's face; he shook his head. "Strangest thing. I suppose you realize what a monstrous tragedy of errors Osborne's subtlety bred. I'm sure he had no idea, in leaving all those backwards things, of involving any one. He probably saw no significance in it at all; merely turned everything around as a cover-up for the collar and missing necktie without grasping the implications.

"But fate was unkind to him. It took hold of several unrelated facts and hurled them at me. I looked for significance in everything. But I looked, as I explained, for the wrong kind of significance. The result was that everything backwards, it seemed to me, about anybody at all required investigation. And there were you, Miss Temple," his gray eyes twinkled, "fresh from China, the abode of the living backwardnesses. Do you blame me for attempting to see significance in the fact that the victim had eaten a tangerine—a Chinese orange—shortly before his death?"

"Oh," she murmured; she seemed disappointed. "Then his eating of the tangerine meant nothing at all? I was hoping for something very clever."

"Nothing," drawled Ellery, "except that he was hungry; and we knew that anyway. I couldn't even squeeze any light out of the fact that he had selected a Chinese orange to appease his hunger rather than the pears or apples or other fruits in the bowl. I like 'em myself, and I've never been nearer China than Chicago. . . . But there's one thing about the Chinese orange that's—well, interesting."

"What's that?" demanded Kirk. He was holding the packet very tightly.

"It illustrates," chuckled Ellery, "the capriciousness and whimsicality of fate. Because, you see, while the Chinese orange he ate had nothing to do with the crime, the Chinese Orange he *brought* had everything to do with it, since it inspired the motive!"

"The Chinese orange he brought?" murmured Miss Temple, puzzled.

"With a capital O," said Ellery. "I mean the stamp. In fact, it makes such a fascinating coincidence that if ever I fictionize the remarkable case of poor Osborne and the smiling little Chinese missionary, I shan't be able to resist the temptation to entitle it *The Chinese Orange Mystery!*"